'You're a peculiar sort of marquess,' Tiffy said in tones of strongest disapproval.

'I beg your pardon?'

'Shabby,' she enlarged indicating his fustian pantaloons, ungaitered half-boots, well-worn shooting-jacket and, most particularly, the shooting-belt not usually worn by those who could afford servants to relieve them of the necessity. 'Are you an eccentric?'

'I don't believe so,' he replied, his voice a little unsteady with amusement.

'Then you should be ashamed of yourself,' she told him severely. 'You are a marquess, which is above an earl and very nearly a duke. Meeting you should be an occasion, but how can it be when you walk around like everybody else? How, pray, is anybody to know who you are?'

His lordship repressed a smile. 'You have the advantage of me still, ma'am. You know my name, but I do not know yours.'

She frowned. 'You must have heard about me. I am Miss Yorke.' When Lord Dalmaine continued to look enquiring rather than shocked, she added ominously, 'The *infamous* Miss Yorke.'

Before settling on the Isle of Wight several years ago to concentrate on writing fiction, Rosina Pyatt worked on various magazines at home and abroad as a feature writer and fiction editor. She has many short stories and novelettes to her credit.

Her eldest son is a reporter, her daughter is writing her first novel, and her youngest son is an art student. She has one compulsive hobby—walking her cross-bred collie, Digby, mainly as a means of escaping the typewriter.

Rosina Pyatt has written two other Masquerade Historical Romances—*To Catch an Earl* and *Silk For a Lady*, which was short-listed for the 1985 Romantic Novel of the Year Award presented by the Romantic Novelists' Association.

THE MARQUESS
AND MISS YORKE

ROSINA PYATT

MILLS & BOON LIMITED
15–16 BROOK'S MEWS
LONDON W1A 1DR

First published in Great Britain 1986
by Mills & Boon Limited

© Rosina Pyatt 1986

Australian copyright 1986
Philippine copyright 1986

ISBN 0 263 75544 4

Set in 10 on 11 pt Linotron Times
04–1086–76,400

Photoset by Rowland Phototypesetting Ltd
Bury St Edmunds, Suffolk
Made and printed in Great Britain by
Cox & Wyman Ltd, Reading

CHAPTER ONE

'GOD DAMN,' breathed the much-tried Miss Yorke, her blasphemy and lilting accent revealing the ramshackle colonial upbringing which, in her English relatives' opinion, made her quite unfit for polite society.

Unrepentantly she repeated the oath, feeling she was owed that much, for the discovery that the log she sat upon was damp was all of a piece with the dark forces ranged against her. She was convinced that these forces, manifested in a fate perverse enough to amount to persecution, would have goaded a saint to strong language.

She raised her head, stared about her and made another discovery. The rustic glade in the midst of the thick wood where she had dismounted to brood on her wrongs, and consider her next move, was totally unknown to her. On top of everything, it seemed, she was lost.

Moreover, the wintry sunlight shafting through the trees was becoming less frequent. Although barely noon, it was growing darker and chillier, causing the little glade to lose its attractiveness and take on the forbidding aspect of the wood.

Miss Yorke suspected that the changeable skies over this southern country of Kent were once more preparing to weep, and had she been made of less stern stuff, she would have wept with them. As it was, she stood up. There was nothing for it but to find her way out of this strange wood and seek some familiar landmark to guide her home. Once there, she must face with whatever fortitude she could muster the starch-faced disapproval of her relatives.

This prospect did nothing to raise her wilting spirits. Her present predicament was caused by fleeing, midway through its delivery, a stern homily on her previous misdeeds. Nor could she deny that her fortitude, when mustered in the past, had never proved sufficient to refute the accusation that her tongue was as unruly as her behaviour. When reproached, she never failed to defend herself, and in such a fiery manner that her relatives feared the devil already had her in his grasp.

Her very features conspired to give her a look of mischief, even when she was trying to be good. Her little nose was retroussé to the point of cheekiness. Her full soft lips tilted at the corners as if perpetually hovering on the brink of a smile, which could not be commended, for too much levity in a female was held to be a deplorable trait. That her cheekbones and eyebrows continued this upward slant was also objected to, on the grounds that it was exotic and therefore un-English.

Also, when Miss Yorke laughed, only one of her cheeks was dimpled. A second dimple she certainly possessed but, as if her countenance was determined to display the contrariness that was so much part of her character, it was placed unexpectedly and sensuously in her chin.

Nature, having assembled this odd assortment of features in one rather small face, then apparently repented and bestowed upon her large violet eyes of such magnificence that they triumphed over all the rest. They were so expressive, mirroring her every mood, that she frequently needed the thick black lashes framing them to screen her thoughts from the world. When her eyes were downcast, it was not a sign of maidenly modesty but that she had something to hide.

Under normal circumstances her thick black hair was her second claim to admiration, but it was not at its best right then, needing time to recover from a cropping so ruthless and inexpert that her glossy waves had disintegrated into a mass of riotous curls.

Miss Yorke, glumly aware she lacked classical beauty, had still to realise that she possessed the far more potent power of a born enchantress. Her relatives were not so naïve, hence their vigorous efforts to tame her waywardness before history repeated itself and the family was plunged once more into a dreadful scandal.

She was a daughter of Sin, and they never let her forget it. Miss Yorke, never having encountered disapproval before her precipitate arrival in England some months earlier, indignantly fought back, stating unequivocally that she was damned if she was going to be turned into a prosy bore by a parcel of dowds. Battle fairly enjoined, it raged unabated while the last weeks of the year 1812, which had been the most traumatic of her life, slid with little celebration into 1813, which so far had proved little better. By the time Miss Yorke found herself lost in the wood, she had succeeded in setting that quiet corner of Kent by the ears, and it was freely whispered that there was nothing she would not do to prove she was dead to all sense of shame.

In truth, however, she looked more woebegone than wanton as she retrieved her purloined horse and climbed on to the damp log to re-mount more easily. She was about to place her foot in the stirrup when the roar of a gun discharged close at hand shattered the tranquillity of the wood. The horse's shrill whinny of alarm and her own scream blended in the moment before they parted company physically. The horse reared and bolted, throwing her backwards into a bush, whose thick and wiry branches at first absorbed and then repulsed her.

She lay where she fell, stunned by the suddenness of the incident rather than by injury, until the rapidly receding hoofbeats of her horse made it clear she would have to walk home. Her hands curled into fists and she beat upon the ground in frustration. 'Hell and the devil confound it!' she shouted. 'Will nothing ever go right for me?'

Her outburst was lost in the squawks of the birds winging away in panic from the wood, and in the closer rustling and twig-snapping flight of earthbound creatures. A weasel and several rabbits, unnatural companions, burst from the deeply shadowed bushes and shot across the glade with a more formidable animal in close pursuit, judging by the noise it made.

Miss Yorke, not too sure what manner of beasts lurked in seemingly innocent English woods, seized a stick from the ground, scrambled to her feet and prepared to defend herself. She was in such a temper that she felt no relief when the shape that emerged was that of a man and not a beast. She saw he carried a gun. So! She had survived all else, to fall foul of a gamekeeper.

She exploded angrily, 'You misbegotten son of a bitch! If you have come to gloat over my lifeless body you are premature, for you have neither shot me nor broken my neck. And if you think that entitles you to carry me off to the magistrate, I will not go! I'll be damned if I'll be hanged or transported when I am *not* a trespasser or a poacher or even a horse-thief, whatever that odious toad Tarleton might say.'

She broke off to draw breath, then continued with renewed fury, 'Perhaps I did not ask permission to borrow his horse, but what would have been the use when I know he would have refused! Heaven knows I am more sinned against than sinning, whatever *anyone* might say. However, I expect no justice. How can I, considering the crosses I am called upon to bear, which is the greatest injustice of all, for surely that is a Christian's duty, and I am generally held to be a pagan! Well, I have had enough and will endure no more persecution, so be warned!'

Miss Yorke backed up her challenge by brandishing

the stick, then striking it against her thigh in a threatening manner. Its damp-rotted interior could not sustain such rough treatment and crumbled to pieces. She flung away the fragment remaining in her hand and exclaimed in disgust, 'Was there ever such luck! I swear I was never more tempted to sell my soul to the devil. He is supposed to look after his own, which is something!'

Her outraged feelings partially relieved, she resumed her seat on the log, lifted her skirt, rolled up a leg of her drawers and examined the knee that had borne the brunt of her fall.

The fury of her tirade, its heavy emphasis and incoherence, had held the man motionless. Like one emerging from a trance, he leaned his gun against a tree and dropped to his knees beside her to say, 'You are in shock, I believe, but how thankful I am you have taken no serious injury! I would never have fired my gun had I suspected I was not alone in the wood. When I heard you scream and your horse galloping away, I feared a dreadful accident. Pray tell me how I may help you?'

Miss Yorke, disdaining to raise her eyes from her knee, retorted sarcastically, 'Help me? After nearly murdering me? What do you offer next, the coup de grâce? Indeed . . .'

She broke off, as the refined accent and courteous manner with which she had been addressed belatedly penetrated her preoccupation with her damaged knee. Her head jerked up. 'You are no gamekeeper. Good God!' Her eyes widened as she saw his countenance for the first time. 'You are—you must be—Dalmaine!'

Courteney de Lucey Sinclair Harwood, sixth Marquess of Dalmaine, a Captain of Hussars lately invalided home from the Peninsular War and one of the richest landowners in the kingdom, had been too concerned with the young lady's welfare to spare a thought for himself. Now, however, a habit acquired over many painful weeks reasserted itself. He averted his face so that she might be spared the embarrassment of averting hers.

His tact was lost on Miss Yorke. She put her hand under his chin and turned his face back, staring shamelessly at the scar caused by a sword-slash to his left cheek, and running diagonally from cheekbone to chin. Lord Dalmaine, accustomed to far more deferential treatment, was held captive more by her audacity than by her hand.

He was further startled when she presently pronounced, 'What a cheat! After the ghoulish tales I have heard, I expected to be most deliciously frightened if we should chance to meet, and I am no such thing. All gossips should be hanged by their tongues, for I was never more taken in. Scarred you certainly are, but not—mangled. Why, you do not even make me shudder,' she ended, making it sound like an accusation.

'Your disappointment naturally devastates me,' the Marquess replied with awful irony.

That, too, was lost on Miss Yorke, and she answered crossly, 'Oh, don't play off the airs of a martyr on me. I am martyred enough on my own account, only my wounds do not show.'

Silence fell between them. She resumed rubbing her knee while he studied her with fresh interest. He had survived his wounds, the crude treatment of his doctors, the subsequent fever that was responsible for his eventually being carried home little more than a corpse, only to find heartbreak awaiting him. That, too, he had weathered, for all his sympathies were with his beloved, and yet his trials were not over. These past weeks, while he was fighting his way back to health and strength, he had had to bear the sympathy of his friends and well-wishers, and his powers of endurance had never been more severely tested.

Had he been less sensitive, he could have played the autocrat and consigned them all to the devil, but that was not his way. To spare them the painful stratagems they adopted to avoid looking him in the face, he had learned to keep his left cheek averted. He accepted that he was scarred, but it was impossible for him to forget about it when every pair of eyes meeting his were full of ill-suppressed pity.

Except, of course, the gloriously unsympathetic eyes of this young lady. He wondered who she was, certain he would have remembered her had they met before. The violet colouring of her eyes was distinctive, although, his heart being lost to a blue pair set in a face of angelic fairness, their effect on him was necessarily muted. Indeed, she inspired no romantic thoughts, for she seemed to him the most complete tomboy, and a wilful one at that. Yet there was a wistfulness about her face and a certain fragility about her slight figure that troubled a protective chord in him.

Her riding-habit had faded with the wear of several seasons and he was very sure it had originally been fashioned for a more robust figure, for it all but swamped her. Her circumstances, then, were not affluent, a fact borne out by her shabby gloves and scuffed boots. He also noticed with amusement that there wasn't a scrap of modesty about the way she rolled down the leg of her drawers, flicked her skirt back in place and raised her head.

Neither was she dismayed to find herself being closely scrutinised, readily subjecting him to a far more blatant appraisal. His thick fair hair was cut shorter than usual, and owed its dishevelled appearance to natural circum-stances rather than to fashionable brushing. His nose, chin and mouth were strongly formed and sufficiently regular to be accounted handsome, though not in a spectacular way. He had particularly fine grey eyes, clear and steady, and eyelashes a good deal darker than his hair. He looked what he was, an aristocrat, and although this would have been enough to interest most young ladies, he lacked whatever vital ingredient was necessary to make Miss Yorke's adolescent heart beat faster.

Eventually, making up her mind about him, she said in tones of strongest disapproval, 'You're a peculiar sort of marquess.'

'I beg your pardon?'

'Shabby,' she enlarged, indicating his fustian pantaloons, ungaitered half-boots, well-worn shooting-jacket and, most particularly, the shooting-belt not usually worn by those who could afford servants to relieve them of the necessity. 'Are you an eccentric?'

'I don't believe so,' he replied, his voice a little unsteady with amusement.

'Then you should be ashamed of yourself,' she told him severely. 'You are a marquess, which is above an earl and very nearly a duke. Meeting you should be an occasion, but how can it be when you walk around like everybody else? I thought noblemen never moved an inch without an army of flunkeys to impress the world with their consequence, and you have neither loaders nor beaters! What a *poor* way for a marquess to go out shooting. How, pray, is anybody to know who you are?'

'I have my scar,' Lord Dalmaine reminded her wryly.

Miss Yorke stiffened. 'That, I collect, is your way of telling me I have been impudent. Do you demand an apology?'

He smiled. 'For being honest? I am still enjoying the novelty of it.'

'You, an Englishman, praising honesty!' she exclaimed. 'I have been punished for it ever since I arrived in this country.'

'You are not English? I have noticed you speak with a . . .'

'Don't you dare say "brogue"! Nothing puts me in more of a rage except, perhaps, when it is said I was reared in the colonies. America was an independent country before I was born there. Nor am I acquainted with any feathered savages, let alone being raised among them, whatever anyone might say!'

'Ah, America,' Lord Dalmaine breathed, as though that explained a great many things. 'But you have the advantage of me still. You know my name, but I do not know yours.'

She frowned. 'You must have heard about me.'

'Believe me, I haven't.'

'You must have,' she insisted. 'My name will remind you of it. Then you will not wish to know me any more.

'You are judging me in advance. If I promise not to do the same with you, will you tell me?'

'Oh, very well. I am Miss Yorke.' When Lord Dalmaine continued to look enquiring rather than shocked, she added ominously, 'The *infamous* Miss Yorke.'

'How very exciting,' he murmured. 'You must be quite out of the common way.'

'What do you mean?' she asked suspiciously.

'Only that the young ladies of my acquaintance are better described as insipid. I cannot think of a single one meriting anything as distinguished as *infamous*.'

'You are laughing at me,' she accused.

'Yes. Do you mind?'

For a moment the issue was clearly in doubt, then her frown vanished and she burst out laughing. 'Oh, I like you,' she exclaimed impulsively. 'You are not like all the rest.'

'Neither, Miss Yorke, are you,' he assured her, then held out his hand. 'We have discovered a bond. Shall we shake hands on it?'

She did not hesitate. She placed her small hand in his strong one with a trust he found touching, and then she sniffed as her eyes unexpectedly misted over.

'Whatever have I said to upset you?' Lord Dalmaine asked in consternation.

'I am not upset,' she responded fiercely. 'I know there is nothing a gentleman loathes more than to be wept at. I *never* do so. At least, almost never. I shall be better directly. It is just that finding a friend after everybody has been so horrid, almost—almost unmans me.'

'Violets in the dew,' he murmured. 'I can't think of a better recommendation for crying.'

'I beg your pardon?'

'Violets in the dew,' he repeated. 'Your eyes when you are crying—or, rather, when you are determined not to.'

'Oh! What a beautiful thing to say,' she wailed, searching frantically for a handkerchief as her tears spilled over. 'I swear you are the best of good fellows.'

Lord Dalmaine repressed a smile and offered his own handkerchief. 'You are more accustomed to male than female company, Miss Yorke?'

'Yes, my papa's, for my mama died when I was eight.' She took his handkerchief, mopped her cheeks and blew her nose. 'How did you guess?'

'The expressions you use.'

'Well, Papa never stood on ceremony with me, and he could never find a governess willing to undertake our wandering kind of life. Only pray call me Tiffy. He always did so. He said I lacked the dignity to support my given names, although he laughed when he said so, which quite took the sting out of it, if you understand.'

Lord Dalmaine did, but asked, 'Your given names?'

'Theodora Ianthe Felicia Francine Yorke. The initials spell Tiffy.' She moved along the log and patted the place beside her. 'Please sit down. Your knees will be as bruised as mine if you kneel much longer, and were you not also wounded in the leg? I should have remembered sooner, but, to tell the truth, I have been a little preoccupied with my own troubles.'

'I am quite recovered, thank you,' Lord Dalmaine replied, but he sat beside her and added with his characteristic kindness, 'I am sure you will grow to support the dignity of your name.'

'I shall be satisfied if I prove to be well named. Theodora and Ianthe are from the Greek, meaning "God's gift"—the sweetest sentiment!—and "violet flower", after my eyes, of course, which made your comment just now so very apt. Felicia is from the Latin, meaning "lucky", which makes my present misfortune quite incomprehensible. Mama chose Francine, for Papa's name was Francis and she wished to compensate him for not producing a boy, although he always said he would rather have me than a *dozen* sons. He had your knack, my lord, for saying beautiful things. My relatives never do so, and yet they dare to malign him. Are you similarly burdened?'

'With relatives?'

'No, with names! I am aware only of your title.'

'So you are. I am Courteney de Lucey Sinclair Harwood, but I fear my names were chosen only to commemorate some of my ancestors.'

'A piece of walking history! You really should try to look more the part,' she scolded. 'I know I must not call you Courteney, for you are so much older and more distinguished than myself, but I shall think of you as such, to remind me that we share a bond. Papa told me we sprang from a Saxon line. Did you come over with the Normans?'

He smiled. 'Yes. Does that stand against me?'

'It might have done several hundred years ago, but I am not one to bear a grudge that long,' she told him. 'How strange, though, that you should be Saxon fair and I Norman dark. The strains must have become very mixed. A mercy when you think of it, my lord, for it enables us to speak the same language.'

Lord Dalmaine burst out laughing. 'Tiffy, I never know what you are going to say next.'

'Nobody does, and that is held to be deplorable,' she said ruefully.

'I find it delightful.'

'Then I wish you were my uncle. He is the Reverend Hector Everett, and he has the living at Honivale. Poor Mama was his sister. He disapproves of her. I can't do anything right, either. He and his wife and daughter, a snivelling sneak called Cassy, believe I am incorrigible. That means,' she added, not without pride, 'depraved beyond reform. I know, because I looked it up.'

'Then you are not, as I supposed, related to the—er —odious toad you referred to earlier? I took that to be young Tarleton Creighton, Sir Geoffrey's son, from the Hall.'

'Related to that tailor's pattern-card?' Tiffy responded in disgust. 'No, that is one affliction I have been spared. It is bad enough having to call Cassy my cousin. Tarleton has the vapours if he gets a speck of mud on his boots. Such fustian! The way he minces and lisps and puffs off his consequence, one would think *he* were a real live marquess instead of a mere baronet's son. When he called at the vicarage this morning and I borrowed his horse, he called after me, "Stop, thief", as though I were a common brigand. I suppose the fact that it was not saddled for a lady will be added to my crimes, and the list is long enough already.'

She picked at a loose cotton on her glove as she spoke and Lord Dalmaine watched with amusement as an extra violent tug caused a seam to part, revealing one pale finger.

'What shoddy workmanship, and I shall be blamed for it,' she grumbled. 'As if I were accustomed to wearing clothes that fall off my back, and I am not! Only our funds were at low tide when Papa died so suddenly. It was necessary for me to leave America with no more than I could carry, so that I am obliged to wear Cassy's cast-offs like a wretched pauper brat. It is insupportable!'

Her magnificent eyes flashed and then settled moodily on his face, causing him unconsciously to avert it. 'Stop doing that!' she snapped, again turning his face back to hers. 'Anyone would think you had need of a pretty face, which is ridiculous, for you are a man—and a marquess besides. You could look like the devil himself, and still people would come to you.'

'Is that supposed to be a comfort?'

'It is a fact. Besides, I don't like to be insulted.'

'Insulted?' he repeated in astonishment.

'Certainly. I don't know what sort of company you keep, but they must be a poor lot if their friendship depends upon the way you look. Mine does not, and pray remember it, for it makes me very cross when you turn your face away. I shall slap you if you do it again. You demean both of us!'

Lord Dalmaine was a good deal touched. 'Forgive me, Tiffy, but you are such a rarity that I have not become accustomed to you yet. Most people, you see, will do anything except look at my face, so that I have fallen into the habit of sparing them the embarrassment.'

'Well, I think it is a great deal of fuss to make over what is, after all, a simple scar. I shouldn't be surprised if you came to be grateful to it—for giving a distinguished touch to what would otherwise be a very ordinary sort of face.'

His lordship's laughter rang out. He stood up and held out his hand to her. 'Tiffy, you are a gem, and I should be taking better care of you. This log is definitely damp and it would be too bad if, after escaping serious injury, I allowed you to succumb to inflammation of the lungs. I must get you home. Will your bruises allow you to walk, or shall I carry you?

'I can walk.' She stood up reluctantly. 'I never thought

I would be sorry to see the last of this horrid log, but I am because I have been happy here with you. Not once have you preached at me, or scolded. You have smiled and laughed as—as—Papa used to, and made me feel quite like—like—my old self. But of course it must end. Before my horse bolted I knew I had to return home, only I was in disgrace when I left, so I must be past redemption now. The truth, my lord, is that I am in *such* a scrape.'

'I rather thought you were,' he told her gently, 'but the home I was referring to was mine. I shall take you back to Honivale by carriage when you are rested and refreshed.'

'I am to go to Dalmaine Castle?' Tiffy's gloom dropped from her, and she flung her arms round him and hugged him. 'Oh, what a treat! And just as I was thinking nothing good would ever happen to me again. Cassy will be sick with envy, and if you will come back with me to—to—stand buff, you will save me from *such* a lecture. I dare say I shall turn out to be a heroine. The thing is, my relatives revere the nobility almost as much as they do the Lord, although they would send me supperless to bed for saying so. Yet it is true, for they fawn all over Sir Geoffrey when he visits and, as I have said, he is only a baronet.'

Wondering what his uninhibited protegée would say next, Lord Dalmaine suggested tactfully, 'Shall we walk as we talk? I don't wish to rush you, but the rain will not hold off much longer. It shouldn't take us above fifteen minutes by the short cut, although the path is sadly overgrown.'

'I shan't care a jot for that. Let us go *immediately* and by the *shortest* route,' she urged. 'A castle! Only imagine.'

'I fear you will be disappointed. Not much of it remains,' he warned as he retrieved his gun, pushed through the bushes and held them apart so that she could follow. 'Castles may sound romantic but they are deuced draughty. My ancestors built more comfortable wings once the need for fortification had passed. When my grandfather added the last, he renamed the entire pile Dalmaine Park, but custom dies hard and it is still known as the Castle.'

'I should think so,' Tiffy remarked, walking behind him until he stopped to pick up the game-bag he had dropped when hearing her scream. 'Deer can live in a park, but one expects a castle for a marquess. What are you looking for?'

'The rabbit I shot.'

'Perhaps you missed it.'

'I never miss,' he replied, and proved himself right when he found it.'

Tiffy surveyed the body dispassionately as he put it in his game-bag. 'A sorry sight I would have looked if you had hit me. Not,' she added mournfully, 'that anybody would have been sorry if I had been killed.'

'I would have been exceedingly sorry. I don't, as a general rule, encourage corpses in my home wood.'

'But you wouldn't have mourned me because you wouldn't have known me,' she argued, then grinned impishly. 'A rare pleasure missed?'

He laughed. 'I am beginning to think you are indestructible, Tiffy.'

'I only hope you never regret meeting me,' she responded, tucking her arm companionably in his as they walked on.

There was some disparity in their heights, Tiffy being diminutive and the marquess over six feet tall, so that when he looked down at her all he could see was the top of her curly head, and he smiled as he said, 'I am sure I shall never do so.'

'When you know my history, you might think I am not—not—quite the thing,' she answered doubtfully.

'You are not obliged to tell me anything you don't

wish to, and you may be sure I will not listen to any unkind things that might be said of you.'

'Oh! How kind. Or is that merely *noblesse oblige*?'

'It is friendship. I cannot offer you anything less than you have offered me.'

Tiffy's throat tightened and once more she was obliged to resort to his hankerchief, blowing her nose and looking up at him with a watery smile. 'You are *such* a comfort. Usually I am judged in advance, and by standards I do not understand. It makes me worse, not better.'

'I am sure it does, although, to be honest, I fail to understand how anybody as young as you could be infamous. I think you are teasing me.'

'I am not! I never knew I had anything to be ashamed of until I came to England, but Papa's brother, my uncle Yorke, repulsed me because I was an *embarrassment*, and so Mama's brother and his wife took me in because I am their *Christian duty*. You have no idea how lowering that is, particularly when one doesn't wish to be anybody's duty, Christian or otherwise, but only wanted. Which I am not.'

'Poor Tiffy,' he murmured, looking down once more at her shining curls.

'You might well say so,' she agreed vehemently, 'because the Everetts are Evangelists and against everything that makes life worth living. Gambling, the theatre —even playing cricket on Sundays, for fear it should incite the passions. I find that quite extraordinary, for when Papa was *incited*, he did not play cricket but visited his mistress, although only after Mama died, of course. The worst is that they are nagging at me to become an Evangelist also. They get so cross when I tell them Papa would not turn in his grave at the thought—he would *spin*, loathing all bores as he did, especially pious ones!'

Her slight bosom heaved with indignation. 'They call me insolent, and have the *impudence* to say I lack the delicacy of mind that distinguishes a well-bred female. I, Papa's daughter, and he a *true* gentleman! On top of that, if you please, I am rag-mannered, selfish and ungrateful, and unless I repent of my wicked ways I shall be eternally damned. Such humbug! I told them this morning that if their next world is as miserable as the one they have made for themselves in this, then I for one will go to the devil with a song on my lips. Are you very much shocked, my lord?'

Lord Dalmaine, bending to untangle a briar from her skirt, did not answer for a moment, then said carefully, 'I can understand why you are in a scrape. What puzzles me is why this conflict started. Did you deliberately antagonise them?'

'Lord, no! I did not have to. The fact that I exist was enough. I am the result, you see, of Papa and Mama succumbing to a grand passion, and my aunt and uncle fear I will tread the same thorny path. They won't listen when I tell them it was more fun than thorns, and say I need saving from myself. Well, I don't wish to be saved. Indeed, I cannot wait for a grand passion of my own, for I never knew two merrier people than my parents, but as I am only sixteen, I suppose I shall have to wait a while.'

Lord Dalmaine was silent. He found Tiffy as invigorating as a breath of fresh air but was worldly enough to realise that her artless confidences would, in a conventional setting, be as explosive as dynamite. The father she obviously adored had much to answer for, because what he had laughed at in the child would be condemned in the young lady. Already, it seemed, she was a target for gossip. Unless something was done, she faced the bleak future of a social outcast.

A wise man would have drawn back at this juncture, divining that if Tiffy Yorke did not deserve to be called infamous now, she very soon would be. Yet Lord Dalmaine could no more abandon her to her fate than if she had been a puppy he had found lost in his woods.

Moreover, he had pledged friendship, and he was too honourable to recant.

Also, he was convinced she spoke outrageously not because she was steeped in sin, but because she was totally innocent of it. She simply accepted as common-place circumstances which were, to others, scandalous. Never having been schooled against giving offence, she was unaware she did so. It was little wonder that her relatives' condemnation should make her resentful, for their attitude must be totally incomprehensible to her.

The problem was that he, a bachelor, could not throw his mantle of protection over her without causing the kind of gossip that would damn her for ever. Had she been younger . . . But at sixteen, no! He had, whichever way he looked at it, got himself in the devil of a fix. On the one hand he could not abandon her, on the other he could not protect her. For her own sake he should really sever the bond he had spoken of, and quickly. Better to dishonour himself by recanting, than dishonour her.

Just as he had reached this painful decision, Tiffy totally disarmed him by looking up with eyes full of concern. 'You are limping, my lord. Your wound is troubling you.'

'It is nothing. This uphill slope, now that we are clear of the wood, is good exercise for my leg.'

'You are in pain, I know it, and when was pain ever any good for anybody? You must have suffered enough already. You will not suffer any more if I can help it. Let me carry that heavy gun and game-bag.'

'Thank you, but there is not the slightest need. I am quite comfortable.'

'I have not *once* lied to you,' she retorted. 'Have the goodness not to lie to me.'

He couldn't help smiling. 'What a firecracker you are! Nevertheless, I am perfectly capable of carrying my own load.'

Tiffy abandoned argument for action. She slipped her

arm out of his, then placed his arm across her shoulders. 'There, you may lean on me as much as you wish. *Please*, my lord. I am amazingly sturdy, I promise you, for all I don't look it. No, don't frown at me. Pride, between friends, will surely permit a compromise?'

She smiled so warmly up at him that the marquess capitulated and allowed her to bear some of his weight. It would take a harder man than himself, he acknowledged ruefully, to repulse Tiffy Yorke.

'There's a good fellow,' she told him approvingly, as if he were a child who had been coaxed into sharing a treat. 'If it wasn't so cold we'd be quite cosy, wouldn't we?'

Lord Dalmaine laughed at her absurdity, and she laughed with him. And by some subtle means, as they toiled on up the hill to the castle, the bond between them strengthened beyond all possibility of severance.

CHAPTER TWO

'I AM NOT a bastard, you know,' Tiffy quite floored Courteney by remarking conversationally, 'so you need not blush to introduce me to your relatives. The gossips are quite wrong about that part of my history. My parents married and regularised me, as Papa put it, before I was much above three years old. They could not marry when they eloped, since Mama was unfortunately the wife of another gentleman and a divorce takes an interminable time. I'm sure it's not to be wondered at that I arrived first. That is why Theodora is such a special name, although I do not care for it.'

She glanced up, saw the furrow caused by his brows snapping together, and explained, 'God's gift. It signifies that they were pleased to have me, whatever anybody else might think. They were so passionately in love that I believe they should be commended for running away. However, it is a wickedly censorious world we live in, where respectability is put above happiness. There was a very great scandal.'

'Society is not kind to those who break its rules,' Courteney admitted.

'Precisely, and a great love cannot be bound by convention, can it? I hope I may prove as spirited when my turn comes, however inconvenient it might be.'

'Inconvenient?' Even by Tiffy's standards it seemed a masterpiece of understatement.

'Yes, for not only was Mama already married, but Papa was in the dragoons. He had to resign his commission, which left him without a career, and there was Napoleon to contend with as well.'

'Napoleon? Ah, you mean the war. They could not flee to France.'

'That's it, and Papa believed his talents would have flowered more fully in Europe. However, it had to be America, where there was less scope for a man of his genius.'

'Genius? Forgive me sounding like a parrot, but I do not follow.'

'Papa was a *brilliant* gambler,' Tiffy explained. 'His family made him a yearly allowance never to return to England, but it was insufficient to support a gentleman of his great style. He turned his talent into a profession, and it answered splendidly. Sometimes Mama had to sell her jewels, but she never minded. He always bought her more when he was flush again! When his luck was out past all understanding he painted portraits, so we never starved or came anywhere near it. I have inherited his talent for gambling and painting. I'm sure they will be useful, though I'd exchange them for a tenth of Mama's beauty,' she ended with a sigh.

Courteney was framing a diplomatic response when she spared him the necessity by asking, 'Tell me frankly, my lord, what impression did you gain of me when we first met?'

'Frankly, Tiffy, I thought you looked the most complete urchin.'

'If that doesn't beat all!' she exclaimed. 'For that is what I thought when I ran away to sign on board ship as a cabin boy. Such pains I went to, paying the gardener's son sixpence for the most disreputable set of clothes, and cutting my hair, and dirtying my face so that nothing about me looked female —only the captain wasn't fooled.'

'Good God! Anything might have happened to you.'

'*Anything* would have been better than living with the Everetts,' she responded feelingly. 'It was the kitten that was my undoing. It followed me all along the quay and on board ship, and there was something in the way I tried to persuade it to go home that told the captain I was female. I was put in the roundhouse and held there until my uncle arrived to collect me, and *such* a scold I got! It was the same when I ran after the gipsies who passed through Honivale, thinking they would let me live with them, only they took me back for a reward. But that's the way my luck has been running, ever away from me, and why I should be punished for trying to relieve the Everetts of my *unwanted* presence, I do not know!'

'What an exciting time you have had in England,' Courteney murmured.

'It is the dullest time of my life, and I cannot and will not support it,' she retorted passionately. 'But we were discussing my looks, my lord. Have you observed that when I smile only one of my cheeks is dimpled?' She looked up at him and demonstrated.

'Yes, and found it charming.'

'Oh!' Her false smile became a real one. 'I shall tell Cassy so. She says my smile is lopsided, the cat! And this dimple in my chin is not, as she maintains, a cleft?'

He studied her upthrust chin and decided, 'Merely a dimple. Most definitely not a cleft.'

'I knew as much,' she said with satisfaction, then added more dolefully, 'I think there is little point in discussing my nose. It will always turn up too much.'

Courteney, glancing at the offending feature, thought the day was not too far off when a gentleman would come into her life who found kissing such a cheeky little nose quite irresistible, but it was not his place to say so.

'My eyes, of course, are incomparable,' Tiffy continued. 'If that sounds insufferably vain, you can't deny I need *something* to be complacent about. Your own eyes, my lord, are remarkably fine.'

'Tiffy, it is my turn to be unmanned.'

'I wish I might see the day,' she told him roundly. 'For

one who doesn't say much, it's my belief you tease a great deal. Do you think I talk too much?'

'No, but sometimes unguardedly.'

'Fiddlesticks! I refuse to become a canting hypocrite, and will speak my mind, come what may. Besides, what need have I to guard myself from a friend?'

'None, but there are those who would tear you apart for your frankness.'

'I wish they might try! They would find me more than a match for them. Small I might be, but . . .' Tiffy broke off and started on another tack. 'That reminds me, do you think I might grow some more? You will have noticed my head reaches nowhere near your shoulder, and I should hate to be thought of all my life as a poor little dab of a creature.'

The smile she was beginning to know touched Courteney's eyes and mouth. 'Nobody could possibly think of you in such terms. What you lack in stature, you make up in spirit. It gives you a very positive impact that no poor little dab of a creature could hope to achieve.'

Tiffy, entranced by this new view of herself, said warmly, 'How pleased I am you nearly shot me, for otherwise I might have spent my entire life believing all the English are horrid.'

'You are English yourself,' he pointed out.

'By blood, but not by inclination. I feel very foreign. Indeed, the longer I am here, the surer I am that Papa's grand plan for me would not have worked at all.' She wrinkled the nose she disliked so much as a large drop of rain splashed on it. 'We are going to get wet, after all. Why do you have to live on top of a hill?'

'It was thought the right place to put a castle at the time. Tiffy, what was your father's grand plan?'

'To bring me to England when I was seventeen so that I could make a splendid marriage. Only the thought of being buckled for life makes me feel quite claustrophobic. I get bored so easily. If I married young, then ten to one I'd do as Mama did and fall madly in love with somebody else. All in all, my lord, I believe my temperament is more suited to being a mistress than a wife.'

'Tiffy!' Courteney remonstrated, and felt rather than saw the shrug of her shoulders.

'Oh, I know,' she sighed. 'Young ladies are not supposed to know about such things, but there's no gainsaying that I do know. After Mama died, Papa had a succession of mistresses, and very dashing creatures they were. He never wished to marry again, for he said he could never love any woman as he loved Mama, and so his liaisons never lasted long. There wasn't time for boredom, which makes me think I'd make a very good mistress.'

'Had your father wished such a career for you, he would never have turned your thoughts to marriage.'

'He wouldn't have wished me to be miserable as a wife,' she countered. 'And I can't be expected to waste my life waiting to fall in love. I wouldn't mind running a gaming-house, but one needs such a vast sum to get started. There is always the possibility of a run on the bank!'

'No!'

'It will have to be the stage, then. Some actresses, I believe, are respectable.' Seeing disapproval still written on his face, she asked suspiciously, 'You're not a damned Evangelist, are you?'

'I am not, Tiffy, but whereas gentlemen can misspend their youths and be forgiven for it, ladies never are.'

'Then I am at *point non plus*. If I cannot run away to sea, or be a gypsy or a courtesan or an actress, what else is there?' she asked. 'I cannot remain at the vicarage. It is a living death for one accustomed, as I am, to a life of adventure.'

'Is it not possible that the friction at the vicarage is

caused by your being as intolerant of your relatives as they are of you?'

'Lord, yes,' she agreed cheerfully, 'but don't expect me to feel guilty about it. The one virtue I have is that I don't *pretend* to be a saint.'

Courteney knew he should not laugh, but he couldn't help it. 'Tiffy, you are a rogue!'

'Of course I am, and mean to remain one, but I shall never take advantage of your friendship,' she promised, then quite spoiled her effect by adding, 'at least, not very often.'

The half-hearted raindrops increased now, encouraging them to once more step up their pace. Tiffy's bruised knees were beginning to stiffen and she was hard put not to limp also, guessing that if the marquess suspected she was struggling, he would refuse what little aid she was able to give him. To take her mind off her discomfort, she remembered another piece of gossip she had heard, and remarked in her usual blunt fashion, 'You have had as little luck in love as you have had in war, my lord. Perhaps you should take up gambling, for everybody is entitled to be lucky at something. Or do you count yourself fortunate to discover *before* you married her what a miserable wretch your fiancée was?'

He stiffened, and his arm dropped from her shoulder. 'Miss Hunt is above reproach. I will not have her name bandied about in common gossip.'

'Hoity-toity,' Tiffy mocked, rushing in, as ever, where angels feared to tread. 'I heard she all but knocked the last nails in your coffin. Is it not true that you were so close to expiring when you were brought home from Portugal that Miss Hunt was summoned in a last desperate attempt to rally you? But when she saw you wasted to the bone by fever and with your face unhealed, she screamed and fainted and so robbed you of your will to live? Very pretty behaviour, I must say! If she did not love you, she should at least have known what was due to one of England's heroes. Above reproach, indeed! I never heard of anything shabbier in my life. Or is it all lies?'

Courteney's mouth tightened with an anguish far worse than physical pain. He was re-living the day Eleanor had been brought to him during one of his rare periods of clarity between bouts of fever. He recalled the great yearning that had filled him, and summoning all his strength he had stretched out a hand to her. She had recoiled, shock and revulsion on her face, and screamed. He also remembered wanting to die—but, against all the odds, he had lived.

'Well, my lord, is it all lies?' Tiffy prompted.

'It is grossly exaggerated. Miss Hunt was never my fiancée. An understanding existed between us, that is all,' Courteney replied curtly. 'She is an only child, and much loved. She has been so much protected from the harsh realities of life that it would have been remarkable if she had not fainted when presented with what was, after all, little more than a living corpse.'

'But it was you!'

'I was not in a recognisable condition.'

'You are now, and where is she?'

'Jamaica. Her father has estates there. It was thought she needed time to recover from her shock, and I from my wounds, before we met again.'

'What piffle! She needed her ears boxed. I am glad she is gone. You deserve better.'

'On the contrary, she is far more than I deserve.'

'If you believe that, you will believe anything. You seem a sensible man, so obviously you are besotted still. Don't glare at me so! I know it is as well to argue with a bedpost as with a man in love, so I shall say no more.' She put his arm back across her shoulder and smiled. 'There. Now we can be comfortable again.'

'Tiffy, you could talk your way into a noose and out of it again.'

She took this as a compliment, explaining, 'If Papa was an adventurer, then I am an adventuress, and a ready tongue is essential for survival. I did not mean to upset you, but it grieves me to see you unhappy. You are so nice! If Miss Hunt is vital to your happiness and you win her back, I shall be the first to wish you happy—and I'll try *very* hard to mean it. I can't be fairer than that, can I?'

Courteney smiled, but he still looked troubled. Tiffy raised her hand to cover his one resting on her shoulder, and squeezed it. 'My own life is very black at the moment, but I don't despair. Neither must you.'

Again he was a great deal touched and, to shake off the shadows of the past, he changed the subject. 'Not much further, Tiffy. You will not mind entering by the back door?'

'Indeed I shall,' she bridled. 'I am not a tradesman! Are you ashamed of me?'

'I am merely anxious to get you out of this cold and rain as quickly as possible. It is the entrance I always use when I am shooting in the home wood.'

'If your dignity isn't offended, I don't suppose mine should be,' she replied, although she was far from mollified. Her disappointment, however, swiftly vanished when she realised that the 'back door' was gained by passing through the portcullis entrance in the old castle walls. 'How deliciously medieval! What fun it would be to be thrown into a dungeon,' she said with a shudder of delight.

'It could be arranged, but it is almost time for luncheon and the servants are averse to serving meals in the dungeons. I dare say it is the cobwebs that puts them off. Or, perhaps, the ghosts of prisoners calling out for justice against the dastardly Harwoods.'

Tiffy glanced uncertainly at him, made up her mind and said with an unladylike snort, 'You will be crying out for justice if you don't stop teasing me.'

Courteney laughed and the sound reached the stable block where Tobias Wade was working. He was a bull-necked man somewhat below average height with massive arms, powerful shoulders, and a round, ruddy and incongruously cherubic face. His sparse greying hair was cropped short, a style he had adopted when he'd accompanied the marquess to the Peninsula and found himself much troubled by lice.

Tobias had the distinction of being the only servant the marquess referred to by his Christian name. He was his lordship's personal groom, and although he looked as clumsy as an ox, it had been largely due to his deft and dedicated nursing that his master had returned home alive.

He was as aware as any of his lordship's misery since Miss Hunt had so let him down, and the novelty of hearing him laugh in his old carefree way brought Tobias to the door of the tack-room. It was raining heavily. He had to repress the instinct to rush out and offer his aid when he saw the marquess was limping and leaning on a strange female, for none knew better than he how his master hated to be fussed. And so he watched and fretted and silently thanked the girl for causing his lordship to laugh like that. He wondered who she was.

The footman in splendid Dalmaine livery of blue and yellow who had been posted to watch for the marquess's return also wondered. The 'back door' Courteney had referred to was, in fact, the magnificently carved oak front door of a fine Tudor mansion that incorporated all that was left of the medieval keep, and it was flung open as its noble owner approached.

Tiffy, breathless and dripping, shook water from her like a dog that had received an unwelcome ducking and stared about her with appreciative eyes. She was in a great hall adorned with suits of armour, ancient weaponry, polished chests and tables and with a fine oak staircase leading to a minstrels' gallery above. 'Well!'

she exclaimed, well pleased. 'If this is the back entrance, I cannot wait to see the front. I would like above all things to try on one of those suits of armour. Did you ever do so when you were a boy?'

Courteney, relinquishing his gun and game-bag to the footman, smiled. 'Many times, with my brother Rolf. It was one of our favourite games until I got stuck fast in a helmet and needed a blacksmith to prise me out. My father put a stop to it after that.'

'Your father . . . Has he had been dead long? Or have you been a marquess only a little while?'

'He was killed fighting the French some years ago. I enlisted, of course.'

'I don't know about the "of course". I'm damned if I'd risk losing all this in some chancy campaign,' Tiffy responded, looking round.

A second footman, lingering longer than he ought, was recalled to his duties by the marquess beginning to lead his guest across the great hall. He sped away to warn all interested parties that the master had returned, soaked to the skin and accompanied by a young person whose respectability he could not vouch for since she was unescorted by maid or groom.

He left open the many doors separating the ancient wing of the house from the modern, and these were closed by the first footman, following his master at a discreet distance.

'What a rabbit-warren! I'm surprised you do not do your shooting here,' Tiffy commented, as Courteney led her through a labyrinth of passages, ignoring many she would have loved to explore had she not been so cold and wet. 'Will I meet your brother, my lord?'

The smile with which he greeted her earlier remark died from his eyes. They took on a faraway look, and he replied after a pause, 'He was killed in the Peninsula almost eighteen months ago.'

Instead of uttering the usual commiserations, Tiffy

exclaimed, 'Good gracious, are the French conducting a personal vendetta against you?'

'We are a military family. We have learned to bear our losses with our gains.' His hand indicated the grandeur of his home.

'Well, you have done your duty and lived to tell the tale. You will be selling out, I take it?'

'Not until the French are beaten.'

'You have been grievously wounded, and if you do not take that as a Grim Warning, you must have windmills in your head. There is, perhaps, insanity in your family? I believe it is often so with the highly bred.'

Amusement quivered in his voice as he replied, 'Some of my ancestors were noted for a certain—er—volatility of character, but I can't recall any of them ever being locked in the turrets.'

'That's something, at any rate, though why you must meddle in a war when you have so much to lose is quite beyond me.' Her opinion delivered, Tiffy's attention was diverted as they came to the end of the twisting passages and reached a long broad corridor.

In former times it had been a picture gallery, but now it served as a storehouse for relics from the Harwoods' acquisitive past that were out of favour with the modern generation. It was so crammed with display cabinets full of outmoded china and curios that Tiffy, casting a knowledgeable eye over the clutter, remarked, 'I trust you are in funds, my lord. I would hate to do your packing if you found yourself obliged to leave in a hurry.'

The footman behind them choked, but the sound was lost in Courteney's laughter. Tiffy said severely, 'It is no joke deciding what to take and what to leave when the bailiffs are at the door.'

'Don't fret for me. My estates are sufficient to support my style of life,' Courteney reassured her with masterly understatement.

'Rich, are you? How Papa would have loved to gamble with you. He once won the sweetest farm in New Hampshire. I *so* wanted to live there, just for a little while, but neither he nor Mama were suited to the rustic life. Which was just as well,' she added philosophically, 'for his luck turned, and he lost it again.'

There was no time for any more, since they now entered the inhabited wing of the house, where a reception committee awaited them. It comprised Farley, his lordship's butler, supported by a footman, and Mrs Royston, his housekeeper, supported by two maids. The marquess was observed to be wet and limping, and none of his retainers had the slightest difficulty in blaming the unknown female with him for this reprehensible state of affairs. They fixed their disapproving glances on her in a manner intended to shrivel her upon the spot.

If Tiffy had merited being described as an urchin a short while before, she had by now deteriorated into a rapscallion. Her shabby riding-habit was soaked and liberally splashed with mud, the rain had caused her cropped hair to curl more wildly than ever, and her cheeks were flushed. What was more, she met their critical eyes with the total unconcern of one who didn't give a hang what anybody thought about her.

Farley, relieving his master of the soaked shooting-jacket, paused for an infinitesimal moment to exchange an indignant look with Mrs Royston as the marquess quickly explained the circumstances of the accident which had caused Miss Yorke's presence here. By reason of a scullery maid at the castle having a sister employed in the same capacity at Honivale vicarage, the gossip surrounding the infamous Miss Yorke was well known to the Dalmaine servants.

His lordship, however, clearly expected the girl to be treated as a respectable guest. He ordered a groom to be sent to Creighton Hall, where he presumed Tarleton's horse would have returned by now, and to the vicarage, to say that Tiffy was safe and would be returned home later that day. Then, since her teeth were beginning to chatter as her chilled body reacted to the warmer atmosphere, he consigned her to Mrs Royston's care, assuring her she would be brought down to luncheon as soon as she was feeling more the thing.

Mrs Royston might be disapproving, but the marquess's word was law, so she led Tiffy up a secondary staircase and into a bedchamber where a fire had been lit. Tiffy ran towards the welcome warmth with hands outstretched, a position she tried to maintain against the odds as one maid stripped her and wrapped her in a towel while another departed for hot water. The fact that Tiffy was neither embarrassed nor overawed by all this attention, but responded as though she were accustomed to it, caused Mrs Royston to thaw slightly. Miss Yorke certainly wasn't behaving as if she had been raised among savages.

By the time she was arrayed in a high-waisted green gown with a demure collar and long sleeves, she was warm enough for hunger pangs to make rejoining his lordship downstairs of the highest priority. A slight hitch occurred when Tiffy refused point blank to wear the only shoes that could be found to fit her tiny feet. They were red, and *nothing* would induce her to wear them with green, but this difficulty was overcome when she said that an over-large brown pair would serve, provided she remembered to take small steps to reduce the possibility of them falling off.

Mrs Royston, with her own hands draping a large paisley shawl around Tiffy's shoulders, bore her off to rejoin his lordship, this time by the main staircase. It was a very grand one, sweeping in a gracious curve down to a hall paved with marble and adorned with busts on marble pillars, for this wing was built in the neo-classical Palladian style. Tiffy was impressed, and felt she was no longer in a castle but a palace.

There was a sudden commotion, and a gentleman in the fully glory of scarlet regimentals swept through the hall at such a pace that Farley and a footman almost had to run to keep up with him. He glanced up, saw Tiffy on the staircase, and paused.

The hall, which he had brought to life, now stilled, and her heart with it. Her cheeks flushed and her lips parted as the power of the man struck her. Cynical brown eyes set in a dangerously handsome face surveyed her in such a way that she felt as if she were being stripped. For some unaccountable reason her toes within her over-large shoes curled, and she felt he could see that, too.

A lesser girl would have flinched and cowered away from the implications of such a calculating and insolent gaze, but some age-old instinct within Tiffy recognised and rose proudly to meet the challenge. Her back stiffened, her chin lifted and she met his eyes with equal arrogance, quite unafraid.

The spell was broken when, his minute examination of her completed, he drawled, 'Good God, this must be Dalmaine's latest waif—or is it a stray?' He threw up a restraining hand as Mrs Royston opened her mouth to speak. 'No, I beg you not to introduce me. I do not share my noble cousin's chivalrous impulses, and I have already suffered enough ordeals for one day.'

He turned away, but swung back when Tiffy, who should have been annihilated, instead said coolly, 'So, too, have I. Permit me to thank you for sparing me another.'

'Don't cross swords with me, miss,' he warned softly. 'You would lose.'

'It's a poor gambler who counts the game won or lost before it has even begun!'

'True, but the stake has to be sufficiently tempting to get the game started, and you, alas, have nothing to offer beyond a remarkable pair of eyes. Most unusual, I grant you, but not enough for me to hazard one moment more of my time.'

He strode on with a clinking of spurs, pausing just long enough for Farley to hand him his gloves and shako and to settle a short military cape over his strong shoulders; then the footman was throwing open the doors.

Tiffy caught a brief glimpse of a groom struggling to hold a spirited horse in the driveway before the dominating scarlet figure blotted out the picture as he went through the door. It closed behind him.

He was gone, without so much as a backward wave, but his eyes and words continued to burn into Tiffy. Far from dying of humiliation, she breathed—with all the satisfaction of one who had discovered what she had been born for—'He's mine.'

CHAPTER THREE

No YOUNG lady teetering on the bridge between child-
hood and womanhood ever plunged more willingly into
the turbulent waters of love than Tiffy. She sensed that
she had found her natural element. No longer did she
wish to run away to sea or live like a gipsy. Within the
space of a few frantic heartbeats, her horizons had
widened to encompass delights far greater than any
offered by childish schemes of adventure.

No wonder Mama had run away with Papa! It had
been as inevitable as night following day. Tiffy herself
would have followed the man with cynical brown eyes
anywhere, had he but lifted a finger. That he had not
done so did not daunt her. She felt excited, invigorated,
reborn, and such heady emotions could not be thwarted.

Her eyes glinted, and a smile of anticipatory pleasure
curved her lips. *Dalmaine's waif*, indeed! How she
would teach him. And toy and tantalise. She wasn't
precisely sure how a woman managed these things,
but she would learn. She felt the power within her,
just as she had felt *his* power. Eagerness for their next
encounter caused her to demand with all the single-
mindedness in her nature, 'Who is he?'

Mrs Royston answered repressively, 'Mr Jago, miss.'

'Jago . . .' Tiffy murmured the name experimentally
and decided that she liked it. Nothing as mundane as
George or Frederick would do for *her* man. She added
abruptly, 'He looks a devil. Is he?'

Mrs Royston stiffened. She wasn't a tall woman, and
her round face was as homely as her plump figure, but
hers was a high position in this great household and she
had her dignity. She was not accustomed to being cross-

questioned in such a peremptory manner, particularly by a Nobody.

She continued her descent of the staircase, and the rustling of her black silk dress and the clinking of the keys hanging from the chatelaine at her waist seemed to echo her disapproval. She replied, when she felt a suitable length of time had passed, 'Mr Jago is a Harwood.' She managed to imply that this circumstance explained and, if necessary, forgave everything.

'A Harwood . . .' Tiffy seized on the vital scrap of information, and casting a shrewd look at Mrs Royston, fenced for more. 'That is sufficient, then, for him to act as if he owns this house?'

'Not yet he doesn't,' the housekeeper snapped, forgetting her hauteur in the heat of the moment because Tiffy had, by pure chance, discovered a chink in her armour. With her defences thus breached, she became very much more human and released a flood of further information.

'Mr Jago is his lordship's cousin, and his heir since Lord Rolf was killed, God rest his soul, and a curse on all tyrants who want to rule the world, French or otherwise. And now, if you please, his lordship is set on going back to that terrible war that is robbing us of all our best and finest men, and what is going to become of us all if he is killed?'

'I told him he had windmills in his head, but he wouldn't listen.'

'No, miss, he won't, even though he knows how much is at stake. We live by tradition here. For centuries the title has passed through the direct line from father to son, or brother to brother, and each of them bred to the responsibility. Now that Lord Rolf's gone, if his lordship dies without a son, the tradition will be broken.'

'A cousin is a very close relationship,' Tiffy pointed out.

'Not close enough for us. We're safe with his lordship. We don't have to fear our security will be thrown away on the gaming-tables, as has happened to so many other distinguished families, but it's no secret that Mr Jago is a rake and pursues a ruinous way of life. It's all very well for his lordship to say the responsibility of the marquisate would soon settle him down if, God forbid, the worst should happen—but that doesn't alter the fact that Mr Jago is not what we're used to and not what we want. We all pray that his lordship will not again risk himself abroad!'

'Mr Jago must be in similar danger! He was in uniform. Isn't he also on leave from the Peninsula?'

'No, miss. He's in the Volunteers, and he's down from London for the exercises that are going on in the neighbourhood this week. He will be called out only if the French should invade, and our navy isn't likely to let that happen, not after all these years of keeping them out. No, he's safe enough. The Volunteers do not serve abroad.'

Tiffy sighed with relief. So . . . he would remain within her orbit, this man she meant to make her own. Her satisfaction was short-lived, however, when she realised that once Courteney went abroad, her tenuous link with Jago would be cut.

She had so much to accomplish, and time and circumstance were against her. The green dress she was wearing might be more presentable than her riding-habit, but it was very childish. Mrs Royston had told her it belonged to Lady Augusta, Courteney's sister, who was married and living in Gloucestershire. Unfortunately, Lady Augusta was several inches taller than Tiffy, and nothing she had worn at a comparable age had fitted.

It was little wonder, Tiffy mused, that Jago had not been impressed by her. She was determined that the next time they met she would be very much in the mode.

Quite how this transformation was to be effected was not immediately clear, but she did not despair. Some means would present itself.

She was bubbling over with optimism when Mrs Royston led her into a spacious salon elegantly furnished in the French style of the previous century, announced her, and then curtsied and withdrew. Courteney was standing by the fireplace. He had changed his shooting garb for pale pantaloons, a dark blue waistcoat and a long-tailed coat of blue superfine which revealed to Tiffy for the first time that he had the same broad-shouldered, slim-hipped and athletic frame as his cousin. There the similarity ended, however, for there were dramatic differences in their colouring, manner and degree of good looks.

'Now I can believe you are a marquess!' she exclaimed, hurrying impetuously towards him with her hands outstretched. 'And look at me . . . Quite respectable! I don't mind losing my gamekeeper if you don't mind losing your waif.'

Courteney smiled, and clasped her hands. 'I never called you that.'

Tiffy wrinkled her pert nose. 'Your cousin did. *Dalmaine's waif*, to be exact. Furthermore, he commanded Mrs Royston not to introduce me because he had already endured enough today. Is he always so rude?'

The clasp on her hands tightened. 'He can be very charming, but I'm afraid he was not in the best of tempers. We had some business to discuss that was not quite to his liking. You must permit me to beg your pardon for him.'

'No fear! He can do his own apologising—one day.'

'Then *I* must beg your pardon. I would not for the world have had you upset while you are under my roof.'

'Poof! I am not in the least upset. I am fortunate

enough not to suffer from the excess of sensibility so many females are afflicted with.'

'He does not visit often. I doubt if you will be bothered by him again.'

This reassurance was the last thing Tiffy wanted, and she answered forcefully, 'I want to be bothered! I found him most diverting.'

'Bah!'

This derisory exclamation, coming from another part of the room, startled Tiffy into releasing Courteney's hands and swinging round. Her eyes widened in amazement as she took in the awesome glory of an ancient lady sitting bolt upright on a delicate giltwood sofa.

Lady Janetta, Dowager Marchioness of Dalmaine, disdaining to wear the flimsy high-waisted gowns she had no hesitation in denouncing as indecent, clung to the discomfort of the grand style of over thirty years before. She wore a quilted jacket over a low-cut gown of striped silk taffeta, its full skirt spread over a false rump and then looped up to reveal a quilted petticoat. Her thin hands clutched a malacca cane, her silk shoes had high heels, and her whole person seemed ablaze with jewels. On her head was an enormous turban of the same striking taffeta, so it was not surprising that Tiffy, for once, was struck speechless.

She was not to know that Lady Janetta was universally regarded as a holy terror, or that she gloried in her notoriety. She affected a blunt and ungrammatical mode of speech, delivered in the hunting-cry tones peculiar to some high-bred ladies. She normally resided at Bath, but that fashionable spa had been relieved of her intimidating presence when the news had been brought to her that Courteney was likely to follow his younger brother to the grave. She had returned post-haste to the castle to do battle with all and sundry, and Death in particular, avowing that over her own dead body would Courteney leave this life before providing Dalmaine with an heir.

It was not that she disapproved of Jago—indeed, he was her favourite grandson—but she was as great a traditionalist as Mrs Royston and believed the marquess should put his duty to his family before his duty to his country. She had approved of Eleanor Hunt as a match on grounds of breeding, fortune and malleability. But it was also she who had abused Eleanor so scornfully when she had recoiled from the desperately-ill marquess that the wretched girl had fled all the way to Jamaica.

Lady Janetta, seeing Courteney sink before her eyes, had then flung out all the fashionable doctors, hurled their leeches and bleeding-cups after them, and taken charge herself. With Tobias's help, she had nursed him back to life on a sturdy diet of beef and home-brewed ale. As the weeks passed, it became obvious that the emotional scars caused by Eleanor's inability to conceal her revulsion from Courteney would not heal as readily as his physical ones. Lady Janetta had stayed on at the castle in the hope that Eleanor's flight would be followed by an equally speedy return. If he would consider no substitute for her, and an heir to the title being of paramount importance, his lady-love had somehow to be coaxed back into the fold.

Lady Janetta had no sooner come to this conclusion when Courteney, having written to tell Eleanor he perfectly understood her behaviour and did not blame her for it, announced his intention of returning to the Peninsula in time for the spring campaign. This bombshell reduced Lady Janetta to near apoplexy, but since he was one of the few people who were not afraid of her, and was so rich himself that the promise of inheriting her own estates could not sway him, she was powerless to prevent his going.

When the news had been brought to her that his lordship had returned from a shooting expedition with an unaccompanied young lady who was the scandal of the neighbourhood, Lady Janetta had bestirred herself.

It was not her habit to go downstairs for luncheon, but spoiling for a fight and sensing a natural prey, she had surprised Courteney by joining him in the salon. The stony silence with which she listened to his entertaining account of his meeting with the dubious young lady had deepened into hostility when she had seen the affection-ate way in which Tiffy had held out her hands and rushed to him, and her outrage had finally been voiced in her derisory 'Bah!'

Having got the attention such an exclamation deserved, she promptly sought to put Tiffy out of countenance by going on to demand, 'What are you staring at, girl?'

Tiffy's hand fluttered to her heart, and she released her breath in a whoosh of relief. 'I thought you were a ghost!'

Lady Janetta's bosom swelled within the confines of her stiff bodice, but Courteney, betrayed into a chuckle, took Tiffy's hand and led her forward. 'Grandmama, permit me to present Miss Theodora Yorke. If she likes you, she will allow you to call her Tiffy. If she doesn't, she will very likely swear at you.'

'Will she, indeed? Then send her to the stables, where she'll doubtless feel at home. Nobody swears in this house.'

'Except yourself,' Courteney pointed out.

'I was sired by a duke and wedded to a marquess, so it ain't for me to mince my words,' Lady Janetta retorted. 'You know what, Dalmaine? It's my belief that fever turned your brain. When your own servants hold up their noses at a person, you shouldn't need telling she ain't fit to be presented to your grandmother.'

'Tiffy is my friend. If that isn't sufficient for you to feel a kindness for her, you can at least be civil,' Courteney answered with unruffled calm. 'Much as I dote on you, Grandmama, I cannot permit you to insult her.'

'Cannot permit . . . That's rich! As if you don't know I

can't abide the underbred and ain't likely to change my ways at my time of life. A friend! Bah! A fast baggage, if ever there was one. You're twenty-six, not sixteen. Too old to be taken in by the likes of her.'

'Well, if that isn't the outside of enough!' Tiffy exclaimed. 'If this is polite society, I hope I may never be around when it becomes impolite. And if rank carries with it the licence to be so shockingly rude when one hasn't been the least provoked, I can only say I'm glad to be a miss and not a marchioness. I am not positively sure what a fast baggage is, but I'm certain it must be preferable to being an antiquated fright!'

'Gallows-born brat!'

'Bigot!'

'Ladies . . .' Courteney began, wishing he had had time to warn Tiffy about his grandmother, and preparing to rescue her from the consequences of his oversight.

The glare he received from her flashing violet eyes, however, showed him that she stood in no such need of rescue, and Lady Janetta's resentment was equally evident when she commanded him to hold his tongue. Courteney, torn between the amusement that had touched all his dealings with Tiffy and his affectionate indulgence of his grandmother, retired from the lists like a seasoned campaigner who knew when the odds were against him.

Satisfied, they withdrew their attention from him, and Lady Janetta resumed the battle by snapping irritably, 'I forget where we were.'

'I called you a bigot,' Tiffy reminded her with relish.

'So you did—devil's spawn!'

Tiffy capped this by uttering what she considered the worst oath of all, 'Damned Evangelist!'

'Damned *what*? Lady Janetta thundered, her jewels quivering with outrage. 'Don't you dare class me with those sanctimonious spoilsports! I ain't no dog in the manger.'

'Then I beg your pardon,' Tiffy offered, willing to be fair to anybody who did not side with her relations. 'I'll think of something else.'

'What made you think I was one in the first place?' Lady Janetta demanded, seriously ruffled.

'Because you don't like me, and they don't, either. They think I am evil.'

'A pox on their opinions! Well, well! If they don't like you, maybe you ain't such a bad girl, after all.'

'Don't think to patronise me,' Tiffy retorted huffily.

'If I chose to patronise you, brat, you can count yourself fortunate—but don't think me won over yet. Just because Dalmaine chooses to hobnob with any brazen hussy he finds lurking in his woods . . .'

'I was not *lurking*!'

'. . . it don't follow that I choose to,' Lady Janetta continued. 'I don't hear you denying that you're a brazen hussy.'

'Why should I? It sounds exciting.'

'If that don't beat all!' Lady Janetta turned to Courteney. 'You better put her back where you found her. It's my belief she's dicked in the nob.'

The marquess smiled. 'I warned you Tiffy was un- usual. If she is insane, I can only say I wish there were more like her.'

'That's all very well, but it don't excuse bringing an unknown female into the house.'

'She is not unknown,' Courteney replied with un- impaired patience. 'She is, as you know well enough, Miss Theodora Yorke.'

'Of Swayle,' Tiffy supplied unexpectedly.

This piece of information meant nothing to the mar- quess, but it caused his grandmother to sit up even straighter. She stared at Tiffy as if seeing her for the first time, then demanded, 'Your father's name?'

'Francis.'

'Your grandfather's?'

'Julian,' Tiffy replied, her eyebrows puckering in bewilderment. 'He was a baron, and his title was Lord Swayle.'

'Good God,' Lady Janetta exclaimed faintly. 'You might have been my granddaughter . . .'

She had been surprised into referring to an indiscreet *affaire de coeur* that had been hushed up over forty years before, and regretted her words the instant they were uttered.

Tiffy echoed, 'Might have been your granddaughter? How could that be? Did you once intend to marry my grandfather?'

'A duke's daughter with a marquess on her string don't tie herself to a penniless baron,' Lady Janetta scoffed, taking the high line that had won her many an argument.

'Then why did you say what you did? Besides, my grandfather was not penniless. He was very young when he inherited the family title and became Lord Swayle; and the estate in Suffolk is a respectable one.'

'Penniless in comparison with the Dalmaine holdings,' the dowager maintained loftily. 'Quite apart from the question of rank. A baron, in case you're ignorant of the fact, is the fifth and lowest grade of the peerage.'

'None of which would have mattered a jot if he was as dashing and charming as my papa,' Tiffy answered with a shrewdness born of her meeting with Jago. 'A *princess* would have been glad to marry him. You did not—but say I might have been your granddaughter. You are hiding something. I know! You wanted him, but he didn't want you. Weren't you pretty enough? Or did he jilt you?'

'Jilt me?' Lady Janetta howled, her rouged cheeks taking on a purple hue. 'The damned rake ran off with me!'

'My grandfather kidnapped you?' Tiffy exclaimed.

'We-ell,' the dowager prevaricated. Then, realising

she had been betrayed into a further disastrous admission, snapped her mouth shut.

But she had said enough. Tiffy's face changed. She clapped her hands delightedly, dragged forward another giltwood chair and sat in it so that she could lean conspiratorily towards the affronted old lady. 'You were willing! I *adore* romances, especially when they lead to elopements. Was there a shocking scandal?'

'No there wasn't, nor is there anything to talk about!'

Tiffy, however, was not to be put off, and she guessed wildly, 'Your parents disapproved of my grandfather's character—that part *must* be right because *all* the Yorkes are unsteady—but he was your own true love and so you ran away with him. You were caught and dragged back before the knot was tied and forcibly parted. Poor Grandpapa was left to nurse a broken heart, and you were married off to the odious marquess to save your name.'

Courteney, quite unable to picture his grandmother in the role Tiffy had painted for her but deeply amused none the less, put in mildly, 'I have no wish to spoil a good story, but I don't believe my grandfather was odious. A trifle crusty upon occasion, perhaps, but otherwise a perfectly likeable man.'

'Oh, what do you men understand of anything?' Tiffy replied dismissively. 'He must have been odious to a bride who was crying her eyes out for another man.'

'Crying my eyes out?' Lady Janetta repeated. 'Let me tell you, my girl, that I was in high gig when I married Dalmaine! He was the catch of the season.'

'What about my grandfather? Did you abandon love for worldly considerations?'

'A girl don't stay green for ever, if that's what you mean. It's true my parents parted me from Julian, but it was only to be for a year or two while I had my come-out. I grew up and soon realised that Julian and I would never have suited, so I wed Dalmaine. He gave me the wealth and position I'm accustomed to, and that outlasts passion.'

'What a sorry ending,' Tiffy said disgustedly. 'I hope I never grow up if it makes one so *tame*. Did you never spare a thought for poor Grandpapa?'

Lady Janetta gave a crack of laughter. 'As often as he spared a thought for me. He wasted his inheritance with his gambling and gallivanting, then married a girl with enough money to sweeten her sour face. He was nearly in the suds again when a stroke put paid to his high jinks. From what I've heard, your father was no better.'

'My father had the good fortune to fall in love with a lady who, unlike you, was as constant as she was loving,' Tiffy retorted.

Lady Janetta mocked, 'I wonder if her husband thought so?'

'You,' Tiffy breathed, 'are a cat. I will not have my mother maligned!'

'Talking pays no tolls. Whatever your mother was, she did you no favours. You're a penniless brat, when all is said and done.'

'If you ran off with my grandfather, you're no better than you should be!'

'Stop raking over old coals. It ain't something I care to talk about,' Lady Janetta snapped.

'*Most* understandable,' Tiffy replied sweetly. 'Don't worry, your secret is perfectly safe with me. *I* do not gossip with the servants. I leave that sort of thing to dowagers and drapers.'

'Touché,' Courteney murmured, drawing an outraged glance from his grandmother, but she was robbed of her right to reply by Farley entering to announce that luncheon was served.

Courteney tactfully separated the ruffled ladies by placing himself between them and offering an arm to each. They maintained a dignified silence while they were led from the salon, but this was soon broken by

Lady Janetta saying irritably, 'What are you shuffling for, girl? Ain't you been taught to pick up your feet?'

'I am wearing borrowed shoes, and they fall off if I walk properly,' Tiffy defended herself.

Lady Janetta smirked, and remarked to Courteney, 'I suppose you'll go the whole hog next and turn the place into a poorhouse.'

'I am not a pauper,' Tiffy denied hotly. 'My own boots were soaked, and Mrs Royston fetched me an old pair of Lady Augusta's. It's not my fault she has such big feet.'

'The females in this family are renowned for their dainty feet,' the dowager returned indignantly.

'Dainty! A ploughman would be proud of these shoes. Oh!' Tiffy drew in her breath in a gasp and tugged at Courteney's arm. 'I did not mean to insult your sister. It was my accursed temper talking.'

He smiled reassuringly down at her. 'Augusta won't mind you using her big feet to score a point off our grandmother. She has felt the rough edge of her tongue too many times herself.'

'Don't talk about me as if I ain't here!' Lady Janetta swished herself and her voluminous skirts into the small room generally known as the breakfast parlour, where it was the marquess's whim to eat informal meals rather than in one of the grander dining-rooms. A cheerful fire burned in the grate, and three places were set at the oval table.

'How pleasant this is,' Tiffy remarked. 'Your home is very splendid, my lord, but it's a mystery to me how you manage to live in such state without contracting pneumonia.'

'It would be. You ain't bred to it,' Lady Janetta barked, then scowled around the room. 'If you were, you wouldn't think this room pleasant. It's cramped. There ain't room to swing a cat.'

'How gratifying for the cat,' Tiffy observed, her attention on the fine ham Courteney was carving. She smiled her approval of the generous slices he put on her plate.

The dowager ignored her. 'Dalmaine, what's this I hear about you ordering the five-acre field to be put under the plough next spring? That's pasture land, and always has been.'

They fell into an agricultural discussion of which Tiffy had no understanding, and less interest, and she was only too happy to give her full attention to the meal. Luncheon was normally a cold collation of cooked meats and fruit, but the cook, learning that the dowager and a female guest meant to grace the table, also sent in omelets delicately flavoured with herbs, and a trifle.

Tiffy was ravenous, and to Courteney's private delight, applied herself to all the treats set before her with gusto. Only when she was on her second portion of trifle did it occur to her that crossing swords with the dowager was the worst possible thing she could have done, and scarcely assisted her intention of entrenching herself with the Harwoods so that she might meet Jago again.

Courteney at that moment was dismissing the servants, and no sooner had the door closed behind them than Tiffy, swallowing hard, made her first sacrifice for love. The strain on her pride made her more curt than conciliatory, but she looked directly at the dowager and said without preamble, 'I was wrong to call you a fright and—and those other things. I have shown none of the courtesy due from a guest, and afforded you none of the deference and respect due to your age and rank. I beg your pardon.'

'Bravo, Tiffy,' Courteney said quietly.

But Lady Janetta merely snorted, 'If you think that is an apology, I take leave to tell you it ain't half of one.'

Tiffy's good intentions foundered on a flash of temper. 'Nobody could accuse you of generosity of spirit!'

'I'm glad to hear it. Dalmaine's got enough of that foolishness for one family.'

Tiffy's chair scraped along the polished floor as she thrust it back and jumped to her feet. 'How *dare* you call his lordship foolish! He is the best person I have ever met, and how he came to be one of you *insufferable* English I shall never know.'

'Tiffy!' Courteney broke in.

'Will you be quiet!' she shouted, rounding on him, and then her face became a picture of dismay. '*Never* interrupt me when I am speaking my mind. No good ever comes of it. I end up quarrelling with everybody, and you have not given me the least cause to be cross with you. Indeed,' she added, determined to make a clean breast of it, 'I am sorry I ever called you a misbegotten son of a bitch. I can only plead that I had no knowledge of your family then. It should have been *grandson* of a bitch.'

It was Lady Janetta's painted face that became a picture, but Courteney, struggling to keep his own face straight, merely demurred, 'Not misbegotten, Tiffy, please. I do have the look of the Harwoods. I have no reason to suspect I came to my honours by the—er —back door, so to speak.'

'Oh, you know what I mean,' she answered. 'You are a wretch to interpret literally an expression uttered in the heat of the moment. Damn! I am being rude again, and I truly never meant to be. It is your grandmother's fault for bringing out the beast in me when I was determined to be on my best behaviour. It's my belief she *enjoys* being disagreeable!'

But Tiffy had unexpectedly and unknowingly risen in Lady Janetta's esteem, and she was repeating with deep appreciation, 'Misbegotten son of a bitch. I ain't heard that one before, and I thought I knew 'em all. I don't mean to forget it, either. Fits like a glove a good dozen people I don't like. Sit down, girl, and pass me that trifle. There might be a scrap left that's escaped your attention.'

'There is a great deal left. I am not a pig.' Tiffy put the dish before the dowager but she did not sit down, saying instead to Courteney, 'What do you wish me to do, my lord? If you regret bringing me home, say so, and I shall leave.'

Courteney stood up and came round the table to her. He surprised her, and caused his grandmother to stare, by raising her hand to his lips and kissing it lightly. Then he resettled her in her chair, saying with a rueful smile, 'Half the world is terrified of my grandmother, and with good reason. You have fought her to a draw, and entertained her, I believe, as much as you have entertained me. Don't run away now and leave me at her mercy. I would rather face a brigade of French Dragoons!'

'If you are not ashamed of me, I would face a brigade of *grandmothers* for your sake,' she assured him stoutly.

'I knew I might depend on you.' He rested a hand on her shoulder in an unconsciously protective gesture and looked across the table at the dowager. 'Oblige me by ceasing to bait Tiffy. She has defended herself against enough unmerited insults.'

'What about the insults she has hurled at me!'

'You cannot complain at having your own weapons used against you. I am declaring a truce, so that she can finish her meal in peace.'

'A truce. Bah! I don't believe in 'em,' Lady Janetta replied with all her usual contempt but less of her usual conviction. She recognised a gauntlet when it was flung down and, for once, declined to pick it up. Her caution was due to a certain tone in Courteney's voice. It told her she was not dealing with her grandson but with the Marquess of Dalmaine, the head of his house and the ultimate authority in the family.

He was, in effect, pulling rank on her, and up until this moment she had believed there was no limit to his indulgence of her. To find that this was not so was a nasty shock, and she transferred her attention to the girl who was the cause of it. Tiffy Yorke. Bah! She was all eyes and impudence and nothing more—or was she? The danger was in the name. *Yorke!*

If Tiffy had inherited the charm of the Yorkes, and learned how to use it, that was a different matter. Lady Janetta could not forget how she herself had been prepared to outrage her parents and throw away her dazzling marriage prospects just to lie in Julian Yorke's arms.

Courteney loved Eleanor Hunt, of that there was no doubt, but she didn't miss the significance of the protective hand he had laid on Tiffy's shoulder. Nor was she blind to the special quality of the smile they exchanged before he once more took his place at the table. The girl must be watched. She must be watched very closely indeed.

CHAPTER FOUR

IT COULD NOT be hoped that a few words of rebuke would reduce a lady of the dowager's mettle to silence but for the moment it suited her purpose to let Tiffy dominate the conversation. Given enough rope, the chit would surely hang herself.

Dalmaine was the very model of propriety. Anybody as outrageously unconventional as Tiffy Yorke could not hope to hold his regard for long, and the amusement with which he currently regarded her would presently turn to disgust.

It was a novel experience for the marchioness to feel grateful for Dalmaine's staidness. Up until this point it had been a constant source of mystery and disappointment to her that one of her grandsons—and the most important one at that!—could have turned out to be such a dull dog.

Generally, all Harwoods lived to excess and settled down only on marriage to retrench and provide for the pleasures of the succeeding generation. Jago, now, was a proper Harwood. So, too, had young Rolf been. But Dalmaine, upon whom the reputation and traditions of the Harwoods ultimately depended, had never, to the dowager's chagrin, been known to take one step from the path of duty and decorum. In addition, he was full of the most ridiculous middle-class scruples which, more than anything, put her out of all patience with him.

Lady Janetta properly believed that *noblesse oblige* extended no further than subscribing to fashionable charities when one was reminded of them, seeing that one's tenants were properly housed, and ensuring that one's entire workforce was inoculated against the smallpox, whether willing or not. Anything in excess of this ceased to be obligation, and deteriorated into meddling in matters which were beneath one's notice.

Yet, no matter how many times she told Dalmaine that no good ever came of meddling, meddle he would! He had a soft heart, and she could more readily have forgiven him for having a soft head. The casualties of war, for example, when invalided out of the army or navy, could generally be expected to earn a living begging in the streets if they could not find proper work, yet Dalmaine had seen fit to employ hordes of them on his various estates. One could scarcely take a drive round his lands on a pleasant afternoon without being startled half to death by a one-eyed, one-legged or one-armed veteran snapping to attention and grinning fit to bust.

It was true that Dalmaine's championing of Tiffy Yorke could not quite be classed with the duty he felt towards these deplorable relics of England's military glory, but the principle was the same. He never knew where to draw the line between civility and charity, and so his good nature was imposed upon.

One question at least was resolved by the time they had left the breakfast parlour and were re-established in the salon. Tiffy *had* inherited her full share of the Yorke charm, and it was all the more effective because she was entirely unconscious of it. At the moment she was entertaining Dalmaine with an account of her passage to England when, purse-pinched, she had travelled steerage class and would have starved had she not earned her bread by singing bawdy songs for the sailors and hymns and soulful ballads for the more respectable passengers. She appeared to have no idea that a young lady, reduced to such dire levels, would afterwards have died rather than utter one word about it. Tiffy was all laughter and appeared to relish the experience.

Lady Janetta observed, 'They say the road to the

gallows is a merry one! Enjoy yourself while you can, brat.'

Tiffy responded with an infectious grin, 'I mean to.'

'Hmph! There ain't a horse faster than the devil rides. Why ain't you still in Suffolk? Don't the Yorkes recognise you?'

'Yes, but preferably from a distance. My uncle Yorke, the present Lord Swayle, said one more skeleton rattling around the family cupboard wouldn't make much difference, but his wife did not like me. She gives herself a great many airs and graces and said she couldn't be expected to have the living reminder of a dreadful family scandal under her roof, and I must go. She fell into *such* a rage when I offered to return to America if they transferred to me the yearly remittance paid to my father to stay abroad. It seems that although it is perfectly acceptable to banish a man, it is quite reprehensible to do so to an orphan girl, even if she wants to be banished.'

Tiffy paused, shrugged, and sighed. 'The upshot was I was packed off to the Everetts, with the Swayles paying for my keep, although considering the *rags* I have to wear, one would never think it. The Everetts do not like me any better than Lady Swayle, but, as they are Evangelists and committed to helping the needy, it would cast them in a bad light to shun me. I am saving their Christian faces while they save my Christian soul, or some such nonsense.'

Courteney smiled. He was seated on the same sofa as Tiffy, and when she glanced at him, he slipped unawares into his habit of turning his face away.

She leaned forward swiftly and slapped his scarred cheek, the sound seeming to echo in that quiet and gracious room. 'Stop behaving as though that scar matters. I am a girl of my word, and you must learn not to offend me unless you want a very sore cheek indeed!'

Courteney, catching hold of her fingers and holding

them lightly for a moment, replied ruefully, 'I trust I have no other habits you find offensive.'

'Nary a one, and pray don't pay me back by relating mine. I have dozens of them, including my blasphemous speech.'

'Some of your expressions don't sound pretty on a young girl's lips,' he agreed, expecting her to glower at the criticism.

But she merely looked much struck. He could not know it, but with Jago to impress, his words worked powerfully on her. She asked intently, 'Does my accent also distress you?'

'No, I find it charming.'

She looked pleased. 'First the pill and then the sugar. The Everetts could learn a great deal from you. I will try to think before I speak. *Pray* don't slap me when I err, though, because it is bound to be often, and I don't care for having my ears boxed. A look will be enough. Do we have a pact?'

'We do.'

'To go with the bond?'

'Bond, what bond?' Lady Janetta demanded, misliking the sound of that.

'It would take too long to explain,' Courteney answered.

'I'm not sure that I could,' Tiffy put in, looking thoughtful. 'It is one of those things that Papa always described as Life's Intangibles. It is something that is *felt*, not understood. One cannot explain what one cannot understand, only accept it. Do you see?'

Lady Janetta didn't, but Courteney finished the discussion by rising and going over to pull the bell-rope beside the fireplace. 'I must take you home, Tiffy. My coachman knows the road well, but I cannot expect him to drive in the dark.'

The animation fled from Tiffy's face. She looked at the window and saw that the short January afternoon was almost spent, then said wistfully, 'I hope I may come back. The vicarage will seem drearier than ever now.'

'It ain't good manners to invite yourself,' Lady Janetta reproved her, then told Courteney, 'if you're mad enough to invite her, for pity's sake make sure her relations ain't with her. It's a close-run thing, but all in all, I prefer the poor to the pious.'

'I wish you would stop calling me poor,' Tiffy interjected indignantly. 'I might be at a stand, but I don't mean to remain so.'

'If you're thinking of holding up a carriage, make sure it ain't mine. My coachman will shoot you.'

'Grandmama, please don't put any more wild ideas in her head,' Courteney begged. 'She has enough already.'

'Oh, I won't break the law,' Tiffy assured him. 'Papa says it never answers. I shall think of something perfectly legal—or as near as makes no difference.'

Farley, entering in response to his lordship's summons, put an end to private conversation, and soon Mrs Royston arrived to take charge of Tiffy.

The room seemed curiously empty after she had gone, and Lady Janetta said abruptly. 'She's trouble, Dalmaine. I don't say she means to be, but she can't help it. She's a true Yorke. I see it in her careless ways and in that mischievous smile of hers. A deuced attractive lot, the Yorkes, full of the devil's own charm, but they're unruly. They go far beyond what is permissible, my word on it.'

Courteney was once more standing by the fire. 'You knew her grandfather. If he was such a rake, why did he exile his son for following in his own footsteps?'

'It ain't a puzzle when you think of it. Julian had had the stroke that put paid to his high living by that time. They do say there's nothing as bad as a reformed rake, and remember that the reformation was forced on Julian. Besides, Francis was a younger son and not very important.'

'Even so, it seems unfair.'

Lady Janetta laughed. 'Not if you know the Yorkes. They're a selfish brood and make no secret of it, so one forgives 'em, I'm not sure why. Tiffy's father was expensive and a nuisance. There was nothing for it but to send him packing when he eloped with a married lady —and a poor one at that. One can't countenance a scandal with *no* mitigating circumstances. Well, Julian and Francis are dead and gone, and better forgotten, but that ain't likely now this chit has turned up. What do you mean to do about her?'

'I was rather hoping you would do something.'

'It's my body that's senile, not my brains. I got too much sense to get involved in her games, and don't think she ain't playing any, because she is.'

Courteney stirred the logs with his booted foot, causing one to crumble and send a shower of sparks up the chimney. 'She is trying to escape the vicarage, and I don't think she can be blamed for that. I believe the gossip-mongers call her infamous, yet the true infamy is to blame her for her parents' misdeeds. She has had a rough time since her father died and has borne it with the most amazing fortitude and humour. I want to make life pleasanter for her, and I need your help. The gossips would be busier than ever if I befriended her, but nothing would be said if you took an interest in her.'

'A great deal would be said,' Lady Janetta snorted. 'Me, befriend a penniless waif, when everybody knows I ain't charitably inclined! It would be thought very odd indeed.'

The marquess smiled slightly. 'You are thought very odd already.'

'Thank you,' the dowager replied with awful politeness. 'But I ain't odd enough to sponsor Tiffy Yorke along the road to the devil, and that's the route she'll take, you mark my words.'

Courteney eyed her set face for several moments,

then changed tactics. 'There is the matter of the five-acre field. If you really wish me to oblige you by cancelling my orders to have it ploughed up for grain, you will oblige me in this matter of Tiffy.'

Lady Janetta thumped her cane on the floor. 'That's blackmail.'

'I would prefer to call it an arrangement to our mutual benefit. The five-acre field remains pasture, and Tiffy's life is brightened a little.'

'You may call it what you please, but I want no part of it.'

Courteney argued no further. He bowed politely and strode towards the door. The dowager snapped, 'What do you mean to do now?'

He paused and glanced at her. 'Help Tiffy, naturally.'

'I don't see what's natural about it. You'll cause a scandal, and that's *unnatural* for you,' Lady Janetta scoffed. 'You ain't Jago.'

'No,' Courteney agreed quietly, 'but I am a Harwood, and I rather think the time has come for me to prove it . . .'

'God save us, Dalmaine! Your own back yard ain't the place to kick up a lark. Nor can you treat a baron's niece like a bit of muslin. If you're feeling that way inclined, get up to Town and choose a woman who knows what she's about, not a schoolroom miss whose relatives will see that right is done by her. If you're hot for Tiffy Yorke, let someone else ruin her first, then you can safely indulge yourself. You won't be kept on the fret for long.'

Courteney, the easiest-going of men, stiffened with hauteur. 'Kindly rid yourself of the notion that there is anything disreputable in my relationship with Tiffy. She is more child than woman and, in my hands, will remain so.'

'Stuff! Deceive yourself if you like, but I'm too long in the tooth to be taken in. Don't get on your high ropes with me, neither. You can't say you're going to prove you're a Harwood one moment and play the saint the next.'

'One doesn't have to be scandalous to be a Harwood, merely selfish. It is an accusation you made against the Yorkes, and I can only wonder at it because there is no family where the trait is more ingrained than our own. And I mean to be very selfish over Tiffy. I need her . . .'

'I knew it!' Lady Janetta broke in. 'The girl's bewitched you. It's those great eyes of hers. No wonder she's got her relations all of a'twitter.'

Courteney continued inexorably, 'I need her . . .'

'And I'm telling you that you can't have her. Not yet.'

'. . . to laugh at me,' he concluded.

'*What?*'

The austerity vanished from the marquess's expression and his eyes lit with laughter. 'It's what's so precious about Tiffy—the way she scoffs at all the puffed-up nonsense this society of ours calls good breeding. We've become over-civilised, Grandmother. We need someone like Tiffy to make us laugh at ourselves.'

'I don't see any joke in being laughed at, and I don't intend to. She's impertinent enough without you encouraging her.'

'I don't mean to encourage her, but I do mean to enjoy her.'

'What do you mean by that?' Lady Janetta asked, her eyes narrowing.

'Bring a sacred cow within Tiffy's reach, and she will most certainly kick it. My scarred face was something of a sacred cow, you know, with everybody afraid to look at it or even mention it. Then I met Tiffy. She was so patently unimpressed by my person, my consequence or my scar that I could not help but see how I had allowed my setbacks to become swollen out of all proportion to their importance. There was she, in worse circumstances than mine, wringing what she could from life—and there was I, with so much, moping because I had to exist at all. Tiffy is a tonic better than any physician could possibly prescribe, and I owe her far more than I can possibly repay.'

It took the dowager a few moments to digest this, then she said, 'I take it you mean to make her one of your charity cases?'

Courteney frowned. 'If you think that, you haven't understood a word I've said, and I can only beg you not to put the notion into Tiffy's head. She has a proud spirit that has been bruised enough already.'

'Don't give her feelings another thought. She ain't got any, or, if she has, she won't let them stand in the way of her advancement. As for her present predicament, you didn't cause it, so it's not for you to cure. You've too many scruples and too little sense. The chit is like a cat. Fling her whichever way you please, and she will land on her feet.'

'Understand me, Grandmother. If you will not lend respectability to my friendship with Tiffy, I shall enlist the aid of one of our female relations who will. It's a pity Augusta was so recently confined. She would be the very person.'

'You'd get your own sister mixed up in your intrigues?'

Courteney stifled his exasperation. 'There is no intrigue. Cousin Almeria could come at short notice.'

'The minute that woman steps into this house, I step out of it,' the dowager threatened. 'She sniffs.'

'Aunt Verity, then.'

'Never! She's shabby-genteel and there ain't no hiding it. Prices everything down to the last penny like a cursed tradesman. And don't go through the rest of the dirty dishes among our relations, because I don't approve of any of them.'

'Nevertheless, one of them will be installed within a very few days. It would grieve me to make your stay here unhappy, but the remedy is in your hands.'

Lady Janetta's jaw dropped. 'You would send me packing to gratify Tiffy Yorke? Is that all the thanks I get for saving you from sticking your spoon into the wall?'

'I am, and always shall be, aware of what I owe you—but I am also aware of your motives. You were saving the marquess, not the man. You have a secure place in my affections but I know I have no similar place in yours. I am not reproaching you, merely stating a fact, because I understand what a disappointment I am to you. Jago has always been Jago, but since I inherited the title, you have never called me anything other than Dalmaine.'

'That's tradition,' the dowager blustered.

'How very cold tradition is.'

The dowager was silenced, but not for long. 'It ain't that I don't like you, it's just that you've got some dashed queer notions. You don't seem to know how a marquess should behave.'

He laughed. 'Tiffy will teach me. She also thinks I'm a sorry speciman. If style and luxury is what she wants to make her forget the miserable time she has had, then style and luxury she shall have. Will you not stay, Grandmother, to observe how full of my own consequence I am about to become? You might be vastly entertained.'

Lady Janetta fought a silent struggle with herself. She had no wish to encourage Tiffy, but even less was she willing to stand aside while Dalmaine ruined himself. 'Oh, very well,' she snapped finally. 'You may invite the minx here in my name.'

'Thank you, Grandmother. You won't have to bestir yourself to entertain her. I shall see to that.' He raised her thin fingers to his lips, and kissed them.

'Very pretty, when you have blackmailed and badgered me into submission. I don't approve, mind, and neither will Eleanor if she hears of it. Unless——'

her eyes brightened suddenly '—you are playing a deep game. Is this a ruse to bring Eleanor to heel?'

'No,' Courteney replied, and walked to the door to make good his escape before they fell to quarrelling again.

A few minutes later, Tiffy came down the grand staircase for the second time that day. She had changed out of Lady Augusta's dress and was again wearing her riding-habit. The mud had been sponged from it, and it had been dried, but no amount of refurbishing could make it look anything other than dowdy. Her spirits drooped because she knew that if Jago should chance once more to come through the hall, he would be as unimpressed by her as he had the first time.

This lowering reflection did not stop her heart skipping a beat when she heard movement below, nor could it prevent her leaning over the banister. It was not Jago with his magnetic aura of danger who stood by the front door, however. It was Courteney, who could not look dangerous if he tried.

She resumed her descent, watching Farley help his master into a greatcoat and then hand him a high-crowned beaver hat. Courteney, predictably, set it at a precise angle on his fair head and then accepted gloves of York tan and a short malacca cane from a footman powdered and liveried in the flamboyant style of Lady Janetta's youth.

'You have your waif back,' she said, giving her faded skirt a disconsolate twitch when she joined him.

'Poor Tiffy. Down in the dumps again?' Courteney asked.

'Anyone would be, going back to the vicarage,' she grumbled, but when the door was flung open her spirits rose mercurially. Awaiting her pleasure was a highly polished chaise with the Dalmaine crest painted and gilded upon the door panel, and harnessed to it was a team of four splendidly matched greys. Beside the

coachman in his cocked hat and many-caped driving coat
sat Tobias.

Courteney, as he led Tiffy down the steps to the
carriage, had the satisfaction of watching a glow of
pleasure spread across her face. She breathed ecstati-
cally, 'What a bang-up turn-out. How the Everetts will
stare!' She glanced back over her shoulder. 'I suppose
we couldn't take a footman with us?'

It was with difficulty that Courteney kept a straight
face as he handed her into the carriage and replied, 'I'm
afraid not.'

A hot brick was placed at her feet, a thick rug spread
across her knees, but she was not prepared to give up her
footman without a fight. 'Just one,' she wheedled. 'It
would be such a triumph for me, the despised Tiffy
Yorke, to walk into the vicarage with a footman in
attendance. Only think of Cassy's face!'

Only think of mine, Courteney thought, but replied,
'You'll have to make do with a marquess, peculiar as I
am.'

Tiffy's slanting eyebrows drew together. 'Who called
you peculiar?'

'You did.' He smiled reminiscently. 'And shabby.'

'Oh! Well, we both know I am liable to say anything
when I am in a mood. What's more, I think it is shocking
of you to remind me of it. If I were cursed with sensibility, I might feel obliged to blush. However, I will forgive
you if I might have a footman. Why, when you have been
such a *honey* about everything else, can't I?'

Courteney told her as tactfully as he could, 'It is vulgar
to display too much ostentation, Tiffy.'

She looked horrified. 'How good of you to tell me.
Papa taught me that vulgarity is the one unforgivable
sin, and must be shunned at all times. The thing is,' she
added naïvely, 'I didn't know a marquess *could* be
vulgar. One lives and learns. Pray tip me the wink if I
should say or do anything that is not good *ton*. I don't at

all mind being depraved, but I must never be uncouth.'

Keeping his reflections on her strange standards to himself, the marquess rapped on the roof with his cane. The carriage started, and they settled back on the blue velvet squabs to be driven through the miles of parkland that separated the estate from the road. Courteney, uninterested in the scenery on that damp January afternoon, contented himself with watching the various expressions that flitted across her face.

The frown that presently descended on her brow prompted him to remark, 'You're looking very fierce.'

'I am at a stand. I have been trying to think of a way I might invite myself back without seeming encroaching or underbred, and there is no such way.'

'Then you have been biting your lip for nothing. My grandmother charges me to ask the Everetts if you may spend tomorrow with her.'

Tiffy stared. 'Nothing but the rack could have wrung such an invitation from her! She hates me. This must be your doing.'

'She doesn't hate you, or nothing could have compelled her to oblige me. You must understand that the clock stopped for her when Grandfather died. She has disapproved of everything that has happened ever since. It started with my mother being set in her place when my father succeeded to the title. She turned her back on the world and has fought a heavy rearguard action ever since. I admire her tremendously, but my cousin Jago is the only person outside her own generation she actually likes. He has the knack of treating her as if she were still a great belle.'

Tiffy, delighted that the conversation had turned to Jago, fished, 'You said he could be charming. Is that what you meant?'

'He is certainly popular with the ladies.'

'He is not a rival for Eleanor—I mean, Miss Hunt?' Tiffy exclaimed, sitting upright.

'Fortunately Miss Hunt is the one lady immune to his charm.' Mistaking Tiffy's alarm for concern for his own chances, he added, 'You must not worry on my behalf. I am capable of fighting my own battles.'

'I'm sure you are,' she murmured, privately thinking that in matters of the heart he would stand a poor chance against Jago. 'Is your cousin's interest fixed on somebody else?'

'If it is, it won't be for long.'

Tiffy, well pleased that she had no particular rival, suggested, 'No doubt he will settle down when he meets the right lady.'

'If such a lady exists.'

She exists all right, Tiffy thought, but afraid of arousing his suspicions, she let the subject drop.

A diversion was caused by the carriage slowing as it approached the main gates. A man ran out from the gatehouse to open them, and bowed as the carriage passed. When they once more picked up speed, she turned her brilliant eyes on Courteney and said anxiously, 'My lord, pray *try* to be more intimidating when you meet my uncle. He is in love with the sound of his own voice, and nothing will stop him talking unless he is totally overawed. Do you think, for a little while, you could be more like your grandmother?'

'Not unless I borrowed her turban.'

Tiffy giggled. 'Do be serious! I am in disgrace for leaving my room before serving my full week's punishment for running off with the gipsies, then for quarrelling with my uncle and taking Tarleton's horse. I fear my uncle might not let me visit you tomorrow. It all boils down to whom he fears displeasing most, an earthly lord like you or——' she pointed a finger upwards '——the one up there.'

Courteney grinned. 'I am out of the contest. It is my grandmother who invites you. It would be difficult to refuse her without giving offence. Had I invited you myself, it would have been necessary to invite your aunt or cousin to accompany you, and I knew you wouldn't like that.'

''Strewth, no! I don't mean to share you with the Everetts if I can help it. The only reason I am puffing you off now is to save me from a scold and another week's incarceration in my room. Cassy has crowed over me for so long that now I have the chance to crow back, I shall make her *squirm*! Yes, I know it is shocking of me, but I never pretended to have any virtues.'

'Save the virtue of honesty?' Courteney quizzed.

'Don't stake your shirt upon it, my lord. You must remember I am an adventuress and never *wholly* to be trusted. I like you enormously, but that would not stop me doing something you might think reprehensible if it suited me.'

'You put me in a quake. Are you going to rob Lady Janetta's carriage, after all?'

'Is that your grandmother's name? How very pretty. She must have merited it once, for she is still very taking when she is not frowning, although that is not often. But, no, I don't intend anything as *blatant* as robbery—and I wish you would stop smiling when I am giving you a most *serious* warning to be on your guard against me.'

Courteney, perceiving that she was indeed serious, asked, 'Why do so, then, when it is surely against your best interests?'

'You have been very fair with me, and I wish to be fair with you. I am also,' Tiffy added on a less high-minded plane, 'clearing my conscience. If I should find myself forced—and I would have to be *forced*, mind!—to serve you a mean trick, I need not feel so badly about it now I have put you on your guard.'

'Whenever I have my guard up against you, Tiffy, you have the habit of slipping under it.'

She favoured him with her warmest smile. 'What an

encouraging thing to say. It makes me think I am born to succeed.'

'It makes me think my safest course is to set you down by the wayside and forget I ever knew you.'

Far from displaying alarm, Tiffy chuckled. 'Yes, but only think how poor spirited! For all your quietness *nothing*, my lord, will persuade me you are easily put in a *quake*, as you called it. On the contrary, I think you showed a great deal of bottom in standing up to Lady Janetta as you did, considering that you have to live with her and I do not.' She broke off as the marquess's shoulders began to shake, and exclaimed, 'Now what have I said?'

'Enough to convince me that your friendship is worth all the risks it entails,' Courteney assured her. 'Only, Tiffy, in any company other than mine own pray do not mention "bottom" to signify courage. It is an expression used only by gentlemen.'

'Oh? I can't think why, but I will remember.' Then, noticing the slackening pace of the horses, she glanced out of the window and saw they had almost reached the vicarage. This prompted her to change the subject abruptly. 'Are you sure you love Eleanor Hunt, my lord?' she asked.

There was an infinitesimal pause while he bit back the snub that rose to his lips before he answered, 'Yes, I'm sure.'

'Good! That will keep you safe from Cassy. She is classically featured, being an Everett like my mother, and it would not suit me at all if you became enamoured of her. Besides, she is a prig, and would be an even worse match for you than your faint-hearted lady. Oh! Pray consider those words unsaid. I have no wish to hurt you. Indeed, whenever I do so I seem also to hurt myself. I don't know why that is, but it is most uncomfortable.'

Her ingenuousness once more disarmed him. When the chaise stopped and Tobias jumped down to open the door and let down the steps, Courteney helped her to descend, then said, 'Lead on, you rogue. The Everetts can say nothing that will take me aback as many times as you have.'

'That's the spirit,' Tiffy approved as they began to walk up the path to the house. Mindful of how very difficult and pedantic her uncle could be in matters involving his cherished Christian duty, she searched her mind for further means to fortify the marquess against his coming ordeal. 'If you should find yourself hard-pressed, do not despair. Just remind yourself that you are very nearly a duke!'

The marquess's step faltered and he began to laugh. 'Thank God I am not! You would very likely want me to bring my butler with me.'

Tiffy, who had been been regarding him anxiously, broke into a relieved smile. 'Oh, you are *laughing*. I thought you were having a fit of the vapours, which is not to be wondered at. I mean, anyone would, having to meet my relations.'

Courteney took her arm and shook her. 'Not another word, Tiffy.' As she opened her mouth to argue, he insisted, 'Not one. Unless you want to ruin everything, you will leave this to me.'

'Well, I never!' she breathed. 'You are doing it!'

'Doing what?'

'Being a proper marquess. Isn't it amazing what one is capable of when one really tries. Now we shall come off all right and tight. In fact,' she added thoughtfully, 'I shouldn't wonder at it if I end up being impressed with you myself. My papa, you know, always maintained that it is as wasteful to underplay oneself as it is one's hand. He was a very wise man, don't you think?'

The marquess did not trust himself to give an opinion on her beloved father, and merely wondered aloud, 'Why didn't I shoot you while I had the chance?'

'You do not like corpses littering your home wood,'

she reminded him impatiently. 'Only do stop funning. You can't have forgotten you are here to rescue me from the *direst* straits, and you must know that if ever you were imperilled, I would do my *damndest* to bring you off safely.'

Courteney regarded her a moment longer. 'I believe you would, too,' he murmured and, once more overwhelmed by the urge to protect her, not least from herself, he began to walk on.

CHAPTER FIVE

THE VICARAGE could not, of course, compete in splendour with the castle, but it was a gracefully proportioned early Georgian structure, its ten bedrooms intended to house a family larger than the single daughter the Everetts had produced. The living at Honivale was a respectable one, being worth £300 a year, and the Reverend Hector possessed a private income that almost doubled this amount, so he was well able to provide his family with the comforts of life. It was rumoured that the showy blood mare he had recently purchased so that his daughter might hack about the countryside in style was worth not a penny less than 200 guineas, and that his wife had expended a comparable amount on new clothes for her. Both rumours were, for once, perfectly true.

Cassy was a year older than Tiffy, and decidedly pretty, and it had not escaped the notice of her devoted parents that Tarleton Creighton was becoming Most Particular in his attentions. High-minded though they were, they were not above doing their worldly best to promote so notable a match. What had escaped their notice, however, was that their own indulgence and Tarleton's attentions had quite turned Cassy's head. She gave Tiffy her cast-off clothing pretty much as a duchess might have distributed largesse among the poor, but Tiffy, neither cowed nor obliging enough to assume the role of grateful pauper, reacted with all the proud contempt of one who had the blood of an ancient barony flowing in her veins.

It was, in truth, Tiffy's strong connection with the nobility that sabotaged Cassy's sense of superiority and made her dislike her cousin so much. Furthermore, attempts to chasten Tiffy by slighting remarks about her parentage awoke no latent inferiority but such immediate and unbridled fury that it was no rare occurrence for Cassy to flee screaming for protection against the savage from across the Atlantic.

Mr and Mrs Everett, had their wisdom matched their goodness, could have eased the situation by using the money provided by the Yorkes for Tiffy's keep to purchase the things she needed, and thus free her from dependence on Cassy's charity. This they were reluctant to do on two counts, the first being that Tiffy's behaviour merited no reward, and the second that if she were allowed to bloom before she had Seen the Light, she might catch some young buck's fancy—with scandalous consequences.

This, then, was the fraught situation Courteney was about to be plunged into, and Tiffy, observing the drawing-room curtains twitch on their approach, felt her bosom swell with triumph. The door was opened by a flustered maid who dropped a deep curtsy, led the way to the drawing-room and announced the marquess in the same awe-filled tones she would have used to announce the Second Coming.

The fetching tableau that met Courteney's and Tiffy's eyes was too rigid to be natural and had, in fact, been most carefully arranged to display the Everett family to best advantage. Mrs Everett, a tall thin woman with grey-flecked hair and a fixed expression of sweetness, had honoured the occasion by donning her very best gown of bronze-green crêpe and was occupied in the artistic arrangement of a bowl of snowdrops. Her husband, wearing the dark clothes of his calling, and with his distinguishing shock of white hair brushed back from his handsome face, was seated in a chair, scholastically absorbed in a leather-bound book of great weight.

Cassy was seated close to the fire, becomingly and

industriously setting stitches in a tapestry supported before her in a free-standing wooden frame. Her fair hair had been curled into ringlets, secured by ribbons to bunch over her ears. If her blue eyes and regular features fell short of true beauty, she was undoubtedly as pretty as her father was handsome.

The Everetts, having swiftly appraised the marquess, just as swiftly removed their gaze from his scarred countenance. Courteney, sensing the storm that was about to burst from the small and wrathful person by his side, pressed Tiffy's arm warningly. He smiled slightly as she glanced up, gave a slight shake of his head, then advanced into the room to offer his hand to each of his hosts in turn—and within a very few minutes had them all eating out of it.

Tiffy was left with nothing to do but marvel. Nobody could doubt they were in the august presence of The Most Honourable the Marquess of Dalmaine, possessor of an earldom besides, and a whole clutch of lesser titles. He was impeccably correct and showed no hint of condescension as he admired Mrs Everett's snowdrop arrangement, inspected Cassy's skill with the wools, and expressed the hope that Mr Everett was not too sadly overworked with such a large and rambling parish in his charge.

He then took upon his own shoulders the blame for Tiffy's prolonged absence from the vicarage, contrived to make her wicked misdeeds appear no more than mischievous pranks, and commended them for undertaking the difficult task of easing her into an entirely new way of life. They were further to be congratulated, he said, for the success they had achieved thus far without damaging her refreshing and highly individualistic spirit.

Before the Everetts could recover from this leveller, he explained that the ducal family of his grandmother, the dowager marchioness, had been intimate with the Yorke family two generations before, and she had been delighted to meet the granddaughter of her old friend. In fact, she had been so taken by Tiffy's natural and unaffected manner that she desired her to visit again tomorrow. A carriage would collect Tiffy at ten and she would be returned before nightfall.

The Reverend Hector, quite dazed by the marquess's eloquence and more used to having a similar effect himself, raised his resonant and cherished voice to moralise on the folly of young females who allowed their minds to be overset by frivolity and social ambition. He might have continued for some time in this vein had not the marquess said he need have no fears on Tiffy's behalf, since the dowager was renowned for her disapproval of rackety females.

This, in view of Tiffy's equally renowned rackety behaviour, not unnaturally robbed the Reverend Hector of all power of speech. Courteney, having achieved all he had set out to do and with his gravity in danger of being overset by the unholy glee sparkling in Tiffy's eyes, judged it time to beat a retreat.

He took punctilious leave of the Everetts, clasped Tiffy's hand briefly, bade her rest and tend her bruises so that she would not have to disappoint Lady Janetta by crying off the following day, and departed in the devout hope that her whispered, 'Masterly, my lord. A duke couldn't have done better!' had not reached the ears of her mentors.

If the silence he left behind was prolonged, it was because the Everetts, staring at Tiffy with bewildered eyes, were wondering what an earth such an exalted personage could see in their despised young relation. It was left to Cassy to break the silence, and she did so by remarking soulfully, 'That dreadful scar! What an affliction it must be to the poor man.'

Tiffy's head snapped up. 'Not half such an affliction as having to endure remarks like yours. The scar is not dreadful, and even if it were, it could not lessen such a kindly gentleman. You surprise me, Cassy. I thought your parents raised you not to regard appearances as everything. I know mine did!'

'Well!' Cassy exclaimed, flushing. 'Since when did you become an expert on proper behaviour? In fact, I wish somebody would tell me what the marquess could possibly find to approve in such an improper person as you!'

'He knows that, whatever I am, I fly under my true colours. I do not smile at his face and make rude remarks behind his back.'

'You! You . . . !' Cassy spluttered. 'How dare you criticise me. You are not fit to criticise a *servant*.'

'That is quite enough, Cassy,' her father rebuked. 'A lady should never betray an unbecoming violence of feelings.'

'Blame *her*!' Cassy shouted. 'I must have been contaminated by her presence.'

'Do not raise your voice to your father,' Mrs Everett intervened, shocked.

'She is the hoyden. Scold her,' Cassy flung back, beside herself with anger. 'I don't know what artful or deceitful ways she used to make the marquess and Lady Janetta believe she is worthy of their notice, but we know her better, and such ways will not succeed here.'

Tiffy, thinking with delight that only the deepest jealousy could have made Cassy betray her spiteful side so disastrously, informed her, 'I used no arts or deceit, but was completely honest about myself and my circumstances. I was mindful of your papa's maxim that virtue is its own reward.'

This sign that their diligent teachings were at last beginning to bear fruit had a profound effect on the Reverend Hector and his wife, but Cassy was goaded into sneering, 'Liar! Loathsome, toad-eating, snivelling liar! Your tongue will be all over spots, and that will serve you right. I hate you.'

'Cassandra!' her father thundered in the tone he

adopted for doing direct battle with the devil, and upon his hapless daughter fell a lecture so stern and all-encompassing that she wept.

Only Tiffy, deeply appreciative of each tear that fell, guessed that they were not the cleansing tears of penitence but the bitter tears of rage and chagrin, and she thoroughly enjoyed her cousin's downfall. Presently, and possibly because she had heard the Reverend Hector in full flight so many times before, her mind drifted to where it really wanted to be—with Jago. Her uncle's voice became no more than a background drone as she re-lived every word Jago had spoken to her. She progressed from fact to even more agreeable fantasy, mentally acting out various scenes with him and eventually deciding that her favourite one was where he knelt as an adoring slave at her feet.

The improbability of such an arrogant gentleman as Jago ever kneeling at anybody's feet, adoringly or otherwise, presently dawned on her, and she chuckled at her own absurdity. The background drone ceased. The silence that followed penetrated her private world, and she returned to reality to discover that her uncle's most unwelcome attention was now upon her.

'What have I said to arouse such mirth in you?' he asked in pained reproof.

Cassy raised her bowed head and shot a look of malevolent triumph at her discomfited cousin. It inspired Tiffy to lie as only she could lie when in a very tight spot. 'I was thinking, Uncle, that with your voice you would have made a very fine actor had not you been called upon to do the Lord's work. I dare say you would have been as famous as David Garrick. It is still said of him that his voice commanded attention, just as your does. Only with you disapproving of theatres as sinful places, the notion is ridiculous, which is why I chuckled. I beg your pardon if I interrupted you.'

Cassy's mouth rounded into an 'O' of disbelief, but

Tiffy had touched on one of the little vanities that made the Reverend Hector, at times, quite human. 'Well, well, he said. 'An apology must always be accepted in the spirit in which it is offered. I feared your mind was wandering, but after your accident you must be tired. You may leave the room if you wish to rest before dinner.'

Tiffy went thankfully to the door, only pausing to say, 'Aunt, I think I will take the marquess's advice and tend to my bruises. May I ask Doris to fill a bath for me?'

Cassy jumped up. 'I also want to bathe, so you must wait. Mother, you can't expect me to get into her muddy water! I always go first.'

Her plea, for once, fell upon deaf ears. Mrs Everett, dazzled by the prospect of a social connection with the Harwoods and believing it might make Sir Geoffrey look more kindly on a match between Cassy and Tarleton, was anxious that Tiffy should say nothing to the marquess that would put the Everetts in a bad light. She was not an unkind woman, but she wished belatedly that she had treated Tiffy more like her own daughter. She refused to admit, even to herself, that a goodly proportion of her resentment at having Tiffy thrust upon the family stemmed from a fear that she might one day outshine Cassy.

What amends could be made, however, must be made, and she replied, 'Tiffy will bathe first. It will be a small concession to make after your unchristian remarks this afternoon. In fact, now that you put me in mind of it, I believe it would be fairer in future if you girls took turns in bathing first.'

Cassy appealed to her father. 'Tiffy is the wicked, blasphemous one. Am I to be scolded and punished while she escapes scot-free? It isn't fair, Papa. You know it isn't!'

The Reverend Hector did know but didn't care to have the fact pointed out to him, nor could he tolerate criticism from his daughter. 'Go to your room, and while

Tiffy is bathing you can reflect on the impropriety of defying your parents by thought, word or deed. There is, as Lord Dalmaine pointed out, some excuse for Tiffy's behaviour since she is new to a Christian and civilised way of life. There is no excuse for yours. Reflect and repent, Cassy, so that you might return to the path of righteousness.'

Cassy stormed through the door Tiffy was holding open, and when the girls were alone in the passage, she hissed, 'You little worm! Don't think you can queen it over me just because you've met a marquess and his silly grandmother has taken a fancy to you.'

Tiffy grinned. 'Green eyes.'

Cassy stamped her foot. 'You'll come to a bad end!'

'It will be in the very best of company. The truth is, Cassy, that there are those of us who are born to stay at home and embroider tapestries—and those of us who aren't.'

'I am the one who will be safe!'

'Poor Cassy.'

'Don't pity me,' Cassy said between clenched teeth. 'Pity yourself. I don't dare to guess what will happen to you.'

'But I can tell you,' Tiffy replied, patting her bouncing curls in a new and shockingly provocative manner. 'I am the one who will be loved.'

Having gained an inch in the aristocratic stronghold of the Harwoods, Tiffy naturally took a mile. Although nobody was too sure how it came about, she spent not one but all her days at the castle, where Courteney allowed her to run wild. Her impetuous footsteps, frank comments and ready laughter were heard from the dungeons in the medieval wing to the sumptuous state apartments in the newest, so it was always a matter of conjecture where she would show up next.

This caused much consternation among the stiff-necked senior servants. Inclined as they were to regard anybody born outside the rustic boundaries of Kent as foreigners, they wouldn't have been surprised if she had suddenly produced a tomahawk and broken into a war-dance.

If she disappointed them in this, she amazed their master by showing an unexpected thirst for culture. Not that she had the slightest intention of becoming a blue-stocking; she was merely determined that when the worldly Jago crossed her path again, he would discover 'Dalmaine's waif' was no uneducated hick.

Since the first Harwood had hung a tapestry on his stone walls and set a jewelled goblet on his rough-hewn table, his successors had been dedicated to the embel-lishment of their domain. Consequently, Tiffy was able to compare a Rubens with a Rembrandt, or a Caravag-gio with a Velasquez, from original examples, and to pore over chests full of sketches and etchings.

The long gallery revealed examples of most of the more famous portraitists' work, and Tiffy lingered a long time over the last to be hung, a portrait of Courteney. He was depicted in all the braided and laced magni-ficence of a captain of Hussars. A sash was wound round his waist. A fur-trimmed pelisse slung from one shoulder partially covered his dark blue jacket. His braided trousers disappeared into gleaming Hessian boots, and a heavily carved and wicked-looking sword was clasped in his hand.

The portrait had been painted four years ago, before Courteney had suffered the loss of his brother and so many of his friends, and observing almost with disbelief his then cheerful and unlined countenance, he smiled and said, 'You have my permission, Tiffy, to denounce me as a posturing popinjay.'

'I shouldn't think you were ever that,' she answered thoughtfully. 'But certainly you have improved.'

'*Improved!*'

'Of course.' She raised her hand and touched his scar. 'You *needed* that touch of character carved into your face. There won't be any danger in future of your being outshone by your uniform.'

'What a habit you have of putting me in my place,' he murmured. 'That's my fond memories of once being a splendid young fellow gone for all time.'

'And good riddance to them, too,' she replied cheerfully, tucking her arm in his in her companionable way. 'It's far more profitable to look to the future than to the past. Only think! If you hadn't been wounded and brought home you would never have met me, and we've already agreed that would have been a rare pleasure missed.'

Courteney laughed, as he so often did in her presence, then bore her off to study a collection of miniatures. On other days he taught her to distinguish Sèvres china from Meissen and Dresden, initiated her into the more baffling art of identifying one dynasty from another in Oriental porcelain, or chose books for her to read from the extensive library.

She was not slow, as ever, to air her grievances, and in her usual forthright manner told Courteney of Cassy's refusal to let her ride the showy mare. The Reverend Hector permitted her to ride his ancient hack when he was not using it, but it was a slug, and refused to jump. She was starved, she said, of a decent gallop. Courteney went into consultation with Tobias, and once Tiffy had proved she was as accomplished a rider as she was intrepid, a spirited but viceless grey gelding was selected for her exclusive use. It quite shone down Cassy's mare, and Tiffy's cup of happiness brimmed over, so that she was once more obliged to borrow the marquess's handkerchief. Thereafter they enjoyed a brisk gallop daily, with Tobias accompanying them as an unlikely duenna. The marquess was giving the gossips no opportunity to whisper.

The benefits of her daily absence from the be-leaguered vicarage were felt immediately. Peace reigned between the hours of ten in the morning and four in the afternoon. Cassy was the only inmate of the vicarage to regard Tiffy's friendship with the Harwoods as the worst thing that could have happened. Jealous from the start, her resentment increased as day followed day without her being included in an invitation to the castle. She became impatient with the leisurely pace of Tarleton's courtship, seeing him as her only chance of reclaiming the centre stage from Tiffy.

A married lady had far more consequence than an unmarried one, and all the prestige of making a brilliant match would be hers. Thirsting for such glory, she employed all the arts she knew to bring Tarleton up to scratch. She became adept at, seemingly accidentally, brushing her soft bosom against his chest as she passed him in the confines of the parlour or passage. She lifted her skirts high enough when she sat down for him to glimpse her shapely ankles, and even grew bold enough to permit him an occasional flash of the pretty lace edging on her long drawers.

Tiffy, preparing in her own way for the role of temp-tress, had no idea her cousin was ahead of her in the field. Although she derived wicked satisfaction from Cassy's jealousy and frustration, she could do little more than leave her to stew in her own juice while she took on a more formidable opponent. Lady Janetta, as cross as crabs, was doing her redoubtable best to oust Tiffy from Dalmaine Castle, and her tactics had all the finesse of a battering-ram. Tiffy, nothing loath, met each onslaught head-on without relinquishing a fraction of the place she had won in Courteney's affections and consequently his home.

These battles took place round the luncheon table where the dowager appeared daily, ostensibly to lend countenance to Courteney's and Tiffy's friendship, but in reality to finish it. The insults and epithets flew, scorching the ears of master and servants alike, and ultimately achieving an effect nobody could have predicted. Lady Janetta and Tiffy, invigorating rather than exhausting each other, became during their clashes the very best of enemies, and at other, quieter, times as thick as thieves.

This came about because the marquess, busy formulating plans for the management of his estates while he was abroad, sometimes had to leave Tiffy to her own devices. It was on one of these occasions that the dowager chanced upon Tiffy in the library throwing dice, playing one hand against the other.

Lady Janetta was far more passionately attached to gaming than she ever had been to her husband or her beaux. She bore Tiffy off to her apartments, where they indulged in a close and earnest game of hazard. As Tiffy was allowed no pin-money, they played for vast but mythical stakes, a fortunate circumstance since both were ruthlessly dedicated to winning, and not always by scrupulous means. Hazard led by natural progression to cards, with Tiffy sometimes, magnanimous after a run of luck, teaching the dowager a sleight-of-hand trick that had not previously come her way. Thus by degrees, and in an entirely different way, the dowager found the young scapegrace from America every bit as entertaining a companion as the marquess did.

Just before Tiffy had thrust herself into the Harwood stronghold, Lady Janetta had been temporarily deprived of her usual companion, an indigent but inoffensive relative on the distaff side, by her being called away to nurse her sister's family through an influenza epidemic. When Tiffy stepped into the breach no other dared to fill, the dowager's temper improved tremendously. The servants noticed, just as they noticed that the marquess had lost his careworn look, but they were conservative diehards down to the meanest scullery maid, and would not readily admit that the presence of the infamous Miss Yorke was proving to be more of a pleasure than a plague.

The first servant of importance to crumble before Tiffy's careless charm was Tobias. He watched her closely, eventually coming to the conclusion that even if she was a scheming little minx as everybody maintained, it didn't matter, because she clearly wasn't scheming to be a marchioness. She neither flattered nor fawned on nor flirted with the marquess. It took him well into the second week of her daily visits to the castle to decide that his master needed no protection from her, and thereafter he unbent towards her. Towards the end of that second week, an incident occurred that won him over completely.

It was one of those mornings when Tiffy was left to amuse herself, Courteney having gone off with his bailiff to inspect a tract of marshland with a view to its possible drainage and conversion to agricultural use. Napoleon's Continental Blockade had brought all but illicit trading with Europe to a halt, and with a rapidly rising population, England needed all the food she could produce.

Since the dowager was a late riser and the morning particularly cold and drizzly, Tiffy had curled up by the fire in the library to fill some of the glaring gaps in her literary education. To sustain her through her study, she had the marquess's promise of a good stiff gallop at noon, when she was to meet him at the stables. If the frequent glances she shot at the elegant French ormolu clock on the mantelpiece was anything to go by, she was very much on the fret to cast her books aside.

At half-past eleven she did so, racing up the grand staircase to the guest-room set aside for her use, and thereby betraying another gap in her education. A well-brought-up lady never arrived anywhere breathless, as Tiffy invariably did. She threw aside her maroon morning dress with its long straight sleeves and single unadorned flounce and changed into her riding-habit which, for convenience's sake, she kept at the castle.

She arrived, still breathless but with a few minutes to spare, at the stables, to find she was ahead of the marquess. The ground was soaked, the driving wind had a keen cutting edge and the drizzle was thrown in gusts at her face, but she scoffed when Tobias said it was a rough day for riding.

'The wind and the rain will drive the cobwebs away. I've spent a dreary morning with the poets—Milton mostly, whom I don't appreciate quite as much as I should since my uncle Everett approves of him so much. However, his lordship said I should read him and so I have, and a good gallop will be my reward.'

'A fine poet, Milton,' Tobias replied. 'Seems to me, Miss Tiffy, you'd be better off reading some more than riding out on a day like this.'

'You may have the poets with my blessing, Tobias. I have a very contrary nature, and the knowledge that I should do something unhappily puts me off. If it hadn't been for this gallop, I couldn't have stuck at it as long as I did. Where *is* his lordship? It isn't like him to be late. Was he driving or riding?'

'He was on foot.' Tobias's voice was heavy with disapproval.

'Hell and damnation! I mean, good gracious, whatever for?'

'He believes in tramping over his own land whenever he is able. He says it gives him a better knowledge of it than he would get on horseback.'

'For all the world as though he were a tenant farmer or a bumpkin of a squire!' Tiffy exclaimed. 'Couldn't you stop him?'

'Bless you, miss, do you think I wouldn't if I could? A very stubborn man, his lordship, and he can't abide being fussed.'

'He's been gone two hours! His injured leg will be hurting him.'

'I fear so, and that marshland down by the river is very heavy going.' His round face and blue eyes were expressionless as he added, 'Not that you have to worry about your gallop, Miss Tiffy. He won't cry off. Not if he was dying he wouldn't, once he's promised. If he's limping, he won't regard it.'

At that moment Courteney rounded the corner of the stable block, and both Tobias and Tiffy saw that he was limping heavily. As if to prove his servant's words, he said, 'A thousand pardons for keeping you waiting, Tiffy. We'll be off immediately. The ground's too soggy for a cracking ride, but if we take the road up to the downs we should get at least a tolerable one.'

Tiffy saw that his face was quite grey and that his smile did not quite erase the lines of pain about his mouth. Her eyes met Tobias's, and she didn't need to be told they were of one mind. She returned her attention to Courteney, and replied, 'I've got a headache. I thought it would pass once I was in the fresh air, but the wind is so cold it's making it worse. Would you think me too shocking a spoilsport if I stayed indoors? There's such a lovely fire in the library. Once you have changed out of those wet things you could join me there, and—and explain some lines of Milton I don't properly understand.'

Forgoing a ride, for whatever reason, was so unlike her that Courteney was completely taken in. He put an arm around her shoulders and began to lead her across the cobbles. 'You shouldn't have stayed out here to wait for me. Come on, it's back to the fire with you.' He looked over his shoulder at Tobias. 'Put the horses away. We won't be needing them today.'

'Yes, my lord.' Tobias's stolid countenance admirably concealed his gratitude at Tiffy's masterly way of sparing the marquess the ordeal of a ride and, knowing what a sacrifice it had been for her, he volunteered, 'If Miss Tiffy's headache should go away, and the weather improve, she could ride back to the vicarage this afternoon if she wanted. I'd go with her and bring the horse back.'

Tiffy peered back over Courteney's arm. 'Thank you, Tobias. I should like that! If this silly headache goes away, of course.'

Tobias nodded, well satisfied.. And shortly afterwards, when he repaired to the servants' hall for lunch, he let it be known that Miss Tiffy was 'all right'.

This, from so phlegmatic a person as Tobias, was high praise indeed. Since he was also the servant closest to the marquess, and quite the fiercest in his protection of him, it had a most dramatic effect. The servants' ranks opened, and when they closed again Tiffy was, metaphorically speaking, safely within the fold. Thereafter, no criticism of her was encouraged, no gossip from outside tolerated. The castle, as it had for centuries, protected its own. Tiffy had no knowledge of the change in her status when, dramatically recovered, she rode home that afternoon with Tobias beside her. Neither of them mentioned her play-acting at the stables at noon, but theirs was the silence of understanding.

When they had galloped the friskiness out of their horses and slowed to a canter, Tiffy's thoughts turned to the one cloud on her horizon—her lack of funds. The problem of how to raise the ready to rig herself out in the first style of fashion was as far from being solved as it had ever been.

Her return to the vicarage was usually observed, but when she said goodbye to Tobias at the gate and watched him ride off with the gelding, the house had a deserted air. She remembered then that the Reverend Hector and his wife were visiting the incumbent of the neighbouring parish, and she assumed that Cassy, unwilling at breakfast, had been persuaded to accompany them. As always, she was reluctant to go into the house; it was like stepping back into a cage. She was dawdling along the path to the front door when she saw Tabitha, the vicarage cat, slink across the yard at the side of the house to the stables.

A few days earlier Tabitha had produced kittens, but Tiffy had not seen them yet, hard as she had searched for the nest. She decided to have another look, and changing direction, crept after the secretive cat. Entering the stables noiselessly, she stood listening. A rustle came from the hayloft above the stalls, and going forward on tiptoe, she went stealthily up the ladder.

As her head came level with the loft she saw, not the cat, but a sight so unexpected that she stopped short. A pair of booted feet were almost in her face. She crept up another rung. The tailored breeches emerging from the boots covered the easily recognisable plump legs and bottom of Tarleton Creighton. His jacket was discarded, his white shirt rumpled and his plump shoulders partially obscured the damsel clasped in his arms.

Tiffy could see only a pair of slipperless feet, a fair stretch of legs and the flounce of a pink gown trimmed with green rosettes. It was enough. She propped her elbows on the ladder, dropped her dimpled chin in her hands, and said with wicked delight, 'Well, well, Cassy! Is this how you do your Christian duty when your parents are away?'

CHAPTER SIX

COLD WATER couldn't have had a more dramatic effect. Cassy and Tarleton jerked apart and set up a great rustling of straw as they scrambled into sitting positions to stare at Tiffy with dropped jaws and appalled eyes. She watched with deep appreciation the guilty colour burning up from their necks to the roots of their dishevelled hair. Oh, life was good! To have caught them so, these paragons of propriety, was more than she could have hoped for. Now The Colonial Cousin, as Cassy so disparagingly called her, could return with interest every slight she had been made to endure.

But, more than that, she recognised that here was the golden opportunity for which she had been waiting. If she played her cards right—and how could Papa's daughter fail?—she would soon be rigged out in fine style for Jago's appreciation.

'What would Mama and Papa say,' she asked provocatively, 'if they could see their saintly daughter now?'

'It—it is not what you think,' Cassy blustered, pushing back her tangled ringlets from her flushed face. 'Tarleton was—was helping me to look for the kittens.'

'Did he expect to find them inside your bodice?' Tiffy's eyes dropped pointedly to her cousin's ample breasts, gleaming with naked paleness in the dim and musty loft.

Cassy followed her gaze, gasped, and made a wild lunge to pull her loosened bodice together. She also abandoned all pretence of innocence. 'You beast! Creeping about and spying on people.'

'I have had such an excellent teacher in you.'

Cassy reddened again. 'How I hate you! This is all your fault. You and your precious marquess. Ha! He will never marry you, but Tarleton will marry me. I shall be Lady Creighton. You will always be nobody!'

'You mean that to become somebody I must first allow myself to be tumbled in the hay like a common strumpet?'

'You . . . You . . .' Cassy stuttered.

Tiffy grinned. 'Careful. Don't tempt me to call you "whore".'

''Pon my soul, it isn't as bad as that,' Tarleton exclaimed, finding his tongue at last. He looked the picture of unhappiness. It was impossible to play off the airs of the exquisite, which he dearly loved to do, while in his shirtsleeves with his high starched collar points wilting and his cravat sadly rumpled. It was no secret that he aspired to become an arbiter of taste and fashion—a latter-day Beau Brummell, in fact—but he was miserably certain the Beau would never have allowed himself to be caught in such a predicament. Or, if he had, he would have brought himself off safely with some witty quip. Lacking the necessary quickness of mind, and certain that ruin stared him in the face, Tarleton could only repeat wretchedly, 'Not as bad as that.'

'I wouldn't wager a groat on Cassy's parents believing you,' Tiffy told him.

In her opinion, he was not much of a man at all. He was a little above average height and tolerably good looking, but an over-fondness for good food and wine, combined with a dislike of physical exertion, was beginning to blur face and figure alike.

He pleaded, 'They must never know! Try to understand. This is the first time Cassy and I have ever been alone together. It—it went to my head.'

'Your loins, surely?' Tiffy corrected sweetly.

Cassy gasped, but Tarleton only groaned and buried his pomaded head in his hands. Tiffy, realising he was too craven to offer real sport, returned her attention to Cassy. 'Pray button your bodice. Your bosom is falling out again, and I don't find the sight as edifying as Tarleton. I shouldn't think your parents would, either, and they will be back soon. What *do* you mean to say to them?'

'They will be delighted to hear I am betrothed,' Cassy retorted defiantly.

Her words alarmed Tarleton out of his dejection. 'Cassy, no! You can't tell them that. It isn't true. I can't declare myself without my father's approval.'

She turned on him. 'Your father, your father, that's all I ever hear! Am I to understand you have only been trifling with me?'

'Lord, no, but dash it, you know my circumstances. You always have. The property is not entailed. My father says he'll leave it to my brother Jack if I marry to disoblige him. He can't stop the title coming to me, but we can't live on that. I'm a gentleman. I don't know how to earn my bread.'

'I will not allow myself to dwindle into an old maid waiting for your father to give us his blessing. You must force it out of him,' Cassy insisted.

'That's easily said,' he retorted, nettled. 'Only show me how it may be done!'

'Elope,' Tiffy broke in mischievously. 'You will have your love to sustain you, even if you have to live in poverty.'

'Elope?' Cassy echoed. 'My character would be ruined!'

'L—live in poverty?' Tarleton faltered. 'I couldn't do that. I mean, I couldn't expect Cassy to.'

Tiffy said in disgust, 'Your lust is stronger than your love; therefore I am left with no alternative but to save you from the consequences of it.'

'What do you mean?' Cassy asked, all suspicion.

'I must tell your parents what I have witnessed, of

course. Indeed, it is my Christian duty to do so. How else can I prevent you cavorting as if you are in season whenever Tarleton comes tom-catting over here?'

'How dare you!' Cassy exploded. 'If you tell, I shall . . . I shall . . .'

'Yes? What will you do?'

Cassy could think of nothing she could do to Tiffy that would equal what would happen to herself if her parents found out, and her defiance collapsed. 'You cannot tell,' she pleaded. 'It would be too dastardly.'

'Pretty talk, coming from you! Since the day I arrived here, you've sneaked on me. When you had no tales to tell, you made them up so that I would be punished. You deserve all that's coming to you.'

'I shall say you are lying. My word will be believed above yours.'

'You are forgetting Tarleton. He's just assured us he's a gentleman, and gentlemen do not lie. He will, in honour, have to support me.'

'He'll say whatever I tell him to say!' Cassy's well-modulated voice rose with anger.

'For pity's sake, don't set up a screech,' Tarleton begged. 'You'll have the servants on us. There will be no hushing up anything then.'

'Cook and Doris? Poof! They could be bribed quickly enough.' Cassy's blue eyes gleamed with sudden hope as she turned them on Tiffy. 'Say nothing, and I shall let you ride my mare whenever you wish.'

Tiffy almost laughed. At last the argument was heading in the right direction, but she shrugged away the offer. 'I prefer Lord Dalmaine's gelding.'

'I'll give you my fur tippet and muff.'

'Paltry moleskin. No, thanks.'

'What do you want, then?'

Tiffy's moment had come. She climbed off the ladder into the hayloft and sat down. 'Nothing from you. My silence might be won, however, if Tarleton could summon up enough manly spirit to perform a small service for me.'

'Name it,' Cassy replied eagerly.

'Here, I say, not so fast,' Tarleton objected. 'If we get mixed up in one of her bacon-brained schemes, we'll be out of the frying-pan and into the fire before we know what's what.'

'We're already in the fire,' Cassy snapped. 'If my father hears of this, he will be impossible! You do not know what he can be like.'

'I do,' Tiffy intervened. 'He will be full of righteous wrath. For my own part, Tarleton, I'd rather take on the devil. It's not my uncle's style to take a whip to you, but he'll batter you half to death with words. When he stops, Mrs Everett will add her mite. The one thunders and the other whines. Then you will have to face your father. Perhaps he will exile you, as my father was exiled for loving imprudently. That *might* be a good thing, because it will get you away from the Reverend Hector—but you will need a taste for adventure to survive.'

Tarleton had no such taste, as Tiffy knew only too well, and he listened to her recital of the horrors in store for him with an expression of ludicrous dismay on his fleshy face. His pallid complexion took on a greenish tinge as he gulped, and grasped the straw she offered. 'I'll—I'll be happy to do anything in my power to be of service to you, Tiffy.'

She became all business, and said briskly, 'I have heard from stable talk at Dalmaine Castle that a card game with high stakes takes place every Friday night at the Tin Flute inn. Have you played there?'

Since it was very much the fashion among a certain clique of young bloods to amuse themselves in low company, and Tarleton was always fashionable, he nodded, albeit mystified.

'Good! You will take me there this Friday and introduce me as a young friend staying in the neighbourhood desirous of an evening's entertainment with the cards.'

'They will never admit a girl!' Tarleton exclaimed.

'I shall be a boy. Meet me in the spinney below Parson's Meadow at nine o'clock. Bring with you a spare horse for me to ride and a suit of your brother's clothes. He's at Harrow, isn't he? We must be much of a size —that is, if he's not as fat as you. You will have to advance me twenty guineas as a stake, but I shall pay you back out of my winnings. Afterwards, we shall ride back to the spinney, where I can change into my own clothes and then walk home with no one any the wiser.'

The neat plan seemed ordinary enough to Tiffy, but it stunned her listeners. Even Tarleton, miserably expecting the worst, was aghast. So much so that it was left to Cassy to gasp eventually, 'You cannot go into a gambling den!'

'Fudge. I was weaned in one.'

'But dressed as a boy . . . wearing breeches . . . showing the shape of your legs . . .'

'You didn't scruple to show the shape of yours not above ten minutes ago. Dammit, you were in greater danger of being ravished here than ever I shall be in public. Besides, people see what they expect to see. Nobody will suspect I am a girl.'

'It's outrageous!'

'Yes, I think it bears my touch, and that is why it will succeed. Papa always said that people are prepared for everything but the outrageous. *That* never occurs to them, and he should know, for he brought off many ruses in splendid fashion. My short hair and slimness will favour my disguise, and to conceal my eyes I shall wear the plain-glass spectacles Papa affected whenever he wished to look scholarly. This time I will not make the mistake of expressing feminine sentiments, as I did when I tried to coax that kitten off the ship.'

'That dreadful American accent of yours will expose

you the moment you open your mouth,' Cassy informed her waspishly.

'Hell's blood!' Tiffy's vehemence acknowledged she had been guilty of an oversight. 'I can't manage your breakteeth English, that goes without saying. I know! I shall be French. An émigré boy. Papa had a French mistress in New Orleans, and I remember very well how she spoke English. She made me wish that I were French.'

Cassy covered her ears with her hands. 'Have you no shame? How many times have you been told not to mention your father's mistresses in my hearing? The man was infamous, just as you are.'

Tiffy's eyes gleamed dangerously. 'Don't you ever dare preach propriety to me again, or malign my father! If he was a rogue, he had the saving grace of spreading happiness about him, not spite and msiery as you do.'

'I refuse to remain here to be insulted,' Cassy said, attempting to crawl past Tiffy to the ladder.

Tiffy thrust her back. 'Stay where you are. Our business is unfinished. Well, Tarleton? Will you do as I say? Or is Cassy's reputation to be ruined and your future blighted?'

Tarleton disliked Tiffy's punishing tongue as much as he disliked her scheme, and he answered peevishly, 'You ask too much. A fine figure I should cut if you were discovered. No gentleman would take a girl disguised as a boy into a gambling den. It isn't even a respectable place. There might be a merchant or two, or perhaps a young blood out for a lark, but mostly they are rough fellows. Thieves . . . cut-throats for all I know.'

'I mean to play cards with them, not dance,' she retorted irritably. 'I am not used to poverty, and this is the best way I can think of to set myself up.'

'What if you lose?'

'I won't. My papa taught me everything he knew.'

'Nothing is sure in a game of chance,' Tarleton fretted.

'That's the fascination of it! Stop panicking, Tarleton, and *think*. The men playing on Friday will see me as naught but an inexperienced stripling with a fistful of golden guineas—a young chicken ripe for plucking, in fact. They will be *eager* to let me play. Their money will be out of their pockets and into mine before they are on their guard. And the Tin Flute is miles away from Honivale.'

She sounded very plausible. Tarleton, because he needed to, was half-way to believing her, yet still he jibbed at committing himself. 'If you are discovered, nothing will excuse my conduct in taking you there.'

Tiffy felt like swearing at him. Restraining her impatience, however, she offered him the lifeline he needed. 'You may say that you met me by chance at the door of the inn and recognised me. Since nothing could dissuade me from my purpose, and you couldn't ruin me by denouncing me in public as a girl, you took the only honourable course open to you. You offered me your gentlemanly protection until you could get me safely away from there.'

'What if the marquess should find out? He might believe I had deliberately led you astray. My father thinks the world of his good opinion, and would never forgive me if I upset him.'

'Nobody will find out,' Tiffy insisted. 'Even so, it would be my neck on the block, not yours. I shall support your story that you were merely trying to extricate me from a situation of my own making. What I shall *not* support is any more argument. You should be thinking less of yourself and more of saving Cassy's reputation.'

Recalled reluctantly to his duty as a gentleman, Tarleton might still have prevaricated had not the sound of an approaching carriage spurred him into recklessness. 'I'll do it,' he blurted out, knowing he had not the courage to face the furore that would otherwise burst about his defenceless head. His decision made, he instantly fell into a fresh panic. 'Quick! We must not be found here. We might still be undone! Where's my coat? Cassy, where's your hair-ribbon? Oh, do move yourself, Tiffy. We can't get to the ladder.'

Tiffy, her purpose gained, surveyed him with amusement. 'Do you never think? My presence here makes yours permissible—unless, of course, you're the sort of libertine who enjoys sporting with two females at once?'

'You know I'm not!' he exclaimed. 'And I'll thank you to curb that curst tongue of yours.'

'Readily, if you'll stop whining. Sit still while I straighten your cravat. You look as if you've just climbed out of bed.'

Tarleton, whose appearance was of paramount importance to him, allowed her to neaten the intricate folds of his neckcloth and to ease him into his tight-fitting jacket. Cassy fished her green ribbon from the straw and tied up her ringlets, after which Tiffy pronounced them both fit to be seen. She led the way down the ladder, then swooped to pluck a piece of straw from Tarleton's carefully ironed shoelaces.

'You think you're so clever, but there's one thing you haven't considered,' Cassy snapped with a sudden return of spirit. 'How do you expect to get out of the house on Friday evening without anybody knowing?'

'Nothing simpler,' Tiffy assured her breezily. 'I shall go to bed early with a headache and climb down the tree outside my window. A child could do it.'

'Only a child would think of it. When are you going to grow up, Tiffy?'

'I have,' was her enigmatic reply. 'That is why I am prepared to risk all to win all.'

'You talk in riddles. I think you're mad!'

Tiffy thought of Jago. Of course she was mad to set her cap at such a man. He had probably forgotten her very existence by now, but she was still intoxicated by the sweet sensations he had aroused in her, and fortune was still on her side. She turned her brilliant eyes on her cousin, surprised to find that she pitied her. 'You poor thing,' she exclaimed. 'I don't believe you will ever know madness such as mine.'

'I profoundly hope I shan't,' Cassy returned stiffly.

Tiffy's sympathy died as suddenly as it had been kindled. 'If your marriage ever comes off, I pity the little Creightons of the future. What a sad time they will have of it, saddled with such a pair!'

Having delivered her final salvo, she walked out of the stables to meet the Everetts descending from their carriage, her thoughts already leaping ahead to Friday. Three whole days to live through between then and now! To Tarleton it was not near enough, but to Tiffy—planning all the new plumage she would buy with her winnings—it seemed an eternity.

Her days at Dalmaine Castle were always so pleasurable that the time between the conception of her plan and its execution did not drag as much as she had feared. In fact, Friday morning found her curled up on the couch in the library looking the very picture of contentment. She was waiting for Courteney to join her when he had finished signing what she referred to as his steward's 'abominable papers', and, as usual, the servants had paid every attention to her comfort.

The log fire burning merrily in the grate being deemed insufficient to protect her from the bitter February cold, a thick shawl had been placed about her shoulders. From time to time she nibbled a macaroon or sipped the lemonade provided for her refreshment, looking as if she hadn't a care in the world—which, indeed, she hadn't. She had all this; soon she would have money;

and it seemed perfectly logical to her that Jago would shortly follow.

Part of her present contentment was because of her absorption in a novel borrowed from Lady Janetta. Had she taken it home to the vicarage to read, it would have been cast upon the fire as unsuitable for a young lady striving to attain refinement and a proper tone of mind.

She was too deeply engrossed to be aware that Courteney had entered the room, until he stood over her. She jumped out of her skin, choked on her macaroon and spluttered indignantly, 'Hell and the devil confound it! What a start you gave me. I thought you were a ghost.'

Courteney ruffled her curls and sat on the end of the couch, smiling at her. 'What a disappointment for you. Did nobody tell you we have trained the Dalmaine spectres never to stray from the dungeons during daylight? A fortunate circumstance, if encountering one would shock you back into bad language.'

'I make no apology for that,' Tiffy retorted, shaking the book at him. 'What did you expect when a cowled monk, glistening as though covered in hoary frost, was creeping up on the heroine. Grief, I nearly died to see you standing there.'

His smile deepened. 'Does your heroine also blaspheme when she is shocked?'

'No, she faints. But, as this is a medieval tale, no doubt her stays are too tight. Oh! I suppose I should not have said that, either.'

'Nor should you be reading this nonsense,' Courteney replied, taking the book from her.

Tiffy pulled a face. 'You sound as if you are about to join my uncle in Holy Orders. I have a better idea. Join me in a good gallop. Tobias says the rain will hold off as long as this wind blows, so we've little fear of getting wet.'

'Presently.' Courteney got to his feet and walked over

to the fire. 'There is something I must talk to you about first.'

Tiffy snuggled down among the cushions, her eyes dancing. 'How ominous you sound! Am I accused of some new misdemeanour? Sliding down the banisters? Stealing the crested silver? Bewitching the kitchen cat? Oh, do smile! The day is gloomy enough without such gloomy looks.

Courteney smiled, but only fleetingly. 'I am not gloomy; merely thoughtful. Do you think you could be serious for a few minutes?'

'I'm in no mood to be serious. I want some fun.' She jumped off the couch and went quickly towards him in her impetuous way, her most engaging smile spreading across her face. She held out her hands and added, 'I will not let you be serious, either, my so-solemn lord. Let us go riding.'

He clasped her hands, but for once did not succumb to her coaxing. 'Not yet. What I have to say affects you very much.'

A premonition chilled her, frightening her more than the novel she had just been reading, and her heart lurched. She pulled her hands out of his grasp and put them over her ears. 'No! Take me riding. I will not listen.'

'Tiffy . . .'

'I don't have to listen,' she shouted. 'I know what you are going to say. You are going back to that dreadful war!'

'Yes,' he began, but once more had no chance to finish because Tiffy was in the grip of a panic she scarcely understood. She had always known, of course, that some time in the future he would go away. What she had *not* known was that when he did so her world would rock, as it was rocking now. Her instinct ever to fight when she felt threatened, she lashed back with all the passionate intensity of her nature.

'You are a fool! A stupid, stupid fool!' she raged. 'Your presence in the Peninsula cannot be needed as much as it is needed here. England has enough dead heroes. Why should you be added to the list? What difference would it make? None!'

'Tiffy, please don't upset yourself. If . . .'

She stamped her foot, and stormed, 'Why should I be upset if you have no more brains than you were born with? Oh, I blame your wretched Eleanor for this. She should be here talking sense to you instead of sulking in Jamaica. You would *have* to listen to her because you love her. Do not look at me in such a way! It won't make me recant. She *is* wretched. Yes, and wicked, too—for it is wicked of her not to make the slightest push to stop you getting yourself killed. I hate her!'

'You cannot hate somebody you do not know. Besides, she could not affect my decision. It is my duty to see this war through. My personal feelings do not come into it.'

'"I could not love thee, dear, so much, Lov'd I not honour more",' she mocked, swinging back to the couch and grabbing the book she had just quoted from. 'A pox on all poets, and those who are taken in by them. I am not.'

She reinforced her views by hurling the book at Courteney. It skimmed past his head, crashed into the mirror above the fireplace and then fell. He bent to pick it up and place it on the mantelshelf.

'No man can be kept against his will.'

Her head tossed, her eyes flashed, and her hands settled on her hips in an eternally feminine stance of challenge. 'I would lay you odds on that, my lord, if I loved you.'

'You would find yourself with half a man. Perhaps less. A man who betrays his principles is nothing.'

'A pox on principles, too, and anything else that

stands in the way of love,' Tiffy retorted comprehensively. 'When one loves, one feels, one doesn't think. You would not do for me, my lord, if you love in such a tepid way that war is more important to you. No wonder Eleanor ran away from you! She must have had a great deal too much to bear.'

'She did,' Courteney replied, his grey eyes sombre.

Contrarily, his words kindled Tiffy to fresh fury. She stamped her foot again, and shouted, 'Don't you dare agree with me! I am being spiteful and horrid. Be horrid back. I hate you when you are so patient. You make me feel such a—a—worm.'

His sombre look vanished. 'Dear Tiffy, I might at times be tempted to call you many things—tigress, shrew, vixen—but never "worm". It's not your way to crawl quietly up to a fellow and take him unawares. You spring at him in full spitting fury.'

'So!' she exclaimed with a certain savage satisfaction. 'You are not wholly blind or stupid. You do know me for what I am. Why, then, do you never protect yourself or strike back?'

Courteney went over to her and put his hands on her shoulders, smiling ruefully down at her. 'If my grandmother hasn't succeeded in provoking me to quarrel with her in all these years, you can hardly expect to. I am, as she will tell you, a dull dog and lack a quarrelsome nature. I suppose you, like she, find that infuriating?'

Tiffy wrenched herself out of his grasp and paced about the room, very much in the manner of the tigress he had likened her to. 'I find it *damnable*!' she ground out between gritted teeth. 'What can one do with a man who will not make a fight of it! At least concede my relations are right when they say I'm uncivilised. You might as well, because there's no taming me. I won't permit it.'

'How fortunate that I like you the way you are,' he murmured.

She glared at him. 'Rubbish! You know the very worst of me.'

'And the very best.'

Her throat constricted. 'Damn you, Courteney,' she whispered, using his Christian name for the first time. 'You make me so ashamed of myself.' Her anger drained away. She shuddered, looking all child again, then rushed towards him and threw herself into his arms. 'I am *afraid*. That is why I am being so horrid.'

Courteney's arms closed comfortingly around her. 'There's not the least need for you to be afraid,' he told her in a rallying tone. 'I shall be back. They say lightning never strikes in the same place twice, you know.'

He won only a muffled groan from her. 'There you go again, crediting me with virtues I don't possess. It is *myself* I am afraid for. Now are you disgusted with me?'

'No, only with myself for tackling this in such a poor way. I meant to reassure you, not upset you.'

Tiffy reached up and tugged at his coat collar in exasperation. 'Stop that! Stop blaming yourself. This fuss is all of my causing. I was so very *lost* in . . . in many ways when you found me and befriended me, and I have been so very *cosy* since that I am afraid of losing you again. You have become my safe place. I suppose that sounds ridiculous to you.'

It didn't. Courteney understood only too well. Tiffy's roving way of life had robbed her of a home to retreat to in times of trouble, and so her security had always been wrapped up in a person. Temporarily, he had become that person—her safe place.

Out of need, he had befriended her, but she, out of a deeper need, had virtually adopted him. It had been an instinctive, childlike response to his uncritical and undemanding affection, but during the past few minutes he had been permitted very positive glimpses of the emergent woman. Her days of dependence upon him were numbered, and if he could only guide her through

the months ahead he was sure none of the direst pre-
dictions of the gossips would come true. Tiffy was bold,
judged by English standards, but he refused to believe
she was bad. Once she had accomplished the difficult
transition from a raffish to a respectable way of life, she
would be safe.

Her head was drooping against his chest again.
"Tiffy, you would be a great deal happier away from the
vicarage, wouldn't you?'

She nodded, but displayed none of the quick interest
he had expected. He was not to know, now her immediate panic had subsided, that she was considering the
wider implications of his departure. The worst and most
obvious would be losing her link with Jago . . . and just
as she was within an ace of getting enough money to
consider ways and means of flaunting herself, modishly
gowned, before him. Was there ever such appalling
timing! Irrationally, and like the dowager before her, she
blamed Courteney for his incorruptible sense of duty.
How dare he go away before her dreams were realised!

Her full lips set in a pout, and she grumbled, 'It would
have saved us both a great deal of trouble if the French
hadn't made such a sorry job of killing you the first time.
I would never have met you, and therefore couldn't have
missed you.'

This piece of selfishness did not appear to bother
Courteney in the least. 'Will you stop sulking if I can get
you away from Honivale? My grandmother returns to
Bath when I sail for Portugal. I must warn you that this is
as yet only an idea, but would you like to go with her?'

Bath! Tiffy could scarcely believe her ears. She had
learned from Lady Janetta that Jago's estate was not
many miles from there, and that he visited her whenever
he was in residence. Fate, then, wasn't playing ducks
and drakes with her. It was actually pushing her in the
right direction. 'Like to go . . .' she gasped. 'It is a
famous scheme. Would she have me?'

'It is possible.' Courteney took her elbow and led her to the couch. When they were seated he smiled into her brilliant eyes, fixed on his with an almost painful intensity, and explained, 'Lady Janetta's companion is not returning. Doubtless she finds helping to look after her sister's offspring less harassing than attending my grandmother. You, however, appear to have the knack. You have become something of a legend among the servants. How, apart from quarrelling with her, do you manage to keep her so well entertained?'

'Hazard,' Tiffy replied tersely. 'Pray go on.'

Courteney looked taken aback; then he laughed. 'I might have known. It had, of course, to be something of that nature to win her over. She was so very much against you at the start, and now she looks forward to your company. That, combined with the loss of her regular companion, encourages me to think she might like you with her. Life with an elderly lady is bound to be tedious at times, but Bath is a fashionable spa.'

'After the vicarage, it would seem like heaven,' Tiffy assured him fervently. 'Have you asked Lady Janetta if I might go with her?'

'No. There was something I had to ask you first.' He looked down at her hands clasped tightly in her lap, and took one of them, holding it gently. 'I have never imposed any conditions on you, Tiffy, knowing how much your spirits have been oppressed at the vicarage, but my grandmother's welfare concerns me greatly. You must promise me your good behaviour will continue and that you will not cause any scandals.'

Much as she was breaking her neck to go to Bath, Tiffy was in a quandary. She could not keep her word unless she gave up her gambling plan for that very evening, and yet her need for money was more urgent than it had ever been. The opportunity to grasp everything she wanted —Jago, clothes, romance—had virtually been dropped into her lap. To be held back by a scruple was unthinkable. *Go for the main chance*, her father had always counselled her. No advice could be more compatible with her nature, and it wasn't as though Courteney hadn't been well and truly warned.

On the other hand, she found it extraordinarily difficult to look directly into his steady grey eyes, and lie. To make matters worse, he put a hand under her chin and tipped up her face so that she couldn't avoid looking at him. 'Tiffy, are you already in a scrape I don't know about?'

'No.' She could answer that honestly. She wasn't. Not yet. Nor would she be if all went well tonight.

'Well, then?'

'I am surprised,' she prevaricated, 'that you should want any word of mine when I have told you I am never wholly to be trusted.'

'I would put my trust in any promise you made to me directly.'

Suddenly a way out occurred to her. Once tonight's gambling escapade was safely behind her, she could give Courteney her word with a clear conscience. So she must delay the issue without arousing his suspicions. It would be no easy task, but she had her charm to help her, and for the first time in her life she used it deliberately. 'Will you give me a little time to consider whether my nature will allow me to be good for any length of time? Then, when I give my word, I shall *have* to keep it, even if it becomes inconvenient to do so. I shall not be able to excuse myself on the ground that the promise was extracted from me on the spur of the moment, without proper thought.'

Courteney was frowning. 'Time is getting short, Tiffy. I am going up to London tomorrow to order new uniforms. I shall be away several days, and sail for the Peninsula in just over two weeks. If you are to go to Bath, there will be a great deal to arrange, including getting the approval of the Everetts and the Yorkes, and Lady Janetta will not like the scheme sprung on her at the last moment. It is her way to see the disadvantages in anything before she can be brought round to seeing the advantages.'

'That's true enough,' Tiffy conceded, momentarily diverted. 'Er . . . will quarrelling and gambling with her be advantages enough?'

He could not help but laugh. 'We must hope so! I shall delay my departure tomorrow until after luncheon so that I have time to talk to her. Will you have examined your conscience sufficiently by then to give me your word?'

'Certainly,' she assured him. 'Thank you for being so understanding, my lord.'

She did not quite like the searching look he gave her, but as he said no more, she was able to congratulate herself on brushing through a difficult situation rather well. Her panic gone and a dazzling future before her, she was swinging round to the thought that it was no bad thing he was going away. To an adventuress like herself he was fast becoming the one thing she couldn't afford. An Achilles heel.

CHAPTER SEVEN

TARLETON WAS NOT happy. He arrived at the rendezvous in the spinney that evening to find his fervent prayers had not been answered. Tiffy, disobligingly, had neither suffered Second Thoughts nor been struck down by a deadly pox. She presented herself in the rudest of health and the highest of spirits. She blithely dismissed his last-minute pleas to abandon her risky masquerade and made short work of changing into his young brother's clothes.

Feeling like a man forced to put his own neck in a noose, Tarleton glumly watched her pocket the purse containing the twenty guineas she had asked for, then mount the horse he had fetched. The very weather was against him. It was bitterly cold, but the wind had chased away the heavy rain-clouds, revealing a moon that made night riding perfectly feasible.

A hunter's moon, Tiffy bracingly called it, and took it as a good omen for her night's work. However, when they entered the homely taproom of the Tin Flute some time later, her confidence suffered a slight shock and Tarleton's disappeared altogether. Tobias Wade, the last person either of them expected to see, was sitting at one of the long narrow tables sinking a pint of home-brewed.

The low doors and ceilings of the ancient inn could not accommodate such a towering man of fashion as Tarleton Creighton. He was forced to remove his high-crowned hat as he entered, but even so he was a sight to behold. His many-caped riding cloak swung open to reveal a green coat, a green-and-orange striped waist-coat, green breeches and knee-high riding-boots adorned with orange tassels, an inspiration he was pleased to acknowledge as his own. In addition, his plump face was trapped between the monstrous height of his starched collar points and supported by an extravagantly folded neckcloth.

The yokels in their smocks and homespuns and gaitered boots gaped at him with all the awe they would have afforded a hobgoblin suddenly appearing in their midst. Normally Tarleton would have derived considerable gratification from such attention, but he was so taken aback himself that he could only gape, in his turn, at Tobias, whom he knew was well acquainted with Tiffy.

She, entering behind him with all the jauntiness to be expected from a schoolboy out for a lark, also held her hat in her hand. Her curls fell with gipsy darkness and dishevelment around her mischievous face, and the glasses perched precariously on her little nose failed to make her look scholarly. She was unobtrusively clad in a warm cloak over a dark coat and breeches. Her shirt was modest, her neckcloth simply tied, and her boots functional rather than fashionable.

She almost walked into Tarleton's back when he stopped so abruptly, but she checked in time and peered round him. Her eyes, for a fraught fraction of a second, met Tobias's. Smartly she changed direction so that Tarleton's bulky form was between them.

'Acknowledge him, you fool,' she hissed at him, gripping his arm and propelling him forward, at the same time contriving to throw a superbly nonchalant '*Bonsoir*' to the landlord behind the counter.

Tarleton, glassy-eyed with horror, managed a stiff nod in Tobias's direction as he was dragged on. Her tactics appeared to answer, though, for no word came from Tobias nor was any move made to stop them. They passed safely out of the taproom, along a narrow passage and into a stuffy back parlour, where the card game was in progress.

Tiffy, jubilant they had got this far, suffered no after-effects from her brush with disaster, and thereafter everything went exactly as she had predicted. Her confidence did not permit suspicion. Nobody doubted she was an émigré boy, and her guineas made her welcome among gamblers eager for fresh victims. When she cheerfully announced that she expected to relieve everybody of their gold before the clock struck twelve, a shout of laughter greeted so absurd a jest. Tiffy also laughed. The role of cheeky innocent suited her well.

When Tarleton had previously honoured the back parlour with his presence, he had been sustained by the knowledge that every fashionable young buck was expected to indulge in an occasional bout of slumming. It was not, however, the done thing for females. It ceased to be dashing and became downright disreputable, as Tarleton, looking round despairingly, was only too well aware.

The scene was certainly one of dissipation. A potman was placing fresh candles on the guttering stumps of the old, adding to an atmosphere already thick with the fumes of cigars and alcohol. Every so often a rogue gust of wind found its way down the chimney, belching out suffocating blue-grey smoke. It was just such a pit of depravity as the Reverend Hector railed against from his pulpit every Sunday, but his niece studied her cards with the absorption of one who was as oblivious to the foul atmosphere as she was to the uncouthness of the shady characters surrounding her.

The game in progress was macao, a form of vingt-et-un which depended equally heavily on chance and skill. It was not what Tiffy would have chosen had she been consulted, but she was as exhilarated by hoodwinking Tobias as Tarleton was shattered. She believed that luck was with her, and was soon proved right.

Tarleton, mentally and emotionally all to pieces, was soon to be financially so. She won all the money he had brought for his own stakes, repaid her loan and promptly won it back again, at the same time making inroads on the purses of the other players. Beginner's luck they called it, with an amused indulgence that experience would eventually sour.

Calling for brandy, Tarleton retired with the bottle to an armchair by the fire, his nerves so desperately in need of the fortifying effects of hard liquor that he downed his first glassful in one incautious gulp. The brandy was atrocious. In no way could it be compared with the excellent cognac that his father, that highly respected Justice of the Peace, purchased from The Gentlemen engaged in the smuggling trade with France. Although his educated palate shuddered at the rawness of the liquor and his fastidious nose wrinkled at its strange bouquet, the one unquestionable quality of the brandy was its potency. On balance, he decided it was beneficial. He risked another glassful, and then another, and pretty soon he was beaming upon the scene that had caused him such disquiet.

Players came and went as the evening wore on, and Tarleton's spirits rose as the level of the brandy in the bottle dropped. Tiffy, casting a knowledgeable eye at him and mindful that she was supposed to be French, asked in heavily accented English what he had drunk with his dinner. On learning it was claret, she observed that her father, who had been very much *au fait* with such things, had warned against putting brandy on top of claret without port in between.

Tarleton giggled and refilled his glass. Tiffy, shrugging in true Gallic fashion, returned her attention to the cards. Some time before midnight Tarleton was having such difficulty in focusing his eyes that he found it necessary to close them altogether. They remained closed. Sometimes he smiled and sometimes he snored, but he bothered nobody. Nor was he bothered himself until the dilapidated clock on the mantelshelf wheezily chimed one o'clock, and he was shaken awake.

Tiffy was standing over him, as alert as he was sleepy. 'Pull yourself together,' she told him briskly. 'Everyone's gone. The sooner we are on our way, the better.'

Tarleton had not out-slept his euphoria, and smiled foolishly at her. 'You're Tiffy. Beat 'em all to flinders, didn't you?'

'That's right. Put your cape on.' She gave it to him, and then fastened her own about her neck. She removed a small pistol from a pocket and placed it on the table.

When Tarleton rose from the chair and struggled into his cape, he had the greatest difficulty in maintaining his balance, which made him laugh. Presently he became aware that Tiffy was filling her pockets with guineas, and exclaimed admiringly, ''Pon my soul, if I ever saw such luck. You've won a mint!'

'This game wasn't as rich as I had hoped. There's not much above two hundred guineas here. By the by, my good fortune was resented. To keep matters sweet, I promised to play again next Friday to give everyone a chance to win back their money. I shan't do so, of course. Pulling the same trick in the same place twice is too risky. If you are asked what's become of me, say I was sent back to school.'

Tarleton, in his confused state, absorbed few of her words. His attention was fixed on something else. He lurched towards the table, his hand outstretched towards the pistol. 'That's a pretty toy.'

Tiffy removed it to the safety of her cape pocket. 'It was my father's, and it's no toy. Its range is short, but it will deter anyone resentful enough to rob me on the way home.'

These words successfully penetrated Tarleton's befuddled brain. 'You're a girl . . . You can't go round shooting people! Not in England. Shocking bad *ton*.'

'Good *ton* or bad, nobody is going steal my money without paying a heavy price for it. How exciting this is! Quite like the old days when Papa and I had such jolly times.'

She sighed nostalgically, thrust his hat at him, picked up her own and walked out of the room. Tarleton lurched after her, and although his shoulders collided with one wall of the passage and then the other, causing him to complain that it had shrunk since he last passed along it, his mood was still buoyant. The joke rudely ended when he followed Tiffy out into the moonlit yard.

A freezing wind almost bowled them over, billowing out their capes and cutting most unkindly through Tarleton's euphoria. He gasped and instinctively turned back to the shelter of the inn. Tiffy, cursing him as as only she could, bullied him across the yard. Weighted down by the coins in her pockets, battling against the wind and obliged to tug Tarleton every step of the way, she was out of breath and patience when they gained the temporary refuge of the decrepit barn where they had left their horses.

The interior was pitch black, save for a few feet where the moonlight was able to penetrate the doorless entrance. Tarleton tottered a step or two inside, stopped and leaned heavily on Tiffy's shoulder, groaning, 'I feel as queer as Dick's hatband.'

'Serves you right for making such a pig of yourself with the brandy. A lot of use you will be if we should find ourselves in a tight fix.'

The words were no sooner out than a sound different from the snuffling of the horses and the creaking of the ancient timbers in the wind made her thrust Tarleton away and turn sharply to her right. He staggered and fell to his knees, while she pulled the pistol from her pocket, cocked it and pointed it towards the direction of the noise, saying imperiously, 'Come out, or I shall shoot!'

'Adone do, Miss Tiffy,' Tobias scolded, coming out of

the shadows. 'It's only me making sure none of them nasty characters you was gambling with hung around to cause you any harm.'

'Oh, my God,' Tarleton moaned. 'We are rumbled. Undone. Ruined. It's all your fault, Tiffy. Tell him so. I can't. I . . .' He broke off and clapped a hand to his mouth.

'If you're about to regret the brandy, do it somewhere else. I don't want my own stomach turned,' she told him sharply.

Tarleton tried to rise, failed, and crawled out of the barn on his hands and knees. He vanished into the night, but sounds of retching proved that he had not got very far before he did, indeed, begin to regret the brandy, and in a most violent manner.

'Stupid fellow,' Tiffy said dismissively. 'I thought I had you fooled, Tobias. What gave me away?'

'You're not an ordinary sort of girl, and you haven't an ordinary sort of face. Them glasses couldn't disguise your eyes. I ain't seen another pair like them, but it wasn't only that. You've a certain way of walking I'd know a mile away. Quick steps, straight back, head high. Make a fine light infantryman you would, if only you was a boy. Which reminds me . . . If that's a real pistol, I'd breathe a mite easier if you pointed it somewhere else.'

'Of course it's real,' she snapped, considerably disgruntled by what he had said. 'What's more, I'd have shot you if you hadn't spoken up so sharply.'

A reluctant smile crossed his face as she uncocked the pistol and returned it to her pocket. 'A proper caution you are, and no mistake! I'd best get you home before you find ourself in more mischief than his lordship can haul you out of.'

'Tobias, you a—a Judas! You're never going to betray me to his lordship?' Tiff exclaimed. 'There will be the devil to pay!'

He sighed heavily. 'I'm sorry, because I like you, but

serving his lordship comes first with me and always will. There's no finer master in the land and I sees it as my duty to guard his back against . . .' He paused.

'Against people like me?' Tiffy suggested through gritted teeth.

'If you like, miss. What if somebody else recognised you, and kept quiet, the same as I did? My reason was to stop a scandal his lordship wouldn't like, but theirs might be to make mischief. A laughing-stock you'll make of his lordship if it gets out. Yes, and his grandmother, too, and he won't like that.'

'It won't get out,' she said, stamping her foot in exasperation.

'I profoundly hopes not, or there will be all manner of gossip. People will say as how the Harwoods was properly taken in by you when anybody with a grain of sense could have seen you ain't respectable. I don't say as how it will happen, only that it might, and that's what I must protect his lordship against. He must be prepared. Just in case.'

'Blast your eyes, Tobias, you can't ruin me on the *off chance* that my identity will leak out! Everybody thinks I am a French schoolboy. Who in their right mind would associate him with the parson's niece?'

'I'm sorry to disoblige you, but his lordship must be told. It's my duty.'

'God damn you English and your sense of duty!' she all but snarled.

Tarleton had staggered back into the barn in time to get the gist of what was being said. He said petulantly, 'A guinea will button his mouth. For pity's sake give it to him so that he will go away. I'm dying.'

'Bribe Tobias to act against his master's best interests?' Tiffy retorted. 'You must be drunker than I thought.'

'Every servant has his price. Stands to reason. Wouldn't be a servant otherwise,' Tarleton persisted.

'He's no different from all the rest. Just holding out for more than a guinea, that's all. Fellow's a leech.'

He should have stayed silent, because Tiffy rounded on him and released all her pent-up frustration over his hapless head. 'Tobias is more than the marquess's servant. He is his friend. Oh, you wouldn't understand. You are so puffed up in your own esteem that you think such a friendship beneath a gentleman's dignity. Well, it isn't, not for a true gentleman like the marquess. He doesn't buy loyalty, he merits it, which is why his servants regard him so highly. You, now, are no more than a dressed-up joke, and jokes are laughed at, not respected. Go away and be sick again. It's all you're good for.'

'You'll cut your throat with that sharp tongue of yours one of these days, you unfeeling little monster. I'm dying, and all you can . . ' He broke off, clutched his stomach and went on in an entirely different tone, 'My God, I *am* dying . . .'

'What an act of mercy that will be, only pray perform it somewhere else. I'm tired of the sight and the sound of you.' She watched as he fled once more into the night, then turned, still glowering, back to Tobias. 'I could willingly consign you to the devil as well, but that's no reason for an idiot like Tarleton to insult you. Don't regard anything he says. He's half flash and half foolish, and both halves drunk.'

'Lord bless you, miss, I know that. What I can't fathom is what you're doing with him, you two not being what I'd call natural companions.'

'We met at the door of the inn. He couldn't dissuade me from my purpose, so he offered me his protection.'

Tobias couldn't imagine a popinjay like Tarleton Creighton doing any such thing, but he said only, 'He should have bundled you on your horse and taken you home, willing or not.'

'Violence is abhorrent to him,' Tiffy improvised. 'He

did what he thought best. I don't want him punished, so
keep quiet about his part in this.'

'I'm sorry again, miss, but it's not my way to tell his
lordship half a story. Whatever made you do it?'

A ghost of a smile crossed her face. 'The role you see
me in now suits me better than that of a poor relation.
I now have a couple of hundred guineas to play with,
whereas before I hadn't tuppence to rub together.'

'His lordship . . .' Tobias began.

'His lordship is my friend,' Tiffy interrupted hotly. 'I
will not become his pensioner.'

Tobias watched with troubled eyes as she went over to
her horse, wishing he did not like her quite so much. He
was blessed if he had ever met anybody with such a talent
for doing all the wrong things for all the right reasons.
When he went forward to help her, she said, 'These
guineas in my pockets weigh me down like millstones. I
can't get into the saddle.'

After she was safely mounted, he climbed on to his
own horse. 'Do we leave young Mr Creighton to find his
own way home?'

'What a temptation but, no, I have need of him still.
This is his horse, and these are his brother's clothes I'm
wearing. He must return them to the Hall tonight.'

'How did you come by the horse and clothes if you met
him only outside the inn?'

There was a brief silence, then, 'I stole them.'

'You have had a busy night,' he observed non-
committally.

Tiffy, wondering if she had been in Tarleton's company long enough to become a fool herself, cursed
herself as comprehensively as she had ever cursed anyone. She would have to be more plausible when she was
called to account by the marquess. To have come so
close to achieving all she had set out to do, only to be
brought down at the last fence, made her chew her lip in
vexation. Courteney might very well decide she was

unfit for a fashionable life in Bath. Jago, the inspiration of all her dreams and endeavours, was once more slipping from her grasp.

As she and Tobias left the barn, desperation made her ask, 'I suppose I was right in assuming you couldn't be bribed?'

'Yes, miss.'

'Damn you, Tobias.'

'Yes, miss.'

The screaming wind prevented further conversation. They found Tarleton weakly clinging to a tree. He had also lost the last lulling effects of the brandy, and was, in fact, most horribly sober. His teeth were chattering, and when Tobias helped to haul him into his saddle, he slumped forward, waiting for death to claim him and uninterested in all else.

If any disgruntled gamblers had planned an ambush, the hostility of the weather or Tobias's intimidating presence must have deterred them, because their journey to the spinney was uneventful. The thick trees afforded some shelter to Tiffy as she dismounted to change into her own clothes while her companions turned their backs.

When Tarleton received the rolled-up bundle of his brother's clothes from her, he said sulkily, 'I wish I'd never listened to you. Everything has gone wrong. The marquess will take me to task, and my father will find out. I am in a worse fix than when you surprised me with . . .'

'Blabbermouth,' Tiffy intervened. 'Hold on to your tongue—and your nerve, if you have one. The marquess is not vindictive, and you know I am pledged to protect you.'

Tarleton, realising he had almost revealed the secret he had gone through so much to conceal, nevertheless felt some satisfaction in saying, 'In any event, there's no saving yourself. You are ruined.'

'If I am, you won't hear me whine about it the way you do. Go home, Tarleton. You are a bore.'

He was in such a huff he needed no further urging, and snatching the reins of his second horse, he galloped away.

'And a hem good riddance to him,' Tobias said, swooping down to pluck Tiffy from her feet and settling her on the rump of his own horse. 'Hold on tight. I'll soon have you home.'

Tiffy clutched at her pockets, fearful of losing her money, and had such difficulty in keeping her seat that she was profoundly grateful when he set her down close to the vicarage. He tethered his horse to a tree and walked with her to the gate in the back garden wall, asking, 'How will you get in?'

'There is a most obliging tree outside my bedroom window.'

Tobias shook his head but wisely kept to himself any thoughts he might have on a young lady who climbed in and out of windows in the dead of night, careered around the countryside dressed as a boy, hobnobbed with rascally gamblers and was ready to shoot anyone foolhardy enough to stand in her way.

His thoughts were checked when Tiffy, about to go through the gate, hesitated and then said abruptly, 'Don't feel a Judas. I was wrong to call you that. I am *glad* his lordship has somebody to watch out for him, however inconvenient it might be for me just now.' She thrust her cold little hand at him. 'No hard feelings, Tobias.'

He clasped it gratefully. 'Thank you, miss.'

She nodded, went through the gate and walked quickly to the house. He glimpsed her climbing the tree, its broad branches winter bare and bathed in moonlight. An upstairs window opened and shut. The house slept on.

Tobias turned away. He was not much acquainted

with irony, but he thought it a shame that he, who truly liked Tiffy, had to be the one to tell the marquess that she was living up to her infamous reputation.

And, unknown to him, before Tiffy had been in bed for five minutes her ever-inventive brain was formulating a way of re-gilding her reputation before it was tarnished beyond repair. She had to steal Tobias's thunder by getting to Courteney first in the morning. To her, then, would go the virtue of making a free confession before one was forced from her.

She knew her marquess. He admired honesty and he was not petty. He would give her a fair hearing. If she explained how poverty had been her goad, was properly penitent and promised exemplary behaviour in future, he would not easily break her heart by denying her the chance to go to Bath. Pleased with her scheme, she decided she would rise at first light and ride over to the castle on Cassy's mare, arriving a good two hours before the carriage normally called for her—and in ample time to forestall Tobias.

Such touching faith did Tiffy have in the feasibility of any plan of her own devising, despite all evidence to the contrary, that she felt sufficiently relieved of her immediate cares to turn her mind to another problem. Twice she had counted her precious guineas before climbing into bed, and twice she could make them amount to no more than two hundred and twenty. That might represent a small fortune to some, but to Tiffy it seemed little more than pin-money. Back-street dressmakers would not do for her. She intended to be gowned and shod by only the finest modistes when she burst upon the fashionable scene and forced Jago to revise his opinion of Dalmaine's waif.

Ah, Jago. Everything began and ended with him. Well, two hundred and twenty guineas was too small a beginning. Two thousand guineas would be more like. Her plans were nothing if not grand.

Tiffy, suffering all the pangs of frustrated passion, was driven to consider another way of raising money she had already thought deeply about and dismissed. There seemed, now, no other way out. Her love for Jago was demanding another sacrifice, and as her eyes closed at last in sleep, she knew that she would make it.

Three circumstances, innocent enough in themselves, combined to wreck Tiffy's plan of reaching Courteney before Tobias. First, she overslept. Second, Courteney, an incurably early riser, visited his stables at first light to inspect a favourite brood mare suspected of forming a spavin. And third, Tobias, hardened to irregular hours, was bustling about his own particular domain when his master arrived.

So while Tiffy slumbered on all unawares, Tobias was acquainting the marquess with the goings-on, as he termed it, at the Tin Flute. It was in Tiffy's favour that he scorned exaggeration or dramatic effect, but the bare facts alone were colourful enough. The escapade was stamped indelibly with Tiffy's distinguishing touch, as Courteney quickly perceived, but Tarleton's involvement puzzled him.

Tobias, puzzled himself, could only reiterate that Miss Tiffy appeared to have a hold over Mr Tarleton. When she called the tune, he danced, for all he didn't want to. Not that my lord need fear there was anything of a romantic nature between them! It was as plain as a pikestaff they couldn't abide each other. Most peculiar it all was, but only Miss Tiffy could enlighten his lordship further on that score.

He repeated the cheerful part of his tale, that she had made such a convincing French boy that no one else had recognised her, so there was unlikely to be a rumpus. Unfortunately, his innate honesty compelled him to add the warning that unless she were stopped, she might do the whole thing over again, being, as she was, game as a pebble and pluck to the backbone.

Courteney scarcely needed telling that in championing Tiffy he had grasped a tiger by the tail, and he replied drily, 'Miss Tiffy would go on a great deal better if she showed less pluck and more propriety.'

Tobias couldn't argue with that, but neither could he resist a further plea on her behalf. 'For all her hey-go-mad ways, my lord, she's a right 'un,' he said earnestly. 'Once she got over her temper, she told me she didn't bear me no grudge. That was generous of her, considering she knew as how I'd be dropping her properly in the soup.'

'When Miss Tiffy is in the soup, anybody within range is likely to get scalded,' Courteney replied grimly. He thought for a moment, then added, 'I'll delay my journey to London until Monday. Keep your ear to the ground, Tobias. If there are any whispers, I'll be on hand to deal with them.'

'I could go to the Tin Flute again tonight,' Tobias offered. 'There's bound to be talk about the boy who cleaned out those cardsharps. So long as it is about a *boy* still, Miss Tiffy will be in the clear.'

'So we must hope.'

When Courteney entered the breakfast parlour some while later, he took his watch from his fob pocket and studied it. Tiffy, for the first time ever, was late. The carriage should have returned by now. He wondered whether she was lying low until the storm blew over, then dismissed the thought as unworthy. For all her sins, Tiffy wouldn't cry craven.

He pocketed his watch and went over to the sideboard. Ignoring a huge ham, a cold game pie and a blushing joint of beef, he made his selection from the steaming contents of the various chafing-dishes. His appetite had improved with his health over the past weeks and he filled his plate most respectably with fillet of sirloin, buttered eggs, lean cuts of bacon, sliced kidneys, and tomatoes from his succession houses. He carried his plate to the table, flanked it with a tankard of ale and a dish of toast, and sat down. Just as he was getting on terms with his steak, slamming doors and hurried footsteps announced the arrival of Tiffy in, from the sound of things, none too sweet a temper.

In this he was correct. Tiffy was furious with herself for oversleeping. She had dressed all by chance, throwing on whatever clothes came first, and cursing all the while her stupidity in not leaving a note for the servants to waken her at dawn.

During the journey from the vicarage to the castle, her normally fertile brain failed to produce a substitute plan of any reliability. Her heart was aching because the hoped-for bridge between herself and Jago seemed likely to vanish, and her exasperation turned to indignation at what she saw as another case of injustice. Why did she have to be punished for doing nothing worse than trying to help herself? By some strange alchemy known only to herself, Tiffy arrived at the castle a fair way towards believing she was the victim, and not the cause, of the misfortunes that befell her.

She was wearing a bonnet with a crown and poke too exaggerated for her small head, and a heavy brown cape that hung in swamping folds from her slender shoulders. Had she chosen, she could have made a touchingly pathetic figure by creeping into the marquess's presence under the guise of a pale and wilting penitent. She did not so choose, and contrived instead to look magnificent. Her huge eyes flashed violet fire, her dimpled chin jutted belligerently, and the way she swung her innocuous knitted reticule round and round by its drawstring imbued it with something of the menace of a medieval mace.

Just in case she wasn't flying enough battle flags, she fired the opening salvo of the encounter by slamming the door behind her. Then she stood, head high, one hand on out-thrust hip, precisely as she had the previous day when she had challenged him to do his worst.

My lord rose courteously to his feet, knowing that, for her own sake, he must be severe with her. But one look at her and the strange bond that existed between them made him sensitive to the distress concealed by so much militancy, causing him to murmur involuntarily, 'Poor Tiffy. In the suds again?'

She stared at him for a second, nonplussed, then with a little cry of thankfulness she threw her bonnet one way, her cape the other, and launched herself across the room into his arms. She hugged him fiercely, buried her face against his chest and gasped, 'Oh, you *darling* man! I should have *known* you wouldn't condemn me out of hand, my one *true* friend.'

Courteney, soothing her crumpled curls, cautioned her, 'Don't run away with the idea that I condone your masquerade. I don't.'

'I never expected you to! I know how staid you are. Only I do thank you for not glaring at me as if I were a serpent's tooth and saying nasty cutting things, which is precisely what my uncle would have done. Oh, and now I must beg your pardon for thinking you would behave like him. A *moment's* calm reflection would have taught me better, only being in a fret is not conducive to clear thinking, my lord.'

'It doesn't appear to have affected the readiness of your tongue.'

'No, nothing does that,' she agreed naïvely.

Courteney eased her out of his arms and shook his head at her. 'Tiffy . . . Tiffy . . . Whatever am I going to do with you?'

She sniffed, and smiled mistily up at him. 'You could lend me your handkerchief. Your kindness—*tolerance!* —has unmanned me again.'

He gave it to her, and as she blew her nose lustily,

breathed almost to himself, 'What formidable weapons you have for one who looks so frail. Your temper, your tongue and—your violets in the dew.'

Tiffy re-emerged from his handkerchief and pocketed it, dealt with her brimming eyes by wiping them with her cuffs, and asked, 'What did you say?'

'Nothing. Beyond wondering what to do with you, of course.'

Her moment of weakness over, she was very much herself again. The worst had not happened, my lord was giving her room to manoeuvre, and her spirits rose mercurially. She replied, as if nothing could be simpler, 'We can talk over my little enterprise at the Tin Flute in a *rational* way, you can ring a peal over me, and we can be comfortable again.'

'Ring a peal? I feel like wringing your neck!'

Far from being daunted by this prospect, she grinned. 'In that case, you must keep your strength up. Pray finish your breakfast! Farley also will be after my blood if you don't, and there is only so much of it to go round. Would you object if I had something to eat, too? I overslept. Only think how mortified you would be if I fainted through lack of nourishment before you had finished scolding me.'

'Tiffy, your behaviour last night wasn't amusing,' Courteney said as he found himself being coaxed back into his chair, 'so don't think you can turn me up sweet this time.'

'You can't blame me for trying!' she answered reasonably. 'But if it doesn't work, I am ready to stand buff. A poor creature I would be if I could not match your generosity of spirit. So! I am prepared to make whatever concessions are necessary to accommodate your point of view.' She paused, then added ingenuously, 'Considering how pig-headed I normally am, you must admit that's handsome of me.'

She did not wait for him to answer, hunger driving her

to the sideboard where she began to inspect the contents of the chafing-dishes, leaving Courteney to muse, 'What a slippery tail you have, my little tiger.'

Tiffy looked over her shoulder at him. 'I beg your pardon?'

'Well you might! You are an unmitigated rogue.'

'Not *unmitigated*. Adventurers have a code, although it must, upon occasion, be flexible.'

'Even invisible?' he suggested.

'Honour is a simple matter for the rich. The rest of us are often obliged to put convenience above conscience, as you'd soon discover if you ever had to fend for yourself.'

'Definitely an unmitigated rogue,' Courteney re-affirmed. 'You would twist anything to suit your own purpose.'

'That's human nature, so I can't be blamed for that, at any event,' Tiffy retorted, returning her attention to the food. 'Mm, another steak. And eggs . . . bacon . . . kidneys. What a famous cook you have! One soldier to feed, and he provides enough for an army. I wish the vicarage cook were half as generous. We have to subsist on cold meats and bread until dinner, gluttony being permitted only once a day since it is, like everything that is jolly, a Deadly Sin.'

She had been serving herself as she talked, and when she sat down at the table, Courteney looked at her generously-laden plate and said, amused, 'You have overlooked the tomatoes.'

'I don't care for them, but I would like some toast if you could put it within my reach.'

Courteney moved the plate towards her and they ate in silence until she asked, 'Can I still go to Bath?'

'That depends on you. Although my grandmother and I have little in common, we do share a great dislike of scandal. Unless you can accept that and behave yourself, there is little more we can do for you.'

A DIAMOND ZIRCONIA NECKLACE ABSOLUTELY FREE!

Dear Susan,

Your special introductory offer of 12 FREE BOOKS is too good to miss. Please will you also reserve a Reader Service Subscription for me so that I will receive 12 brand new Mills & Boon Romances each month for £14.40, post and packing free. If I decide not to subscribe, I shall write to you within 10 days. The free books and necklace will be mine to keep in any case. I understand that I may cancel or suspend my subscription at any time. I am over 18 years of age.

Yours FREE this beautiful diamond zirconia necklace

Name_____

Address_____

_____

_____Postcode_____

10A6TB

Susan Welland
Mills & Boon
Reader Service
FREEPOST
P.O. Box 236
CROYDON
Surrey CR9 9EL

NO
STAMP
NEEDED

Mills & Boon

ROMANCE
Win or Lose
KAY THORPE

ROMANCE
Wild for to Hold
ANNABEL MURRAY

ROMANCE
Escape from the Harem
MARY LYONS

Dear Reader

I think you are what they call an avid reader of love stories: I'm one,
too - so I know that you will find 12 FREE FULL-LENGTH
ROMANCES from Mills & Boon the most wonderful treat.

They're an introduction for you to our regular
subscription - **twelve brand new Romances** a month and
delivered direct to your home free of all post and
packing charges! The friendly Mills & Boon Reader
Service includes a monthly newsletter (competitions and author
bargain book offers, fascinating features and subscription
profiles) and a telephone advice line for a FREE
queries. Your 12 FREE NOVELS are sent with a delicate gold
necklace, a heart-shaped pendant on a delicate card overleaf
chain. Accept them by filling in this card - today. No stamp needed!

and sending it off to me - today.

She reminded him reproachfully, 'On the first day we met, you promised not to listen to unkind things about me.'

'Tobias didn't come to me with gossip. He spoke only the truth.'

'What could be more damning than that! Only it isn't so, not really. I didn't give you my word yesterday to behave myself when—when it would have been *politic* of me to do so. Don't forget that.'

'I haven't. It is the only thing that encourages me to believe you may still be saved from ruining yourself. How did you compel Tarleton to help you?'

'I can't tell you. It is a matter of my *questionable* honour. I am pledged to silence, you see.'

Courteney, after giving her a considering look, changed his line of questioning. 'Am I right in assuming that no one except Tarleton, Tobias and myself knows you were at the Tin Flute?'

'One other,' Tiffy conceded, wishing she could bring herself to lie to him. 'I am pledged to silence on that, too.'

'Cassy?' he guessed. When Tiffy threw him a darkling look and did not answer, he persisted, 'I must know. If, as you say, she is no friend of yours, she might make more mischief for you than I can quell.'

'I would rather have a scold than an inquisition!'

'Believe me, Tiffy, I dislike this as much as you. If there is to be a scandal, I can't fight it with half the facts. So, I repeat, is it Cassy?'

Tiffy's lips set in stubborn lines.

'Then it is her,' Courteney decided. 'Can she be bought off?'

Tiffy's eyes flew to his and she exclaimed indignantly, 'I went to that gambling den so that I should not have to hang on your sleeve, so I'll be damned if I'll let her! Besides, there is no need. She cannot ruin me without also ruining herself, and she cherishes her reputation more highly than I cherish mine. She would not *dare* do me a mischief!'

Courteney frowned, and then perceived the answer to the puzzle. He had heard often enough from Tiffy that Tarleton haunted the vicarage in pursuit of her cousin, and that Cassy was hopeful of marrying him if Sir Geoffrey should relent. 'Did you chance upon Tarleton and Cassy in a compromising situation?'

Her lips set more stubbornly than ever.

'Then it would appear that there is indeed no danger of your escapade leaking out,' he said, taking her silence to mean he had solved the puzzle correctly. 'Tiffy, if you want to go to Bath, you must promise me never again to enter a gaming hell.'

'Never? Surely you mean while I am in Lady Janetta's charge?'

'It would be as well for you if you made it a permanent promise.'

'How can you say so, when neither of us knows what might happen in the future? Lady Janetta might tire of my company and turn me out, you might be killed in that stupid war, and then where will I be? I might be forced to gamble to earn my bread. Precious use a spotless reputation will be to me if I am starving to death!'

Courteney smiled. 'I do not foresee such dire happenings.'

'I did not foresee coming to England without my Papa, but he is dead and here I am. Be reasonable, my lord.' She placed a hand over his, and went on, 'I promise faithfully to do nothing that would cause a scandal in Bath, if you can persuade Lady Janetta to take me with her. There! That is the promise I could not make you yesterday.'

He turned his hand to clasp hers. 'Understand me, Tiffy. If you let me down, it will be the end of our friendship. The bond will be broken. Do you still promise?'

She clutched his hand convulsively. 'Don't speak of breaking the bond in that—that—awesome way. You can be sure I shall never willingly break it. Only I know myself, and I don't think it is in me to be an *angel*. Besides, I don't think Lady Janetta would like angelic company. She would be bored before we had unpacked.'

'Very well, we shall accept that you are no angel, but can you contrive to be less of a little devil?'

Tiffy's delightful grin curved her lips and her eyes danced. 'Since I am pledged to cause no scandals, I shall have to be, shan't I? Oh, my lord, isn't it *nice* to be comfortable again?'

CHAPTER EIGHT

HER WORDS caused Courteney to choke on the last of his ale. 'I can think of many words to describe my dealings with you, Tiffy, but comfortable is not one of them!'

'Nonsense. We can be natural when we are together. You can be as staid as you please, and I don't think you boring. I can be wild, and you don't think me depraved. We tolerate each other's little faults—and that, my lord,' she ended triumphantly, 'is *comfortable*.'

'If entering a gaming hell dressed as a boy is one of your little faults, dare I ask you to name one of mine?'

Tiffy was nothing loath, and leaning across to froth more ale into his tankard from the jug, responded severely, 'You tell untruths when it suits you. Oh, yes, you do! The day we met, you said it would be vulgar ostentation if a footman accompanied us to the vicarage. I believed you, and later learned it is perfectly usual to travel with a footman in attendance.'

'Not one rigged out in antiquated state livery! You know how Lady Janetta loathes change, particularly at Dalmaine, so those museum pieces are worn when she is visiting. But flaunt a bewigged and satin-clad footman about the countryside, no, not even for you, Tiffy! In this day and age, believe me, it would be shockingly pretentious.'

She frowned over this, then admitted, 'I didn't properly understand. Does that mean that when I travel in your carriage, I could have a footman dressed in modern livery if I wished?'

'Certainly.'

'Good! I wish for one above all things. I do so love to be grand. Oh, and that reminds me. I have something of the greatest importance to discuss with you. Do you think we might finish our drinks by the fire?'

'What, when we have already established how comfortable we are?'

Tiffy smiled at his teasing, but retorted, 'That is no reason why we shouldn't also be cosy.'

'You have an answer for everything,' he sighed, picking up his tankard and rising when she did.

'Well, I should hope so. Only consider what a sorry pickle I would be in otherwise! But pray be serious. This is a matter of some delicacy.'

'God help me,' Courteney breathed, settling himself into an armchair on one side of the fire. 'Don't tell me you're in more trouble than I know of?'

'No, nothing like that,' she denied, but there was little in her manner to reassure him. She sat bolt upright in the armchair opposite his, her reticule on her lap, her forehead puckered. 'This matter concerns my nature, my lord. I dare say you have noticed it leans towards the frivolous?'

'It would be difficult not to notice,' he admitted.

This appeared to please rather than distress her, for she was emboldened to confess, 'Given half a chance, I would devote my entire life to frivolity. It suits me. In fact, it *is* me, and no amount of preaching will make me any different. What is bred in the bone will come out in the blood, after all. Papa loved high living and Mama adored pretty things, so it is not to be wondered at if I crave both.'

She fell silent for a moment, marshalling her thoughts, and when she began again, her tone was hot with indignation. 'You know how it sinks my spirits to be obliged to wear Cassy's cast-offs. Living in reduced circumstances occasionally is one thing, but poverty as a way of life I cannot endure. My aunt may tell me I am suffering from delusions of grandeur, and my uncle may call the expensive things I am used to the trappings of the damned—but I would rather be deluded and damned than meek and miserable. And that is why I gambled last night. It was not an act of depravity. It was desperation!'

'It was misguided.'

'Inevitable!'

'Yes, that, too,' Courteney conceded. 'The Everetts have made a sad business of managing you, but if only you'd waited . . .'

'I couldn't,' she broke in vehemently. 'My nature is as impatient as it is frivolous. Oh, I knew what I risked, but I stood to gain everything I desired. Or so I thought, except that the stakes were so niggardly I won only two hundred and twenty guineas. Not enough to rig me out in the first stare of fashion. Being respectably clad might do very well for an Everett, but it is not good enough for a Yorke!'

The paralysing candour of this speech, with its strange mixture of naïvety, wantonness and arrogance, might well have confounded anybody less well acquainted with Tiffy than Courteney, but he bore up under it remarkably well, and only asked, 'When were you sixteen?'

'Last December. What has that to do with it?'

'A great deal. Whatever plans you are making, they are premature. You are too young to make a come-out this season.'

'I know if I go to Bath it will be as Lady Janetta's companion and not to make my début. The point is that Bath is modish. I shall be *seen*. I must be at my best! It would be fatal to my chances to appear as a dowd.'

'What chances?' Courteney asked, puzzled.

'Of marriage. I have given the matter *much* thought, and quite see that if I cannot be a courtesan or an actress, then I must marry.'

'Tiffy, you are still premature. You said yourself that an early marriage would be disastrous for you!'

'Poof! I was but a child then,' she scoffed. 'I am quite grown up now. I don't mean to marry just anybody. A red-faced country squire or an indigent curate will never do.'

'Indeed not,' Courteney agreed fervently.

Tiffy chuckled. 'You are thinking I would soon be bored and kicking up larks, and, of course, you are right! No, I have decided on a—a—man of fashion. One who leads the sort of life that suits me best. I could be happy with such a man, I know it! Why are you frowning? I thought you would be delighted I have become so sensible.'

'You are being too hasty. A marriage of convenience would suit you as little as it suited your mama.'

Tiffy's thick lashes swept down to hide her expressive eyes. She could not tell him that her heart had already been lost to Jago. On the rare occasions Courteney referred to his cousin, it was in such a non-committal way that it was evident little love was lost between them.

She saw nothing to wonder at in this, since they were so vastly different, but she feared that the protective side of Courteney's nature, which she had good reason to be thankful for at the moment, might well become a severe hindrance in the future. He was unlikely to regard Jago, most decidedly and deliciously a rake, as a suitable bridegroom.

There was also Lady Janetta to be considered. She would be violently opposed to a Harwood attaching himself to a Yorke. She would never take Tiffy to Bath if she suspected that either of her grandsons stood in such danger. And Jago himself would be in a ticklish position. He was Lady Janetta's favourite and had every expectation of inheriting her fortune, so naturally he would not want to upset her.

Tiffy, sufficiently addicted to novels to know that the path of true love never ran smooth, nevertheless felt she had to pick her way through a veritable quagmire. The only thing she could be certain of was that her passion must remain a secret until Jago was similarly afflicted, and then they could plot their way ahead together.

Courteney, believing her to be dwelling on his last words, prompted, 'Surely you can see that if you have changed so much over these past weeks, you are likely to change a great deal more over the next few years?'

Tiffy saw no such thing, but to humour him she replied, 'Possibly, although it would be madness not to be *ready* if the right man should come along. Besides, it still makes me miserable to be shabby. When I am discontented I fall into scrapes, so if I am to keep my word to be good I must be happy. I shall be, too, with everything about me fine! Clothes from the most fashionable modistes and—and—all the expensive trifles that make up a lady of fashion. Which brings me, my lord, to the point of this discussion.'

She opened her reticule, took out a small object, lovingly unwrapped the silk shielding it, and stared at it for a moment. Then she passed it to him, saying simply, 'My mama.'

Courteney found himself looking at a miniature, delicately executed in oils, of a breathtakingly beautiful woman. Her deep-blue eyes gazed tenderly at him. A smile teased her soft lips. Her fair hair, curling about her forehead and ears, was brought forward over one shoulder to repose in two thick ringlets on her snow-white bosom. Her perfection and angelic fairness reminded him so forcibly of his own Eleanor that he winced.

'What's the matter?' Tiffy asked.

'Such beauty almost—hurts,' he answered lamely.

'It certainly hurts me,' she told him frankly. 'But that is because I don't possess it. Where *did* I get this lamentable nose?'

Dragging his eyes away from the portrait, Courteney protested, 'Tiffy, you do yourself an injustice. As a whole, your face is enchanting.'

'Thank you,' she said in polite disbelief.

'I mean it.'

'Your manners are *always* beautiful, but I am a realist. My eyes are incomparable—the rest of me leaves much to be desired! The lily, my lord, *must* be gilded. I shall be sunk if, in my present state, I find myself in competition with a beauty like my mama. Papa said such beauty is extremely rare, but one never knows. He described Mama as a Diamond of the First Water, and that is why he bought her a diamond necklace as a betrothal present when they eloped. See, she is wearing it in the portrait.'

Courteney looked again at the miniature and studied the circlet of diamonds with three pendant drops that was painted round the smooth white throat. It was pretty and dainty, and he said so.

'Yes,' Tiffy agreed. 'Mama never parted with it, no matter what, nor did Papa ever ask her to. She meant to give it to me on my wedding day, you see, so that I could be certain of some kind of a dowry even if we should be out of funds at the time. When she died, she placed it in Papa's care. He let me wear it sometimes. He would call me his fine lady and say that one day I would marry a prince—only I would rather not, for I believe your English princes are old and fat, besides preferring mistresses to wives.'

She opened her reticule once more and drew out a blue velvet pouch. 'Anyway, two years or so ago he had the necklace cleaned. It has been kept in here ever since, fresh and sparkling as new.' She loosened the pouch's drawstrings and tipped the necklace into her hand. Her fingers closed convulsively around it, but only for a second, and then she was holding it out to him. 'Here, my lord. Take it. I want you to sell it for me.'

'I can't do that!' he exclaimed.

'Why not? The portrait is proof that the necklace is mine to dispose of. That's why I fetched it.'

'Tiffy, take it back,' he ordered, holding out the necklace to her. 'It is a memento of your mother,

and irreplaceable. You will regret all your life selling
it.'

He was so right that she pushed the necklace away and
flared angrily, 'What use are diamonds round my neck if
I have rags on my back?'

'That is the wildest exaggeration.'

'It isn't! I shall *die* if I have to remain a dowd much
longer. I want to be a lady of fashion, and I *will* be.'

'One doesn't cast an heirloom to the winds to satisfy
vanity, Tiffy.'

'Perhaps a Harwood of Dalmaine doesn't, but I am a
Yorke of Swayle and therefore capable of anything!' she
flung at him, then was almost overcome. If only she
could keep the necklace! It meant so much to her, but
Jago meant more, and that was all there was to it.

She swallowed hard and, to cover the struggle going
on within her, smiled in a mocking manner that disturbed him. Neither did he like the cynical note in her
voice when she went on more calmly, 'In my family there
are no such things as heirlooms. Only disposable assets.'

'Then explain to me why this asset has never been
disposed of before?'

He had her there! Like her mama and papa before
her, she had clung to the necklace through the grimmest
times until an overwhelming need to sell it had con-
fronted her—and she could not tell him what that need
was. She bit her lip, realised that by doing so she had
revealed her agitation, and cursed him silently.

'Tiffy, are you swearing under your breath?'

She flung up her hand in the manner of a fencer
acknowledging a hit.

'Good,' Courteney said with satisfaction.

'Good?' Amazement widened her eyes.

'Yes, because now I feel I might be getting close to a
truth I am persuaded you are taking great pains to hide.
Why, Tiffy? You can trust me.'

Alarm bells rang in her head and once more she took

refuge in self-mockery, saying lightly, 'With my life, certainly, but not with my black heart. You are much too *good* to be burdened with that.'

Rare anger chilled his grey eyes, and he said coldly, 'Sometimes you speak the most unadulterated rubbish. I don't want to hear any more about black hearts.'

'But vanity is my reason for selling the necklace, and vanity is a sin, and sins are *always* painted black.' She reflected on this momentarily, then shrugged, and committed a further sin by lying without a blush, 'I am not concealing anything from you. You choose to think so because you will persist in believing me nicer than I am. I am a rogue—though *not* unmitigated. The mitigating circumstance here is that it would be ridiculous to be sentimental when common sense dictates that a dowry is useless unless I have secured a husband.'

She paused for breath, hoping she had convinced him. She wanted the necklace removed from her sight. Once or twice, even while advocating its sale, she had been within an ace of snatching it back. Only by conjuring up an image of the man who teased her dreams had she been able to keep her hands firmly rooted in her lap.

Courteney, looking at her in an uncomfortably intent way, said at last, 'I cannot be a party to the sale of this necklace, nor is it necessary. I intended to ensure your comfort in Bath by making you an allowance. It will be payable through Lady Janetta so that you will not be compromised.'

'I would rather risk ruin in a dozen gaming hells than impose on you in such a way. I have my pride!'

'Such heat—and from you, who once persuaded me that pride, between friends, would permit a compromise.'

'Oh! It must have suited me to say so at the time, but it doesn't suit me now. What you suggest is not a compromise but charity, and I am *sick* of that. I don't mind being obliged to you for advancing me socially, because I cannot do that for myself. However, I can and will fund myself.'

'Sometimes, Tiffy,' Courteney replied, 'I believe you would cut off your nose to spite your face.'

'It is not much of a nose, in any event, as we both know,' she snapped. 'I wouldn't have asked your aid if I could get a fair price for the necklace myself, but experience has taught me that I can't. I was obliged to sell two of Papa's beautiful snuffboxes to pay for my passage to England, and they were worth ten times what I was paid for them. They should have raised enough for me to cross the Atlantic in style, but the jeweller was despicable. He treated me as though I were a thief. He told me I was lucky to be offered anything for them, and I had to take his few miserable pounds! It was imperative for me to board ship before the few possessions I escaped Papa's creditors with were seized to pay his bills. Also, of course, there was all the war talk because you British will keep stopping and searching neutral ships, and I thought I might be stranded. Indeed, the United States declared war a month later, which I hope will teach you that somebody has the nerve to challenge your arrogance on the high seas!'

Courteney smiled at her fervour. 'So speaks my little American—by inclination, if not by blood? British naval policy might have been the States' overt reason for declaring war, but we believe the *covert* one was a grab at Canada, which really has to be discouraged, you know.'

'Oh?' Tiffy exclaimed, her eyes kindling. 'It sounds to me as if you're in for another bloody nose, and—what on earth are we talking about war for?'

'You raised the subject.'

'*I* did? Well, perhaps, but only incidentally. There was no reason for you to take me up on it! All I was trying to do was to explain why I shall be cheated if I sell the necklace myself. Papa paid two thousand pounds for it, and I could set myself up nicely with a comparable sum, only I don't know any reputable dealers. You, however, are going to London and *must* know a jeweller who wouldn't dream of cheating anybody as grand as a marquess. I loathe to badger you, but you can see my predicament, and—and the necklace must be sold.'

To gain a respite from her appealing eyes, and to give himself time to think, Courteney returned his attention to the sparkling necklace and studied it closely. Suddenly he asked, 'Have you ever tried to pawn it?'

'No. I thought about it last night, but it wouldn't answer. One is only advanced a fraction of an item's value, and that wouldn't be enough. Even Papa never popped—I beg your pardon, *pawned*—it because he held it in trust for me, and there was always the slight risk the luck wouldn't turn sufficiently for it to be redeemed.'

'What a hair-raising existence you led, Tiffy!'

'Yes,' she agreed wistfully. 'It was very exciting, never knowing each day whether one's fortune would be made or lost.'

That was not at all what he meant, but he made no comment. After frowning for a few seconds, his brow cleared and he said, 'Tiffy, let me become your—er —pawnbroker.'

She blinked incredulously. '*You?*'

'I shall advance you two thousand pounds, and keep the necklace as security. You can redeem it any time you wish. If you fail to do so, I shall not be out of pocket. Diamonds are always a good investment.'

She jumped to her feet with cheeks and eyes glowing, exclaiming excitedly, 'I shall have the money I need, and the necklace will not be *lost*! When I was *certain* it wasn't possible, too! My lord, you are a *genius*.'

Courteney rose to his feet, smiling at her joy. He slipped the necklace into his pocket, and replied, 'We have been an unconscionable time reaching a satisfactory conclusion. You'd best make haste to change into your riding-habit, if you want to ride before luncheon.' He gave her back the miniature, adding, 'Put this away safely first. It is a fine painting, quite apart from the fact that it is of your mother.'

'Thank you,' she said, glowing anew, as she wrapped the miniature in silk and replaced it in her reticule. 'It was painted by my papa which, of course, makes it doubly precious. I shall put it back in my trunk the minute I get home.'

'In your trunk? Surely you display your mama's portrait?'

'The Everetts will not permit the portrait of a Jezebel to be exhibited in their house. Their words, naturally.'

Courteney, normally careful to take no side in the feud between Tiffy and her relatives, was shocked into saying, 'What cruelty!'

'They called it piety. What I called it is too shockingly blasphemous to be repeated. However, I won't let bad thoughts spoil what is turning out to be an uncommonly good day, nor do I mean to miss my gallop. Thank you once more, my lord, for being so very good to me.' She gave him one of her fierce, impulsive hugs and fairly danced her way towards the door.

As she was opening it, he checked her by saying, 'Tiffy?'

She looked back over her shoulder. 'Yes?'

'When you won that money last night . . . did you cheat?'

'What a question! You surely don't expect me to answer it?' She kissed her fingers at him, giggled and whisked herself out of the room.

Courteney did not linger in the breakfast parlour after Tiffy had departed. While she, skirts held high, hurtled up the stairs two at a time to change her clothes, he succumbed to an impatience of his own and made haste to the library. The post, as he had hoped, had been brought up from the receiving office and was set out neatly on his leather-inlaid desk.

Ignoring the carefully folded newspapers, he picked up the pile of letters and flicked rapidly through them, a daily ritual that was doomed once more to disappointment. The letter he sought was not among them. In vain did he remind himself that the mail from Jamaica depended on many unpredictable factors, not only the weather, for much could happen to a ship flying the colours of a nation at war with France on one side of the Atlantic and with the United States on the other. Sensible reflections had no power to appease the bleakness of searching the mail every day for a letter that never came, but he quickly masked his feelings when the door opened.

Lady Janetta walked in, raised her long malacca cane and shook it at him, snapping as she did so, 'Damn if I don't lay this stick of mine across that pesky brat's shoulders when I catch up with her. She nearly ran me down when I came out of my rooms just now.'

'Tiffy? She would not do that. She was merely in a hurry to change into her riding-habit,' Courteney replied, going forward to kiss her hand and lead her to a chair by the desk.

'As well let loose a hurricane in the house!' Lady Janetta sat down, twitched her skirts to order, and went on, 'I tell you what, Dalmaine. Don't ever take her hunting. She'll be heading off the fox before anybody else is in the saddle.'

Courteney propped himself against his desk, folded his arms, and smiled down at her. 'She wouldn't be expecting you to leave your rooms before luncheon. It's something of a surprise for me, too.'

'Well it might be! It ain't good at my age to stir abroad before the day is properly aired. But something's amiss, and I mean to discover what it is. My woman had it from Farley that you ain't going up to London today. It ain't like you to change your mind for no reason, so what's happened?'

'There were one or two matters I wanted to settle first.' He stood up as he spoke, dislodging some letters from the desk. He bent to retrieve them, and the blue velvet pouch containing the necklace fell unnoticed from his coat pocket. He dropped the letters on the desk, strolled towards the windows and stared out as he considered the best way to broach the Bath scheme to his grandmother.

Lady Janetta, whose gimlet eyes missed little, stared at the pouch and hooked it towards her with her cane. When Courteney turned back to her, the pouch was on her lap, the necklace in her hand and she was scrutinising it closely through her eyeglass.

He went quickly towards her, his hand held out. 'If you please, Grandmama. That is Tiffy's.'

'What are you doing with it, then?'

'She placed it in my care.'

'Whatever for?' Lady Janetta dropped the necklace contemptuously in his hand, then gave him the pouch. 'It ain't worth a groat. It's paste.'

He sighed, but it would have been too much to expect his grandmother not to spot a fake. 'I know,' he admitted, 'but Tiffy doesn't, and I beg you not to tell her. The necklace is very special to her. Her father gave it to her mother as a betrothal present, and she intended it to be something of a dowry for Tiffy. Before she died, she entrusted it to Tiffy's father. According to Tiffy, he had it cleaned a couple of years ago. Most possibly it was then he had it copied, and sold the original.'

'That sounds like a Yorke,' Lady Janetta agreed with a bark of laughter, 'but what has it to do with you?'

'Tiffy never knew. She believes the necklace is genuine and worth two thousand pounds. She is tired of living on her relatives' charity, and now that she is of an age to desire fashionable clothes, she brought it to me to sell for her.'

'You didn't tell her it's a fake?' Lady Janetta asked incredulously, her painted eyebrows arching.

'How could I? It would destroy her faith in her father, and you must know that she reveres him. She has little to cling to but his memory. I couldn't take that away from her.'

'I'll tell you something else you can't do, and that's sell that piece of trumpery. If you can't bring yourself to tell her the truth, give it back to her and say you ain't a damned trader.'

'I can't. She will try to sell the necklace herself, and then she will learn that her father was not worthy of the trust both she and her mother placed in him.'

'God save us, Dalmaine, you turn my stomach with your sickly sentimentality! You can't do this, you can't do that—what do you mean to do?'

'Advance her two thousand pounds and hold the necklace as security.'

'What?' Lady Janetta screeched. 'If that ain't proof you're next door to a moonling, just as I always suspected!'

Courteney smiled. 'I knew I might depend on you to confuse compassion with insanity. However, it is not the bad risk that you think. I know she will redeem the necklace one day.'

'Yes, just as you know the moon is made of cheese, no doubt,' Lady Janetta rasped. 'The chit's wheedled two thousand pounds out of you, and that's all there is to it.'

'You wrong her, Grandmama.'

'Bah! I hope I might live long enough to see it. Assuming—which I don't!—that she does buy back the necklace, what will be the point of all this? It's *possible* she's too ignorant now to tell real diamonds from paste, but she won't stay that way. If she gets the necklace back, sooner or later she will discover the truth.'

'By that time, one must hope that she will have a husband to care for her so that she won't be so dependent on memories of her father. All I am doing is buying her a little time in which to grow up and become less vulnerable,' Courteney told her quietly.

'It's you who are vulnerable. She spotted you as a soft touch, Dalmaine, and sold you a pig in a poke.'

'I can only repeat that you wrong her. I am perfectly satisfied she believes the necklace is genuine.'

'Why didn't she sell it long ago if she don't care to be a pauper brat?' Lady Janetta asked triumphantly.

'The necklace is so important to her that only the most pressing need could persuade her to part with it.'

'What pressing need?'

'Ah.' Courteney returned the necklace to its pouch and put it back into his pocket. 'It's unfortunate we should have to approach the matter in this way, but now to come to the part that affects you.'

'Take a damper,' she retorted. 'None of this affects me. I ain't touched in my cockloft.'

'But you did want to know why I delayed my journey to London,' he pointed out, unruffled. 'It was to discuss with you a scheme I have been turning over in my mind for Tiffy's immediate future. It has been worrying me what will become of her when I go abroad. She is unhappy at the vicarage, and will probably run away, with heaven knows what consequences. You, however, appreciate her in a way the Everetts never will. She entertains you better than any companion you ever had. She likes and respects you, and Tiffy, under those circumstances, is not disruptive but affectionate and loyal. If you will take her to Bath as your companion, I believe you will gain as much as you give.'

'Saddle myself with a brat who's no kin of mine, half wild, and a Yorke to boot?' Lady Janetta exclaimed, giving him an arctic stare. 'Why should I?'

'Because it will amuse you to do so.'

Lady Janetta opened her mouth to utter a choleric denial, then shut it again. She dearly loved to set the cat among the pigeons, and to thrust Tiffy upon the sedate society of Bath would cause just such a flutter as she delighted in. There would be whispers a'plenty about Tiffy's raffish background, but Lady Janetta knew her power and loved to use it.

Another factor in Tiffy's favour occurred to her acute mind. The understanding reached between Eleanor and Dalmaine last winter, while he was home on leave, had not been officially anounced because he was still in mourning for his brother.

Mr and Mrs Hunt, knowing Dalmaine to be a perfect gentleman who would not renege on his word, obviously felt their daughter had all the time in the world in which to recover from the shock of his scarred countenance. They needed to be jolted out of their complacency. A letter from herself, carelessly imparting the news that she had under her wing a ravishing young lady expected to take society by storm, would doubtless shock them into booking their passages to England. The marriage mart held no comparable catch if Eleanor lost Dalmaine! Dotingly fond and over-indulgent parents as they were, the Hunts would not risk Eleanor being superseded, unbetrothed, by a new belle. Anxiety bred anxiety, and they would begin to fear that Dalmaine might feel Eleanor had given him good cause to revoke the understanding.

Lady Janetta knew her world so well that she was confident the summer would see the Hunts safely back in England. That news relayed to Dalmaine would surely urge him to exercise a gentleman's prerogative to return home from the war for the hunting season. A wedding before Christmas and an heir on the way before spring would be ample recompense for any disruption in her life that Tiffy might cause.

It occurred to her that Dalmaine was unaware that, in

consigning Tiffy to her care, he was placing in her hands the very tool to bring his erring bride back to his side. He would, of course, disapprove of such tactics, which caused Lady Janetta to give a sudden crack of laughter, and exclaim, 'I'll do it.'

Courteney, expecting stiff resistance, recovered from his surprise and once more raised her hand to kiss her fingers. 'Thank you, Grandmama. You've taken a weight off my mind. I shall make all the arrangements. You need not fear you will be put to any inconvenience.'

'You don't call Tiffy an inconvenience?' she scoffed, but good-humouredly. 'I do, not that she ain't more to my taste than you are. Look what she's achieved in next to no time! Coaxed two thousand out of you and got me to sponsor her into the first circles. I wonder how far she'll go before she over-reaches herself and comes an almighty cropper?'

'I am depending on you to avert such a disaster,' Courteney replied quickly. 'She is set on marriage as a solution to her future, so I must also depend on you to restrain her in that direction. She is far too young to make a sensible choice.'

Lady Janetta, who had no intention of permitting Tiffy to become entangled and thus remove herself as a threat to Eleanor, replied forcefully, 'I don't tell you how to run your curst brigade. Don't tell me how to manage a schoolroom chit.'

Courteney smiled and bowed. 'I stand corrected. Grandmama, I never intended you to know anything about Tiffy's necklace. It is a private matter between us, and must remain that way. Will you promise not to mention it to her or, indeed, to anybody?'

'Good God, Dalmaine, if you ain't got more hair than wit to ask such a thing,' Lady Janetta barked, lapsing into her customary bad temper. 'I know what's due to the family, so I ain't likely to advertise my grandson's folly to the world, am I?'

CHAPTER NINE

Tiffy was thrilled when she heard the news, nor had she any fault to pick with the speedy way Courteney put his plan into operation. A courier was despatched immediately to Lord and Lady Swayle in Norfolk soliciting their permission for Tiffy to spend the spring and summer months in Bath.

And that very afternoon Courteney accompanied Tiffy to the vicarage to seek similar permission from the Reverend Hector and his wife. There was no difficulty there, the pious pair being more inclined to fall upon his neck in gratitude than raise objections, labouring as they were under the illusion that Lady Janetta had tamed their shrewish charge.

Cassy could have told them better, but she had reached the point of equating happiness with never having to set eyes on her cousin again. When the news was relayed to Tarleton he, too, was overjoyed that his own particular *bête noire* was about to be removed from his immediate vicinity.

Tobias, at the end of that busy weekend, was thankfully able to tell his master that no gossip was circulating about Miss Tiffy at the Tin Flute or elsewhere. Courteney, his mind relieved of its most urgent worry, set out early on Monday for London.

Even the weather was in an optimistic mood, and when Tiffy arrived at the castle later that morning there was real warmth in the sun. The promise of spring in the air was so akin to the promise of love in her heart that she was soon tempted out of doors. She was attracted to the ornamental lake by glimpses through the trees of daffodils beginning to bloom in golden glory along its banks. She idly picked some for the library, her mind preoccupied with thoughts of Jago. When she came upon a clump of snowdrops nestling among the daffodils, she picked a few and sat beside a graceful willow to thread them daisy-fashion into a garland.

Tiffy smiled at the result and put the garland on her head, the silky white bells of the flowers looking more charming than she knew against her glossy dark curls. She sat for a while, gazing round and seeing great beauty where none had existed for her before, such a determined hold had she kept on her former life in America. Time and fresh emotions were beginning to loosen that grip so that she felt less alien. She did not feel at home precisely, but she no longer felt trapped. Courteney had opened the cage for her. Soon she would fly away to Jago.

Tiffy smiled at her fanciful thoughts, but they persisted as she dawdled back to the castle. She entered by a side door and encountered a young footman, who, grinning at the forgotten snowdrops on her head, took her cape and promised to bring a vase of water for the daffodils.

She thanked him and went to the library. When the vase arrived, she decided that a table behind the door was as good a place as any to arrange the daffodils and promptly busied herself with this task. She was a fair way towards making a pretty arrangement when she was startled by the door being flung open. A tall man strode purposefully to the desk without noticing her, picked up a newspaper and turned the pages impatiently until he found what he was seeking and paused to read.

Jago . . .

Gone were the much-remembered scarlet regimentals, but in civilian wear he was scarcely less exciting. A curly-brimmed beaver hat was set at a rakish angle on his handsome dark head and a long multi-caped driving coat of white drab was flung over a blue coat, breeches and white-topped boots.

For several seconds Tiffy drank in all his manly glory, then came down to earth with a thump. It was too soon, this second meeting. She was still a dowd, drearily clad in a dark-blue woollen gown the larger Cassy had discarded years before. If he saw her now, there was no possibility of his recognising her as his own true soulmate. She tried to shrink behind the door, hoping he would leave the room as he had entered, without noticing her. She held her breath, certain he was leaving the castle. Had he just arrived, he would have been relieved of his outdoor clothing by the porter.

Jago, apparently, had read all he wanted to. He tossed the newspaper back on the desk, turned once more to the door, and glimpsed her frozen figure as he did so. His brown eyes flicked over her, taking in her unadorned dark dress, the flower arrangement, and her apprehensive expression.

His mobile eyebrows shot up and he came slowly towards her. 'Don't look so frightened,' he drawled. 'I won't tell the housekeeper I've caught you out of proper uniform. I doubt if she'd appreciate the novelty of a cap of snowdrops instead of lace as much as I do.'

Tiffy, realising indignantly that he had mistaken her for a maid, was about to deny that she was any such thing when he took her dimpled chin in his strong fingers and turned her face up to his. 'Charming,' he said at last. 'And something strangely familiar about those splendid eyes. Do you have an older sister?'

Not knowing whether to be thankful or furious that he didn't remember her, but certain that her accent would jolt his memory, she dumbly shook her head.

'A pity,' he went on. 'But one mustn't miss one's opportunities.' His handsome face came closer and closer and before Tiffy realised what was in his mind, she was being kissed full on her soft lips. She was then quite powerless to do anything. Even after the kiss ended, it took her some seconds to recover from its spell.

She opened her eyes finally to find he was looking down at her in some amusement. 'Am I the first man to kiss you, little abigail? What a slowtop my cousin must be—and his servants. Well, I've given you a standard to judge your future swains by.'

Tiffy, her wits as disordered as her senses, only wished he would stop talking and kiss her again.

But Jago appeared as much in command of himself as ever, for he went on, 'I suppose you will eventually be matched with some clodpole of a footman. What a waste! You respond with such promise that I'm almost tempted . . .'

Tiffy, to her chagrin, was never to learn what he was tempted to do, for footsteps approaching along the corridor outside made him release her and step back. Farley entered with the news that his carriage had been brought to the door. He looked disapprovingly from Jago to Tiffy but made no comment—beyond leaving the door pointedly open as he withdrew.

Jago laughed softly. 'Nobody approves of me in this stiff-necked household—save you, I'll wager. I must be gone now, but don't worry. Sooner or later I'll be back. There's a thought to warm yourself with when you're tired of fumbling footmen.'

He came close to her again, towering above her, so that she felt most deliciously threatened, although he offered her no further molestation beyond flicking her snub nose with a careless finger as he chided, 'No cap, no apron, no curtsy and no defence. You've a lot to learn, little abigail, if you are to survive in this wicked world. Mrs Royston will teach you all you should know, and I shall teach you all you should not. Which of us will you run to, I wonder? No, don't tell me. It will add spice to my next visit. Meanwhile, I claim this as a trophy.'

He lifted the snowdrop garland from her head,

twirled it around a finger and, turning on his heel, strode from the room, his long driving-coat swishing about his booted feet.

If he thought he'd left her in a state of nervous collapse, he mistook his quarry. Tiffy was far too cock-a-hoop to think of swooning. Dreadfully clothed though she was, Jago had thought her old enough and pretty enough to be flirted with!

She looked down at her bosom, half expecting it to have burgeoned into Cassy-like proportions now that she had been kissed by the man she loved. It had not, but she was overwhelmed by the urge to get one last glimpse of him.

She hurried out of the library, ran along the corridor and into the gracious blue salon that overlooked the main approach to the castle. She was just in time to see Jago climbing into a racing curricle, its gleaming black body resting on dashing yellow wheels. What a complete hand he was, she thought exultantly. As he gathered the reins, he glanced up at the window as if he knew she was peering down at him. Their eyes met. He smiled and touched his whip to his hat in a mocking salute.

The grooms holding the heads of a pair of black horses every bit as dangerous looking as their master turned to stare at the window. Tiffy sprang back behind the drapes. When she dared to look again, the grooms were releasing their charges and jumping aside. The horses lunged forward and Jago once more departed from her life.

'The devil,' Tiffy breathed, deeply appreciative. When she went back to the library, curiosity took her to the desk, where she picked up the paper Jago had tossed down. It was open at the society columns, but although she read every word to see what had interested him, none of the people or events mentioned had any significance for her.

As she was putting the paper down, she saw on top of a

pile of post brought up from the receving office that morning a travel-stained letter addressed in a beautiful rounded script to The Most Honourable the Marquess of Dalmaine. It was from Jamaica, and Tiffy snatched it up in excitement. So Eleanor had written at last! How vexatious that her letter should have missed Courteney by a couple of hours. It might lie gathering dust for a week or more. Something must be done immediately, for although the marquess thought he had been discreet in his daily search of the post, there wasn't a person in the entire household who did not know he was burning for a letter from his love. Clutching the letter, she ran out of the room, calling for Farley.

When he approached at his usual dignified pace, she waved the letter at him and exclaimed, 'Miss Hunt has written at last! Have a courier saddle up and take her letter to his lordship immediately.'

Farley demurred, 'The marquess left no such orders.'

'Naturally he didn't. We are not supposed to know how much he is dying to hear from Miss Hunt, but we do know, don't we?'

'Perhaps,' Farley admitted. 'What if it is bad news?'

Tiffy had not thought of that. She turned the letter over and studied the seal. 'Damnation! There will be no breaking that without its being noticed.'

'You mustn't do that,' the man protested.

But Tiffy wasn't attending. She was staring at the letter and tapping it against her other hand. Suddenly her expression cleared, and she said confidentially, 'This isn't bad news. Don't ask me how I know. I can only tell you this is a *good* day, and only good things happen on good days. *Instinct*, Farley. If you will not send a courier after his lordship, I shall ride to London myself.'

'In that case, a courier will be despatched,' Farley replied, taking the letter. 'His lordship might not have left orders, but he certainly won't want you careering off after him.'

'Bless you! Mark my words, when his lordship returns, he will be a great deal more cheerful. Genuinely cheerful, I mean, and not just pretending for our benefit.' Having got her way, Tiffy turned to another important matter. 'I was surprised to see Mr Jago here this morning. I didn't know he was due to visit.'

'None of us did, Miss Tiffy. He is on his way to stay with friends in Sussex and broke his journey here last night. Naturally he had to wish his lordship all that is proper now that his departure for the Peninsula is so close.'

'You don't expect him to return in the immediate future, then?'

'No, not that anyone can anticipate what Mr Jago will do.'

Tiffy smiled, thinking that Jago's unpredictability was half his fascination, but she said only, 'Thank you, Farley. I shall not delay you any longer. You will want to get that letter on its way.'

The library, however, now that it lacked the companionship of Courteney's presence or the vitality of Jago's, seemed deadly dull and Tiffy soon left it. She wandered up the grand staircase and along the main corridor of the principal wing, looking for something to do. When she came to the gilded double doors of the marquess's apartment, she hesitated, for this was bachelor territory and the only place in the great house that was off limits to her. Curiosity fought with decorum, and curiosity won. She opened one of the doors, peeped round it and then slipped in.

Tiffy, accustomed to magnificence by now, was none the less awed by the gilded and painted ceiling and the painted panels upon the walls. The furnishings were of blue, white and gold, and the room was large enough to sleep half a dozen marquesses in comfort. She touched the four-poster bed, sumptuously draped with gold-fringed blue velvet, and her eyes then fell on a cluster of miniatures displayed on the Sheraton chest of drawers beside the bed. She went over and studied them. Closest to the bed was a face she did not know, painted in oils and enclosed in an elaborate gold frame. It was of a young lady whose fair loveliness reminded Tiffy of her mother.

She picked up the miniature and saw the resemblance was in the perfect regularity of features, the blueness of the eyes and the fairness of the hair. The difference was in the spirit animating the portraits. Tiffy's mother's breathed a roguish vitality; this one tranquillity. Eleanor Hunt, it must be. She looked just the kind of girl the quiet Courteney would love *à corps perdu*.

A sound made her swing round guiltily, the miniature still in her hand. She found herself being surveyed reproachfully by an elderly man of extreme thinness, whose dark neat clothes proclaimed his calling. Tiffy recognised him as Marlowe, who had been valet to Courteney's father. He had chosen to remain at the castle after his retirement, emerging to serve Courteney when he was in residence.

Tiffy, summing him up quickly, decided that nothing but frankness would serve her now, and said, 'I am trespassing. I can claim nothing in my defence beyond vulgar curiosity. However, some good might come of it. This is Miss Hunt's likeness, isn't it?'

She held out the miniature, and Marlowe glided wraith-like towards her, as if his spirit had already left his emaciated body. He looked at the portrait and replied, 'That is so, miss.'

'I thought it must be.' She frowned. She wanted to give Courteney a memento of their friendship when he went away, and had been wrestling with the problem of what she could possibly present to a man who already had everything. Now she thought she had the answer.

'Marlowe, may I take this miniature home with me for

a few days while his lordship is away? I am very skilled with water colours. If I do a copy, I can get a jeweller to fit it into my papa's watch—and that will make a splendid keepsake for his lordship to take to the war with him. He has done so much for me that I would like to do some small thing for him, and I am sure he would like nothing more than having Miss Hunt's portrait with him all the time.'

After considerable cogitation, Marlowe replied regretfully, 'A very pretty notion, if I might say so, but I'm afraid the portrait must not be taken from the castle. It is his most prized possession.'

'Yes, but he will have *two* prized possessions if I can borrow it. I can't do an exact copy from memory,' Tiffy argued.

'You could make your copy in the schoolroom, miss. Provided the miniature passes from my hands to yours and back again each day, and never leaves the castle, I don't see that there can be any objection.'

She exclaimed, 'That's brilliant! Just the sort of compromise I appreciate. I shall bring my paints over tomorrow. Thank you, Marlowe. You have helped me solve a very knotty problem.'

'Yes, miss, but no more trespassing,' he chided.

Tiffy laughed. 'It was because I trespassed that I met his lordship in the first place. Sometimes it pays not to be quite as good as one should . . .'

Eleanor Hunt had come to bloom in an age when conscientious mothers taught their daughters that emotions, like spots, must be firmly repressed if they could not be banished altogether. This, no doubt, was to spare the girls being crushed like so many bright but fragile butterflies when they discovered their husbands had mistresses.

Eleanor, as biddable as she was beautiful, believed every word her mother dropped into her attentive ears.

Consequently, her letter to Courteney contained no passionate outpouring of her innermost thoughts, but it was full of the next best thing—hope. She wrote that she feared she was not sufficiently stoic to become the wife of a serving soldier, but hoped, however, that when the war ended and he could with honour resign his commission, their friendship would be found to have endured the stresses imposed upon it. Meanwhile, she would pray for his safety, and looked forward to the day when they might meet again.

For all its restraint and stilted phrases, the letter was one of promise and not of renunciation, and Courteney's spirits soared accordingly. Nothing happened to depress them, either, during his hectic week in the metropolis. When he visited Horse Guards he was pronounced fit to resume his military duties, informed that his promotion to major had come through, and pounced on by many old friends determined to fill his every free hour with some form of dissipation or other. Another piece of cheer was that Scott, his tailor, promised the new uniforms would be ready on time. With this assurance secured, Courteney felt free to visit his sister.

It was more than a mere duty visit. Augusta, Countess of Stanleigh, had much in common with the brother who had preceded her into the world by eighteen months, sharing the same clear grey eyes, thick fair hair, steady character and resolute will. Launched into Society at seventeen, she had firmly faced the stigma of being on the shelf by refusing all her suitors until, at the ripe age of twenty-two, she had met the man upon whom she could bestow her heart as well as her hand. Marcus, Earl of Stanleigh, was fifteen years her senior, and in him she had a doting as well as a conscientious husband.

Her delicate condition had kept her away from Dalmaine Castle while Courteney was so ill, and no sooner had she presented her lord with a lusty, male pledge of affection shortly after Christmas, than

Stanleigh himself was incapacitated by breaking a leg on the hunting field.

Only now, with March already upon her and weeks of stifled vexation behind her, had Lady Augusta felt she could safely travel with her new son and convalescent husband to visit her brother. She had been forestalled by Lady Janetta writing that she had no wish to see the new Stanleigh brat until it had passed the mewling and puking stage, and that it would be more convenient for all concerned if brother and sister met in London.

When the meeting finally took place in Lady Augusta's elegant drawing-room, the eyes she turned towards the door as Courteney was anounced were anxious. Lady Janetta was a blunt and frequent correspondent, and her pithy comments on Eleanor, and then on Courteney himself when his emotional recovery lagged behind his physical improvement, had kept Lady Augusta in a torment for weeks. She had scarcely been reassured when Courteney wrote to her himself, until the name of Tiffy Yorke began to appear in both his and Lady Janetta's letters.

Her enquiries about this unknown Tiffy had resulted in Lady Janetta sending her an account of the young lady's questionable history, and in Courteney's regaling her with amusing anecdotes of his dealings with his little protégée. Augusta, intrigued, felt that more questions had been raised than answered.

She had schooled herself to show no shock when she saw her brother's injured face for the first time. When he strode smilingly towards her, however, it was joyous relief that brought her to her feet and made her exclaim, 'Courteney, my dear, thank God I have seen you with mine own eyes at last! I feared—oh, I'll admit it!—that you might look like Cumberland!'

This comparison with the king's fifth son, who had lost an eye in battle so that his aspect was as sinister as his reputation, broadened Courteney's smile. He embraced his sister warmly, and confessed, 'At one time I thought so, too. Tiffy taught me differently, and now Eleanor has written a letter that has banished the last of my blues. All is *not* ended between us. You can imagine how happy that has made me, Augusta.'

'Yes, indeed.' She took his hands and led him to a sofa. 'Sit down and tell me everything that has happened since last we met. Tell me first about Tiffy, before I die of curiosity.'

This he did readily, for it was not by accident that he had introduced Tiffy's name so early into their conversation. Augusta's good will would stand Tiffy in good stead, particularly when she made her début the following year. This, when she heard him out, Augusta readily gave. It was as obvious to her as it had been to Lady Janetta that, however enchanting he found his little Tiffy, his heart was still firmly in Eleanor's possession. She sighed a little over this, for she was fiercely protective towards the few people she loved, and Eleanor had fallen far short of her exacting standards, but because she wished above all for him to be happy, she confided that his romance might be resumed sooner than he thought.

Stanleigh, a staunch Tory and dedicated advocate of continuing the struggle against Napoleon, had told her that even the opposing and pacific Whigs were beginning to think the end of the war was at last in sight. They were both dwelling on this happy and almost unbelievable prospect after so many years of conflict when Stanleigh joined them, and the conversation became more general. The evening passed so convivially that Courteney visited the Stanleighs whenever possible in the following days, and when he returned home he felt he had once more picked up all the threads of his old life.

Tiffy greeted him rapturously, scolded him for being away eight days instead of seven, then admitted the time had not passed too tediously. The courier to Norfolk had brought back a letter from Lady Swayle so carefully worded that it almost concealed her dismay at having a relative she had repulsed taken up by the élite Harwoods. Fearful that the Polite World would say she had behaved harshly towards her niece, she offered Tiffy shelter at Swayle when the summer ended.

Once Tiffy knew she had permission to go to Bath, she was more interested in the letter Lord Swayle had entrusted to the courier without his wife's knowing. In it he congratulated Tiffy on her good fortune, wished her a merry time and, more practically, enclosed one hundred pounds. She wasted no time in frittering away this unexpected windfall. She bought a carriage dress of fine cambric, an indigo pelisse and matching bonnet the precise colour of her eyes, and ordered both bonnet and pelisse to be trimmed most becomingly with swan's-down. Next she purchased a silver campaign flask which she had engraved: *To my friend Tobias Wade. Good health and cheer. Tiffy Yorke.* To ensure the inscription's success, she had the flask filled with finest brandy.

She selected a black shawl delicately embroidered with silver thread for Mrs Royston, a papier mâché snuffbox with a painted lid for Farley, and hoarded what money remained for vails for the other servants she had most frequently encountered. She might have arrived in Kent without two pennies to rub together, but thanks to her father's example, she knew only two ways to depart from anywhere—one jump ahead of the bailiffs or in grand style. This departure would be very grand!

And departure was on everybody's minds, for after Courteney's return there was too much to do for the familiar pattern of life at the castle to be resumed. The last days sped by. It was Tobias, in smart new livery, who was the first to leave, setting out a full day before the marquess. With two undergrooms to assist him as far as Portsmouth, it was his job to ensure the campaign horses travelled by easy stages so that they would be in tip-

top condition when they were loaded aboard ship.
Courteney, Tiffy, and all the servants gathered in the
stableyard to watch the horses leave. Tiffy presented an
astonished Tobias with the silver flask, bade him take
good care of himself and shook him warmly by the hand.

'You shouldn't have, Miss Tiffy,' Tobias said, the
flask quite dwarfed in his big hands.

'I wouldn't be me if I didn't do things I shouldn't.' She
then shocked the watching servants and thoroughly
discomposed Tobias by kissing him on the cheek. 'That's
not a very English thing to do, but it's to remind you to
take care and that I'll be thinking of you. I don't have so
many friends that I can afford to lose any of them.'

She stepped back. Tobias mumbled, 'You'll always
have a friend in me, Miss Tiffy,' mounted his horse and
took the reins of the two horses he would lead. Receiving a nod from the marquess, he set off, with his two
grooms and their led horses falling in behind him.

The following morning Tiffy, with a glee the Everetts
found very difficult to endure, departed—for ever, she
hoped!—from the vicarage with her small battered
trunk. She was wearing her new indigo pelisse and
bonnet, and as the carriage took her to the castle, she
could scarcely refrain from stroking the luxurious
swan's-down trimming.

She refused the porter's offer to relieve her of her
outer garments, and learning that my lord was in his
much-beloved library, hurried there to be com-
plimented on her new finery. When she tapped on the
door and walked in, surprise rounded her eyes and
halted her hasty footsteps.

A tall, broad-shouldered, slim-hipped, military
stranger was standing with his back to her. He turned,
and she beheld the braided and gilt-laced magnificence
of a major of Hussars. Tiffy blinked and asked, awed,
'Courteney, is it really you?'

The so-familiar lines of humour about his firm mouth

and grey eyes deepened. 'It is too late in our relationship for you to be tactful, Tiffy. You may denounce me as a popinjay with my good will.'

'Oh, no,' she breathed, going towards him to touch the dark blue cloth of his heavily braided jacket and the fur trimming of the equally heavily braided pelisse slung over his left shoulder. She raised her hand further to touch the scar on his face, tracing its course lightly from cheekbone to chin. 'Most truly distinguished. The face fits the uniform. If it were not for the wretched war, I would urge you most strongly to stay in the army. I disapprove of the danger, but *entirely* approve of the plumage!'

Courteney burst out laughing.

'It is no laughing matter. If Eleanor could see you now, she would wed you on the instant and go with you to follow the drum. Any girl would who loved you and—and she does, doesn't she, Courteney? You have seemed so happy since you got her letter.'

He took her hands. 'I am. I believe she returns my feeling. She is waiting, and . . .'

'. . . and beauties do not have to wait for anyone if they don't care to,' Tiffy finished for him. 'Well, see you do not keep her waiting too long. Finish the silly war and then pray make friends with the French. Papa always called Paris his natural home, so you can imagine how I burn to see it. He said, too, that the French understand romance as nobody else does, which makes it shameful that so many years have been lost in nothing more exciting than fighting.'

Courteney regarded her quizzically. 'What a pity Napoleon never had the benefit of your papa's counsel before he embarked on world conquest.'

'Yes, indeed. Never mind. At least *we* met, so some good always happens somewhere. And now we must say goodbye, only I won't. It would be too depressing, and I am resolved on sending you off with a smiling face and no—no violets in the dew! I shall just look forward to saying hello when we meet again.'

'That is a charming idea,' Courteney said, but gave her his handkerchief just the same.

Tiffy clutched it gratefully, mopped her brimming eyes, and gave him a wavering smile. 'I have given all your other handkerchiefs back to Mrs Royston, so may I keep this one as a memento? It isn't robbery, precisely, because I have something for you.'

She put the handkerchief in her reticule and brought out the gold pocket-watch. 'It was my father's, but it is *not* an heirloom, Papa never managing to keep a watch for any length of time. It is rather a fine one, though, and I have done my best to make it personal for you.'

As Courteney took the watch, his thumb felt the inscription on the back. He turned it over and read: *C. de L.S.H. My dearest friend. T.Y.* He was touched by the gift, but this turned to amazement when he opened the smooth gold cover and saw opposite the finely engraved clockface the watercolour of Eleanor that Tiffy had copied with painstaking accuracy.

Tiffy, watching his face anxiously, said, 'Marlowe let me copy the miniature while you were away. I shouldn't ring my own bell, I suppose, but it's true that I can copy anything. The real skill lies in an original work. Are you pleased?'

'I was never more pleased with anything in my life,' Courteney assured her, closing the watch and putting it in his pocket. 'I don't know how to thank you.'

'I can think of a way,' she told him cheekily, stepping back a pace and twirling round. 'You can tell me how splendid I look in my new finery. The lily has been gilded, and you never even noticed!'

'I noticed immediately, and have only been waiting for a moment to tell you how *very* spendid you look.'

'Well, I think so, but it is nice to have it confirmed. I . . .' She broke off as a tap on the door preceded Farley with the information that my lord's travelling chaise was at the door. When he withdrew, Tiffy quite forgot what she had been saying in the rush to inform him, 'I have thought up the neatest scheme to keep you safe. I am going to pray for you. The novelty of me praying for somebody other than myself must ensure I will be listened to. I mean, any improvement must be rewarded, mustn't it, otherwise one would soon get discouraged!'

'Tiffy,' he protested, laughing, 'that is not at all the right frame of mind in which you should pray for anything.'

Her own eyes danced. 'What do you expect from a heathen? I am doing my best. If you wish to return the favour, you can pray that I will grow some more, both upwards and outwards. Praying for oneself doesn't always work, you see, otherwise I would already be twice as splendid as you see me now. That is all I have to say.' She gave him one of her fierce hugs, pulled his face down so that she could rub her smooth cheek against his scarred one, kissed it swiftly and stepped back. 'Until we can say hello again, dearest friend.'

'Until then,' Courteney repeated, kissing her cheek. 'Keep yourself safe, Tiffy.'

She nodded. 'Off you go, then. You have your servants to bid farewell. I shall wait here a little while.'

He went out, quietly closing the door behind him. Tiffy looked round the library. How still it was, how bereft, now that Courteney had gone. Soon the servants would be in here, laying Holland covers over everything until he returned. She shivered.

When she presently went out to the front door, Courteney was climbing into his carriage, every servant from bootblack to steward on the steps to wave farewell. Lady Janetta, her disapproving adieux having been made the previous evening, had not yet stirred from her room.

Tiffy stood on the top step, and keeping her promise to show him a cheerful face, smiled gaily and waved. He smiled and waved back, and then the carriage moved forward and he was lost from her sight. For a little while she felt, like the library, bereft. It was not, fortunately, a feeling that could survive the bustle of her own departure with Lady Janetta to Bath, where, sooner or later, she would encounter the man destined to be so much closer to her than Courteney.

CHAPTER TEN

Two MONTHS after her arrival in Bath, a transformed Tiffy hurried out of Lady Janetta's elegant house in her usual heedless manner and bumped into Jago as he ran up the shallow steps to reach for the door knocker. Tiffy, recoiling first in shock and then delight from the impact, found herself caught in his steadying arms. So, he had arrived at last!

She gave a most artistic gasp and swayed towards him as though still off balance, enjoying the pleasure of his touch. The handsome setdown he undoubtedly deserved for his past treatment of her could wait a few moments more.

He was about to release her with a cursory apology when a swift glance downwards informed him he was clasping the most delectable item of feminine frailty to come his way in many a long day. Predictably, being Jago, his arms tightened rather than loosened about her.

Tiffy slanted a look at him through thick eyelashes, saw the predatory appreciation on his handsome face, and tasted triumph. Not for nothing, then, had she spent endless hours standing like a dressmaker's dummy while her new gowns were pinned and re-pinned about her until the precise effect she demanded was achieved.

Jago found himself supporting in his strong arms neither Dalmaine's waif nor his own snowdrop abigail but a young lady dashingly and most decidedly *à la mode*. She was wearing a blue velvet riding-habit, and lustrous natural waves supported the cockaded riding-hat angled saucily towards her face. The lily had been gilded with a vengeance, giving Tiffy the illusion of beauty that she craved. Her eyes looked larger and more luminous than ever. Her other features, hitherto hovering uncertainly between the awkward and the exotic, had reached a compromise and settled for the impish.

She took it as a tribute to her hard work that Jago clearly did not recognise her, and she prepared to enjoy herself at his expense. He, after all, had enjoyed himself enough at hers! She was given the opportunity when, his leisurely scrutiny of her completed to both their satisfaction, he exclaimed with rare honesty, 'But you are enchanting!'

'It is good to know that I have improved. As I remember, I was merely charming last time.'

Jago's dark eyebrows snapped together. 'I beg your pardon?'

'Well you might,' Tiffy scolded. She disentangled herself from his arms and tapped him reprovingly on the chest with her riding-whip. 'And well for you that I don't bear grudges over trifles. I shall accept your apology, late though it is. Now, if you will remove yourself from my path, my horse is waiting.'

He looked round to where his groom was manoeuvring his curricle past Tiffy's groom, waiting in the roadway with two saddled horses, and swung back to her. 'You speak as if you know me, but I swear I have never set eyes on you before.'

'Which just proves what a shocking flirt you are, Jago Harwood! Or liar.' She saw, with the most unholy glee, the flash of anger in his eyes. Whatever might happen in the future, she had succeeded in stamping her image as indelibly on his brain as his was on hers. She moved to walk past him, certain he would not let her go so easily, and she was not disappointed.

He grasped her arm, and demanded, 'Who the blazes are you?'

She sighed, as if sorely tried, and pointedly freed herself once more. 'Truly, I don't know which is the roughest, your tongue or your touch. Pray believe I have neither the time nor the inclination for dalliance just now.'

Jago looked thunderstruck, and Tiffy, exultant, moved him aside by placing her whip once more on his chest. She went unhurriedly down the steps and allowed her groom to throw her up into her saddle. Only then did she look back at him and add sweetly, 'Don't look so cross. You have missed nothing. I have no trophies for you today, snowdrops being out of season.'

Enlightenment dawned. Tiffy smiled and touched her whip to her hat in mocking salute, just as he had at their last parting. Then, to hammer the lesson home, she rode away without a single backward glance.

Jago, remembering all too well the little abigail with the snowdrop garland on her head, swore fluently. When his feelings were relieved somewhat in this manner, but only somewhat, he also remembered there had been something about the abigail that had teased a memory in him. He recalled that the abigail had not spoken one word, while this modish young lady had spoken a great deal too many. And in the most unusual accent. That, for him, was the real clue, and he had it in a flash. The girl on the stairs at the castle. Dalmaine's waif. He had thought her a charity case. Now, it seemed, she was a lady of quality.

Quite how this metamorphosis had occurred was baffling, and he strode purposefully through the still open door to wrest the answer from his grandmother. All he knew for certain just then was that, as the waif, the girl had crossed swords with him; as the abigail, she had melted into his arms like a born doxy; as the fashionable lady, she had given him a resounding set-down. He tossed his coat, hat and gloves to the porter and ran lightly up the stairs to the drawing-room, thinking of many pleasurable ways in which just punishment could be exacted.

Tiffy, harbouring precious few illusions about her

chosen man, guessed which way his thoughts were running: she had no doubt that retribution in one form or another awaited her return. She felt no dismay, only anticipation. They might fight each other to a standstill, but it would be a fair fight. The situation had altered drastically since their last meeting. Jago could no longer treat her as a nobody.

Courteney's last thoughtful contribution to her consequence had been to provide her with her own maid and groom, and to have the grey gelding conveyed to Bath so that when she wished to ride out she could do so in style, and not on a hired hack. In addition, she had money in her purse, all the fripperies of fashion to embellish her, a powerful backer in Lady Janetta and a host of new friends.

She had become very much a *somebody*. That this had happened so quickly was due entirely to Lady Janetta's cunning and total lack of conscience. She had written to Mrs Hunt to say she had taken under her wing a most unaffected and enchanting girl, lately returned from the Americas, who was the granddaughter of an old friend of hers, alas now sadly deceased. She was grateful to Dalmaine for bringing dear Tiffy to her attention before he had returned to the war, and predicted she would take London by storm when she was presented next year, because she already had Bath at her feet.

She then ensured that the threat to Eleanor would be clarified in letters from other of the Hunts' friends by dropping a few well-chosen words into the ear of her dresser. Miss Pugh, who had been with the dowager for over thirty years, was told in strictest confidence that Tiffy was being groomed for the high position she would one day occupy.

In no time at all it was being whispered everywhere that Lady Janetta, out of duty to the Family, was preparing the American émigrée in her care to become the new marchioness when Dalmaine returned from the Peninsula.

As a campaign, it was masterly. While Tiffy was being shod and hosed and undergoing lessons in singing, dancing and deportment, the gossip was doing Lady Janetta's work for her. And since Society looked for virtues rather than vices in a future marchioness, Tiffy's sometimes paralysing candour was held to stem from an unspoilt nature, her slight form became sylph-like, her liveliness refreshing, her accent charming, her unusual face entrancing and her questionable birth no fault of her own.

As Tiffy, after some half-hour or so, turned her horse towards home, she was dwelling on the certainty that Jago would put up a good fight against her. She had learned a great deal about him since she had been in Bath. If she and Lady Janetta were not exactly confidantes, they were fellow conspirators and discussed many matters that would not normally be raised between so elderly and so young a lady. Jago was one of them, and Tiffy's mind returned to an afternoon a few days earlier when Lady Janetta, scrutinising the society columns through her magnifying glass, had suddenly exclaimed, 'Ha! I knew it couldn't last. Jago will be coming into Somerset on a repairing lease. His estate ain't above eight miles from Bath, and he'll be on our doorstep before the week is out to pay his duty call, if nothing else.'

Tiffy, curled up with a book on a sofa since the afternoon was wet, felt her senses quicken, but she turned a page before asking casually, 'Oh? Does it say so in the newspaper?'

'It don't need to.'

'Then how can you know?'

'Because it says the Burroughs widow has left London to visit her parents in Yorkshire. Bah! That jade wouldn't leave London at the beginning of the Season without good cause. Either Jago's left her, or they ain't been discreet enough and the Strattons have got wind of what's going on.'

'Burroughs widow? Strattons?' Tiffy repeated, bewildered.

'God, girl, do you know nothing? That's what comes of being raised in the Antipodes.'

'America,' Tiffy corrected mechanically, her heart thudding with fear at the thought of Jago being caught in a widow's coils.

'Same thing,' Lady Janetta snorted, with a sublime disregard for geography and a great deal else. 'Maria Burroughs was a Stratton before she married, and the Strattons are too prim by half to countenance her having a loose connection with a rake like Jago. They'll want marriage or nothing, and the whole world knows Jago ain't the marrying kind. She was the reason he went into Sussex a couple of months back. They'd got themselves invited to the same house party. Nothing wrong in that, provided they didn't flaunt their affair in public.'

'Perhaps he's in love with her,' Tiffy faltered, feeling quite sick in her stomach.

'Bah! Jago's a hunter, in love with the game, not the quarry. Once the excitement of the chase is over, he soon gets bored.'

Tiffy digested this priceless piece of information, and then asked, 'Why will he come here?'

'To rusticate until the end of the quarter. Jago don't pinch pennies when he mounts a mistress. He was run off his feet in January when he came to the castle to ask Dalmaine for a loan. He got it, of course, because he's the heir, but he didn't care for the scold that went with it. Left the castle as mad as fire.'

'He's not a rich man, then?'

'Lord, he'll be plump enough in the pocket when he settles down. What man doesn't make too many demands on his estate while he's sowing his wild oats?'

This seemed reasonable enough to Tiffy, but the

prospect of Jago being snatched from her scared her into suggesting, 'If the Burroughs widow—I mean, Mrs Burroughs—is rich, perhaps Jago will marry her to solve his financial problems.'

'Over my dead body! She's a bad breeder. A woman who was wed for five years without producing so much as a daughter ain't any good to this family, not while we've got more Harwoods under the ground than on it. Besides, I told you that Jago is a hunter. If she wanted him permanently, she should have stayed out of his bed.'

'Wed for five years? She must be quite old, then.'

'Twenty-four ain't old for a widow. You're thinking of maidens, and Jago never meddles with them. He keeps a cool head for all his hot blood, so he ain't likely to slip into a snare set by a virgin.'

That had been the end of that highly informative conversation, and as Tiffy pondered on it all the way back to Bath she perceived her task would be no easy one. On the one hand she must stay out of Jago's bed. On the other she mustn't be a virginal bore. There seemed to her precious little safe ground between the two, only the precarious path pursued by a tease. Well, so be it. Jago would have to be teased to distraction while, she hoped, she didn't become too distracted herself.

Jago and Lady Janetta knew each other for what they were. They shared the same ruthless determination to wrest what they wanted from life, regardless of who suffered in the process. Consequentially, Lady Janetta knew she couldn't dupe Jago into believing she was sponsoring Tiffy for any altruistic reason. He would laugh in her face. So, after acquainting him fully with Tiffy's background, she told him her true purpose for bringing the chit to Bath, expecting him to appreciate her tactics.

Jago did not. It didn't suit him to have an adventuress

so close to his grandmother, from whom he had every expectation of inheriting a fortune. Nor was it an object with him to promote Dalmaine's marriage. Jago was a leader of the *ton*, a noted Corinthian who excelled in all the manly sports, a member of the exclusive Four Horse Club and a habitué of all the better gaming establishments.

Such a life was expensive, quite apart from the succession of ladies he found necessary to his comfort. While he remained heir to the marquisate his creditors were patient, particularly as his noble cousin pursued such a risky profession, but when Dalmaine married, he would find himself hard pressed.

All in all, he had no reason to be pleased with Tiffy's appearance on the scene, delectable though she undoubtedly was. While he had good reason to know he could bend her to his will by taking her into his arms, he could scarcely do this while she was under the protection of his grandmother. As far as the world was concerned, he would have to treat her like a young lady of quality, whatever he might know about her privately.

Therefore, when Tiffy presently joined them just before luncheon after changing her riding-habit for a fetching gown of cream muslin with a demi-train, she found herself contending not with an avenging rake but with a polished gentleman whose society manners, when he chose, were second to none. Tiffy, deeply suspicious, nevertheless had to follow his lead. On the surface all was civility, but the underlying tension, of which the dowager was sublimely unaware, frequently gave a double edge to their apparently innocuous remarks. They were like fencers, feinting and riposting, while they searched for an opening neither gave. By the time they had gone into luncheon, and finished it, mutual respect was added to mutual attraction, and each was longing for an opportunity to bring the fight into the open.

Lady Janetta gave it to them. As she rose from the table, she said, 'Jago, you can make yourself useful for once by taking Tiffy for a drive in your curricle. Your taste in all things is known to be excellent. It will do her good if the Bath quizzes see you find her worthy of attention.'

Jago's and Tiffy's eyes met. She said, 'That is, if you find me worthy of attention . . .'

'I'm sure you're worthy of something,' he replied. 'Perhaps the drive will decide quite what.'

'What was that?' the dowager demanded.

'I was just telling Tiffy to put on her prettiest bonnet,' Jago told her blandly. 'I don't want my horses frightened.'

Tiffy laughed and left the room, scarcely able to believe she was to have him all to herself, perhaps for the whole afternoon.

No sooner had the door closed behind her than Lady Janetta said abruptly, 'It's over, then? The Burroughs affair?'

'On the contrary, it flourishes. Maria and I, for the moment, are well suited. She has no more thought of marriage than I have, which makes her as remarkable as she is lovely.'

'Then why has she gone off to Yorkshire?'

'To confound the gossips. Besides, we don't feel the need to live in each other's pockets.'

'Then it's an affair of passion, not the heart?' Lady Janetta questioned, mollified.

'Precisely. The sort of arrangement a man searches for and rarely finds.'

'Enjoy yourself while you may. If Dalmaine disobliges me by getting himself killed, it will be your duty to settle down. The Burroughs widow won't do. She don't breed.'

'How good of you to remind me of another of her admirable qualities.' He laughed at her expression, kissed her fingertips gracefully, and took his leave before she could think up a suitable retort.

When he presently handed Tiffy up into his curricle, he was not smiling and seemed impervious to the picture she made in a braided pelisse of light primrose wool and with her gloves, bonnet, shoes and furled pagoda parasol all of the same delicate shade. Her hopes that they would spend the afternoon together were speedily dashed when, dismissing his groom, Jago told him to hold himself in readiness to return to Belmore, his estate, in an hour.

So, Tiffy thought, she must ensure that the measly hour he alloted her was a memorable one. For the first few minutes she was occupied with waving and bowing to all her new friends as he drove her through the town centre, but as they headed for the outskirts she said affably, 'Are you going to admit you were wrong to call me waif?'

'Certainly. It should have been cuckoo.'

'*Cuckoo?*'

'That is, I believe, the bird that makes itself a home in somebody else's nest.'

'That is a remark worthy of my cousin Cassy,' Tiffy replied. 'She's spiteful, too. I had expected better from you, though I'm sure I can't think why.'

'Neither can I,' he responded, loosening his hands a little on the reins as fields succeeded the last of the houses. 'Be warned, cuckoo. You've picked the wrong nest. Nobody's ever succeeded in plucking Lady Janetta yet. She's much too wily.'

'You speak from experience, naturally,' Tiffy retorted.

Jago drew up the carriage on the top of a hill where they could look down over the neat town. He said, very softly, very dangerously, 'I warned you once not to cross swords with me.'

'Then stop crossing swords with me. Do you fear I will

dip my fingers into the purse that one day will be yours? You wrong me. That is not my game at all.'

'Then what is?'

Tiffy unfurled her parasol. The afternoon in late May was more breezy than sunny, but she knew what a pretty accessory it made, for she had posed with it before her mirror. 'Social advancement,' she replied eventually.

'And?'

She looked sideways at him, smiling beguilingly. 'Does there have to be an "and"?'

'With an adventuress, surely!'

She chuckled. 'Then—also surely!—that's for you to find out.'

'I shall. If you've set your cap at Dalmaine, you will come a cropper. Not the most determined adventuress could detach him from Eleanor. Besides, the Harwoods do not marry cocktails.'

'*Cocktails?*' Tiffy gasped.

'The *ton* refers to the issue from unequal marriages as "cocktails". You, Tiffy, since your father married beneath his class.'

'God rot your malicious tongue! My mother came from a perfectly respectable family.'

'So does the better part of the nation, but, really, one doesn't rub shoulders with the better part of the nation. I shall concede, if it is any comfort to you, that you are an above-average cocktail.'

'I am not a cocktail at all!'

His eyebrows went up. 'Dear me, must I call you bastard?'

Tiffy shut her parasol with a snap. 'You have called me waif, stray, cuckoo and bastard. Are you sure you haven't missed anything out?'

'I believe that had I pressed my pursuit of you when I mistook you for an abigail, you would have proved most accommodating, so naturally "whore" springs to mind.

However, as I don't believe you've progressed thus far, I shall withhold it for the future.'

She lashed out at him. He grasped her wrist, using enough pressure to hold her helpless and make her wince. Then with studied deliberation he kissed the open palm with which she had meant to strike his handsome face. Her fury flamed anew as he said, 'Understand me well, Tiffy. I shall not meddle in your games provided you do not meddle in mine—but, if you get in my way, I shall be forced to remove you.'

'Do you think you can? Or do you over-estimate your power?' She flung back her head and looked up at him, her smouldering eyes full of the most exciting challenge, the dormant enchantress awakening to claim her own.

Jago caught his breath, his quickening pulses urging him to answer the challenge in the only possible way. He wanted—needed!—to crush her into his arms and cover her senuous lips with his.

Tiffy, reading his intent in his burning brown eyes, swayed towards him, spellbound. This was the moment she had striven so hard to make possible, the moment when he in his turn became aware that they were meant for each other.

Then, in an abrupt gesture of renunciation, he released her. 'Oh, no, Tiffy, you might bait the parson's trap most deliciously, but you're not catching me in it. You, a baron's niece, not yet out, and entrusted to my care by my grandmother! Clever, damned clever; but I wasn't that gullible at eighteen, so you'll scarcely snare me at eight and twenty. When Dalmaine failed to succumb to your all too obvious charms, did you see me as the next best thing? One day it might amuse me to take what you are only too ready to offer—but it will be on my terms, not yours.'

Tiffy, feeling that she knew what it was like to be flung out of paradise when she had only just found the door, said bitterly, 'That answers my question clearly enough. You *do* over-estimate your power.'

Jago turned from her and occupied himself with turning the carriage for home. When he had completed this manoeuvre, he answered mockingly, 'I think it is you who have over-estimated yours.'

Her fighting spirit, which would not let her be hurt without striking back, prompted her to retort, 'What a hen-hearted gambler you must be! You throw in your hand as soon as the game becomes interesting.'

Nothing could have stung him more. He swung angrily towards her, his grip slackening on the reins. His high-bred horses, sedately trotting, took this as an invitation to gallop and raced away, the carriage bouncing and swaying wildly.

She stung him again by saying primly, 'Mind your horses, sir. I have no wish to be overturned in a ditch.'

Jago, bringing the team under control, ground out savagely, 'Nothing would give me greater pleasure.'

'And you a famous whip,' she clucked. 'Would your prestige survive such a mishap?'

'To hell with my prestige! It would be worth it if I could be sure you'd break your neck.'

'I'll lay you fifty pounds I'd climb out of the ditch with nothing worse than scratches,' she offered.

That confounded him. 'Is that a serious bet?'

'Certainly. I am not at all hen-hearted like you. I risk all to win all.'

'That's the most encouraging thing I've heard today. You will undoubtedly ruin yourself without any help from me.'

'Would you care for a wager on that?' she asked incorrigibly.

'I'll wager any sum you like that I'll break your neck with my bare hands if you call me hen-hearted again.'

Tiffy chuckled. 'That's what I call a proper manly sentiment. It encourages me to think there's hope for you yet! Don't you think, though, that we should stop calling each other names? I have quite enough of that with Lady Janetta, and it becomes a trifle tedious.' She encountered his swift, disbelieving sideways glance, and smiled. 'I'm sure you do not wish to be thought a bore.'

'By heaven, I never knew a girl ask for punishment quite as much as you do,' he exclaimed.

'If you prefer tame females, you shouldn't tangle with an adventuress,' she chided him, making him long again to break her neck. But, as they were now driving through Bath's more fashionable thoroughfares, they were both obliged to nod once more to their various acquaintances. When he pulled up outside Lady Janetta's house, his groom came running to help Tiffy to alight.

She paused long enough to turn to Jago and say, 'Thank you for a most diverting drive.' Then she politely extended her hand. Jago looked at it, but with his groom watching, felt obliged to shake it. Tiffy smiled. 'Until next time.'

As the groom helped her to descend to the pavement, Jago said, 'Are you so certain there will be a next time?'

Her polite smile became a cheeky grin. 'Oh, yes. Aren't you?'

CHAPTER ELEVEN

JAGO PUNISHED Tiffy for her confidence by staying away for eight interminable days. During this time, her heart leapt whenever a carriage stopped outside or a knock sounded on the door. She was afraid to go out in case she missed him, unable to stay in without arousing Lady Janetta's suspicions.

When he eventually strolled into the drawing-room one afternoon her nerves were frayed, her temper touchy, and his attitude did nothing to improve either. He greeted her coolly, then appeared to forget all about her, preferring to entertain his grandmother with political anecdotes. He left after an hour without exchanging so much as a private word or look with her.

She didn't see him again until several evenings later, when Lady Janetta had pressured him into escorting them to a private party. He arrived looking so very handsome in evening attire that Tiffy, as susceptible as ever, readily forgave him all his sins. She was confident she was looking dazzling enough for him to return the compliment. Narrow lavender velvet ribbon was slotted through lace at the round neckline and high waist of her filmy white muslin gown, and more velvet ribbon was wound artfully through the curls piled on top of her head.

Jago raised his quizzing-glass to study her coiffure, and Tiffy, glaring at him, guessed that he was still far from tamed. She was right. Shortly after their arrival at the party he disappeared into the card-room, counselling her to find what partners she could to caper with her in the country dances. For himself, he danced only the waltz, still banned as too lascivious by Bath's old-fashioned hostesses.

The following day, she returned home from a picnic to learn that Jago had taken his leave of his grandmother and returned to London. Furious, she searched the society columns in that morning's paper and, sure enough, found an item mentioning that Mrs Burroughs had been among the guests at an assembly at Carlton House. So, the widow was back in London, and Jago had gone chasing after her!

She continued the singing and dancing lessons she had begun on her arrival in Bath, added politics to her literary studies, and kept a close eye on the war news. Courteney wrote to her every month, receiving a far more prolific response. He must, she wrote, have remembered her most pressing needs in his prayers as she had asked him to, for she had grown a whole inch taller. Nor was that the end of it, because her bosom was rounding out at last. She did not think it would ever reach Cassy-like proportions, but it was so nice to dispense with the lace, tucks and pleating that had been essential on her bodices up until now.

If Courteney's letters lacked Tiffy's zest, they did not lack sincerity. He wrote little about the actual war but described the Spanish scene and his friends for her, and shared all her little triumphs as a good friend should.

Towards the end of June, a letter arrived for Lady Janetta that put her in a high passion. It was from Mrs Hunt, and its tidings were momentous. She had, she wrote, been so sickly during the past weeks that the family's return to England had had to be delayed. Only now had the cause of her malady been discovered. She was, after nearly twenty sterile years, with child again. Mr Hunt, dear man, was delirious with joy. The Happy Event was expected in September so that the return home would be delayed until the new year. Meanwhile, it was a comfort to know that the understanding between Eleanor and Dalmaine was of an enduring nature.

'God rot the stupid woman!' the dowager raved. 'What's a few more months here or there after twenty years! The best we can hope for is that it's a phantom pregnancy.'

But the ultimate effect of Mrs Hunt's little bombshell was advantageous to Tiffy. The dowager, revising her plans, decided not to send her packing in the autumn but to keep her with her until the new year.

One day in July Tiffy was strolling about the Pump Room when she saw Tarleton Creighton drinking a glass of the famous waters, his face screwed up in distaste. 'What are you doing here?' she demanded, seizing his arm. 'Don't tell me the Everetts are also in town?'

'No,' he replied, smoothing the sleeve she had grabbed. 'Damme, Tiffy, do you have to be so—so physical?'

'That's good, coming from you,' she grinned, her good humour restored now that she knew she was not to have the Everetts frowning upon her. 'Oh, stop pouting! I shall not tease you. Only you mustn't run away from me if you wish to be fashionable. I am all the rage.'

'I know. I've heard talk of nothing but you since I arrived. I hoped we would not meet,' he told her gloomily, leaning forward to stare at the floor.

'Tarleton, you creaked!' Tiffy exclaimed. 'You are wearing a corset.'

He sat up abruptly, threw her a look of loathing, and replied haughtily, 'It is a Brummell Bodice. All the dandies wear them.'

'Those who have to, and I can see you do. Tarleton, you have gone from plump to fat!'

He sighed heavily. 'I have been eating to comfort myself. My father still will not countenance my union with Cassy. It is that which is the cause of all my troubles, only he will not see it. I was forced to go on a reducing diet. It quite knocked me up, and I am here to recover by drinking the waters.'

Tiffy's withers were not wrung, disliking the star-crossed lovers as she did, but Jago's contemptuous comments about her mother's family still rankled with her. It occurred to her that if Cassy were to marry Sir Geoffrey Creighton's heir, it would put a certain gloss on the maternal side of her family.

'Tarleton, didn't you tell me once your father refused to let you join the Volunteers in case the manoeuvres should prove too strenuous for you?' she asked thoughtfully.

'Yes. As a child, my constitution was delicate, and it has not improved,' he replied soulfully, looking the very picture of health. 'My brother is the same. My father is obsessed with our health but not, alas, our happiness.'

'Tell him you mean to join the army,' Tiffy said suddenly.

'Eh? The *fighting* army? My constitution would never survive the rigours of campaigning on the Continent!'

'It will not come to that. Tell him that if he will not consent to your marriage to Cassy, he leaves you with no choice but to seek death in the quickest possible way.'

'I couldn't join the army, not even for my dearest Cassy. I would look such a fool if I had to climb down.'

Tiffy resisted the impulse to tell him he looked a fool whatever he did, telling him instead, 'Then you can tell him that Cassy made you change your mind. She was so distraught, you feared she would go into a decline and die herself if you carried out your threat. Either way, you cut a noble figure.'

His expression showed that he thought so, too, but he hedged, 'I vowed never again to be involved in any of your plots.'

'I shall not be involved,' she pointed out. 'It will all be up to you—and Cassy, naturally. I have merely given you my advice, which you must admit is not to be scoffed at. Only look at what I have achieved with a little resolution.'

Tarleton, striving to be a leading figure in the fashionable world himself and knowing how very difficult it was, took her point. He must also have taken her advice, for he departed from Bath shortly afterwards, and within a week Tiffy was reading a jubilant letter from her aunt announcing Cassy's betrothal to Tarleton.

A day later she was reading the official announcement in the newspaper and feeling well pleased with herself. Even if this most respectable link did not cause Jago to revise his opinion of her mother's family, the betrothal would still work to her advantage. The Everetts would be far too busy planning Cassy's wedding to concern themselves closely with what their pleasure-loving niece was up to.

In August the dowager, as was her custom, removed to Worthing, a few miles along the coast from fashionable Brighton, where Jago spent the weeks of high summer. He rode over regularly—so regularly, in fact, that Tiffy suspected his visits were more than mere duty calls upon his grandmother. Her hopes rose, particularly as each visit meant that Maria Burroughs, also in Brighton, was left to amuse herself.

Tiffy was right in supposing the fierce attraction was mutual, but since neither cared for the other's terms, their relationship was something of an uneasy truce. Had she indeed been an abigail, Jago would have resolved the matter by seducing her. Had she been an heiress, he would have married her. But she was neither, and the resulting stalemate frustrated both of them.

In September Tiffy and Lady Janetta returned to Bath, and the following month Jago went up to Leicestershire for the hunting. It was the dowager's custom to spend autumn and winter sojourning at one great country house after another around the country, so that there were few people of the *haut ton* whom Tiffy did not meet.

Lady Janetta's hopes that Mrs Hunt's pregnancy had been a figment of her imagination were dashed when, in a letter bursting with pride, she wrote that she had been safely delivered of a boy. Mother and son were going on so well that the happy family would be re-established in London in time to replenish Eleanor's wardrobe for the next Season.

Tiffy's mood remained buoyant because, within the small exclusive circle in which she moved, Jago was sometimes a fellow guest at the same house party. Unfortunately, he was engaged to spend Christmas with friends, while Lady Janetta and Tiffy went into Gloucestershire to stay a few weeks with the Earl and Countess of Stanleigh.

It was the first time Tiffy had met Courteney's calm, statuesque sister. Finding them very much alike, she warmed to her instantly. Lady Augusta, already kindly disposed towards Tiffy, succumbed to her unaffected charm and they got on like a house on fire.

'She's a most unusual girl,' Augusta mused to Lady Janetta.

'She'll bring Eleanor up to scratch, that's all I care for,' her grandmother declared.

'It's also a most unusual relationship she has with Courteney. They are full of each other's praises, and yet they are not in love. It's very strange.'

'Freakish,' the dowager replied, 'but I've got used to it. They ain't hot for each other, which is all that matters.'

Privately, Lady Augusta thought it a pity. She liked Tiffy far better than she liked Eleanor. Still, Courteney knew his own heart best. And she mustn't meddle. Looking bleakly across at her grandmother, she thought one meddler was enough for any family.

In January, Tiffy journeyed into Kent to see Cassy

safely married to Tarleton, her dashing appearance causing as much stir as the wedding. She laughed at the strictures of the Everetts, visited her friends at the castle, and three days after her descent on Honivale was posting back to Bath.

Lady Swayle, knowing it was her duty to present Tiffy at Court in the spring, wrote that a sudden infirmity made it impossible for her to undertake the rigours of a London Season. In the event, her services were not needed. The spring was such a momentous one that Lady Janetta was at last able to put Tiffy's usefulness to the test.

With warm April sunshine thawing the severe frost that had gripped the country for several weeks, she set forth for Dalmaine House in Grosvenor Square with an ecstatic Tiffy beside her. It was many years since the dowager had turned her back on the frivolities of London. In her determination to get Courteney married, however, nothing would have made her miss this particular Season.

For one thing, the Hunts were home. For another, Napoleonic France had fallen apart. Paris has surrendered to the Allied armies, causing people all over England to sing and dance in the streets and deck their houses in laurel. The little Emperor's star had finally set.

Courteney would be home before many more weeks had passed. In the meantime, Eleanor would have to contend with Tiffy's bid to become the Belle of the Season, and the only thing that could compensate Eleanor for being toppled from her throne would be a brilliant marriage. Complacently, Lady Janetta considered the knot as good as tied.

In the following weeks, London indulged in a colossal spree that was to make it a Season without parallel. The crowned heads of Europe, their glittering entourages, statesmen and generals flocked to England to celebrate Napoleon's abdication and exile to Elba.

Tiffy, bubbling with the exuberance and stamina of youth, whirled through a non-stop round of Venetian breakfasts, turtle-dinners, picnics, rout-parties, balls, ballets, operas, concerts, plays, spectacles, balloon ascents and military reviews. Thanks to her looks, style, impudence, laughing charm and powerful patron, she was invited everywhere. Once a week she went to that holy of holies, Almack's, enduring its staidness for the sake of its exclusiveness. And one afternoon, wearing a white gown with a train, and with feathers adorning her head, she attended a drawing-room at Carlton House to make her curtsy to Queen Charlotte.

Triumph followed triumph. She flattered the corpulent Prince Regent, flirted with the Tsar of Russia, waltzed with the popular Field Marshal Prince von Blücher of Prussia and sharpened her wits on Beau Brummell. He saluted her candour and effrontery, so akin to his own, by making her a stick of his favourite perfume. It was the supreme accolade from the supreme arbiter of fashion. Tiffy had *arrived*.

There had, of course, to be a fly in the ointment, and it was Jago. He remained as elusive as ever. Sometimes he was all gallantry, at others he scarcely noticed her. Yet it was he who, out of sheer devilment, enabled her to slip her leash to sample some of London's gaudier dissipations, which were much frowned on by the *ton*.

To her delight, instead of driving her to Richmond one afternoon to see the deer, he took her to enjoy the vulgar amusements of Bartholomew's Fair with its market, sideshows, freaks and mummers. And one evening, when she had cried off from a ball on the unlikely grounds of a headache, she donned domino and mask and climbed out of a downstairs window, where he was waiting to whisk her off to a Covent Garden masquerade. There they waltzed until the drink-inspired merriment became too rowdy, even for the wondering Tiffy. He took her home, and kissed her before lifting

her back through the window. No expected declaration
of love accompanied his embrace, and when Tiffy saw
him a few evenings later at an assembly he was cold
rather than conspiratorial, bowing but not approaching her. She shrugged a slender shoulder and gave her
full attention to her usual court of more predictable
admirers.

Tiffy was also cross with Courteney. He had not sold
out. He had allowed himself to be seconded to the Duke
of Wellington's staff and was not expected home with
the Duke until later in the summer. She sent him a
heated missive, saying that if he lost Eleanor to another
suitor, he could blame his own dilatoriness, although she
would do her very best to see that this did not happen.

To keep a close eye on Eleanor, Tiffy became her
most determined friend, much to that gentle young
lady's surprise because they had nothing in common.
When Tiffy wasn't watching Eleanor, she was watching
Maria Burroughs. That dashing widow, to Tiffy's disgust, was much more to her taste than Eleanor. She was
a striking brunette, handsome rather than lovely, with
the merriest eyes and a lively disposition. The connection between her and Jago appeared to be a complaisant
one since she was as often in the company of other men
as he was with other women.

They gave the impression of being good friends rather
than lovers, and Tiffy, in her innocence, thought this
wishy-washy stuff. She had not the experience to
perceive that the rapport they shared out of, as well as
in, bed made the relationship more enduring than Jago's
usual brief and tempestuous affairs.

That year, the Season went on longer than usual. No
sooner had the foreign dignitaries departed than fresh
celebrations were planned for the centenary of the
Hanoverian accession. In the meantime, the Duke of
Wellington returned and there was another burst of
jubilation.

The first Tiffy knew Courteney was home was when she glanced across the floor during a lull in dancing at a ball, and saw him standing in the doorway. All her careful Society manners were abandoned in a flash of joy. She shrieked, 'Courteney!' and ran across the empty floor her with hands outstretched.

Courteney, aware of the sudden hush, none the less was far too kind to repulse her. He held out his hands, but she ran straight into his arms, hugging him, dancing with delight and calling him all manner of rogues for not telling her he was returning.

'You look *marvellous!*' she rushed on. 'Not half so thin, and I am so pleased. It didn't *suit* you to look so gaunt, although I never realised it until now. And what about me? Am I not marvellous, too?'

She stepped back, laughing, and twirled around as unselfconsciously as if no eyes but Courteney's were upon her. In that respect, at least, she hadn't altered, although he dutifully noted all the superficial changes.

'Complete to a shade,' he said.

'Yes,' she sighed blissfully. 'That is what everybody says. It is so *satisfying* to be all the rage.' She tucked her arm in his and strolled across the floor with him, adding laughingly, 'If you were not so polite, you would be telling me to go to the devil! I know very well it is not *me* you came to see. And she is here—see!'

Tiffy led him to where Eleanor was sitting, looking a perfect picture in blue muslin and with her fair hair bunched in ringlets over her ears. As Tiffy stood back to enjoy this reunion, she was dismayed to see two bright spots of colour burning in Eleanor's cheeks and that her normally tranquil blue eyes were glittering.

'Eleanor . . .' Courteney said reverently, and bowed over her hand and kissed it.

'My lord,' she replied in a suffocated voice and then, as another gentleman came up, 'it is good to see you looking so—so well. You must forgive me if I excuse myself. I am engaged to partner Lord Horsley in this quadrille.'

Courteney stepped back as though stung. Eleanor, inclining her head more hurriedly than gracefully, went away with Lord Horsley. Tiffy exclaimed disgustedly, 'Well! I hope she trips over that ridiculous train she is wearing and falls flat on her silly face! I . . .'

'Hush!' Lady Augusta, who was chaperoning Tiffy, arrived with Jago, determined to stop an interesting incident deteriorating into a scene. Tiffy subsided into simmering silence while Augusta embraced her brother, and then looked on while Jago and Courteney shook hands. These niceties accomplished, Augusta commanded, 'Jago, you and Tiffy just have time to make up a set.'

'Delighted to oblige you in anything else, dear coz, but you know I don't caper.'

'Do it!'

Jago's eyebrows flew up. 'The Harwoods are closing ranks? It's a bore, but I suppose even the black sheep must do his bit.' He offered his arm to Tiffy and led her on to the floor.

'I could kill her,' Tiffy said succintly.

Jago's eyebrows rose again. 'Augusta?'

'No, idiot! Eleanor!'

It took him a moment to get over the shock of being called an idiot, and then he said drily, 'I rather think that Eleanor could kill you. Everyone knows she has been waiting for Courteney to come home, and when he does, you rush into his arms as if you are used to being there.'

'But Courteney is my dearest friend! She *knows* that. I have told her so. I was excited to see him, but there is nothing *romantic* between us. There never has been.'

'Indeed?'

Anguished as she was over the rebufff Eleanor had given Courteney, she shot Jago a speculative look. 'Are you jealous?'

'Over you, my sweet? Why should I be? I know you better than most. Certainly well enough to realise that the first—no, the second time—I saw you it would have been more appropriate had you been wearing a garland of nettles rather than snowdrops. Anybody who grasps you must inevitably get stung.'

'Son of a bitch,' she growled.

He looked startled, and then laughed. 'Tiffy, you have your delights as well as your dangers! You must forgive me if I lack my noble cousin's fortitude.'

'Courteney doesn't need fortitude to be my friend,' she snapped. 'He just happens to be nice.'

'And I am not?'

Her frown vanished and her roguish dimple appeared in her cheek. 'Jago, you can't expect me to damn myself for ever by calling you anything as paltry as *nice*.'

'Coquette,' he said appreciatively. 'I think Eleanor was right to be jealous.'

'She was ridiculous!'

The music began, and Tiffy, glancing back, saw that Courteney was surrounded by friends welcoming him home. A scene had been averted, then, but she guessed how his sensitive heart must be aching at his beloved's walking away from him like that.

Jago bore his part in the quadrille with such a look of resignation on his handsome face that by the time he restored Tiffy to Lady Augusta, she was almost as furious with him as she was with Eleanor.

He bowed ironically to Augusta and drawled, 'You must forgive me if I excuse myself, coz. I feel I have endured enough of my family, and——' he flicked a glance at Tiffy '—its encumbrances for one evening.'

Before Augusta could reply, Tiffy intervened, 'I shall not keep you one moment longer from more favoured company. Maria Burroughs is over there!'

'My dear Tiffy, how can you possibly suppose I hadn't

noticed?' With a wicked smile and another bow, he walked away across the floor.

'Damn the man! Damn Eleanor. Damn everybody,' Tiffy exploded.

Augusta looked at her in alarm. 'Good heavens, don't tell me you've been foolish enough to develop a *tendre* for Jago?'

'I don't like anybody at the moment, myself included. Why can't I be a stuffed dummy like all the rest of you?'

'Thank you,' Augusta replied.

Tiffy flung up a hand. 'Oh, my lamentable tongue! It goes with my lamentable nature. They called me *infamous* in Honivale, and I begin to think they were right.'

'Not infamous,' Augusta corrected gently. 'Impetuous.'

'A fatal enough failing in English Society,' Tiffy said bitterly. 'I think I am dogged by a wicked demon. Every time something is going right, it steps in and makes it all go wrong. I have tried so hard to bring Courteney and Eleanor together. I have written him letter after letter urging him to hurry home. I have *persevered* in the most dreary friendship with Eleanor to make sure no other suitor would steal a march on him. Then, when they finally come together, it is I—*I*—who ruin it!'

She swung towards Augusta and added earnestly, 'I was so pleased to see him that I forgot all else. I had such a fear he would be killed, although I prayed for his safety whenever I remembered, which was often, in spite of being so busy. Then to see him so unexpectedly, and looking so well . . .' She broke off, swallowed and ended miserably, 'It's no use. I cannot justify myself. I have ruined his homecoming, and that is that.'

Augusta, moved to see tears sparkling in Tiffy's eyes, touched her arm and tried to rally her. 'Don't blame yourself. You behaved exactly as I would have done had

I not been drilled into being such a *stuffed dummy* before I was old enough to fight back.'

A smile wavered about Tiffy's lips. 'You do not reproach me? No, of course you would not. You are kind, like Courteney. He never reproaches me about anything, and I take advantage of it. Sometimes I think it is that which makes me more infamous than anything else. Well, if I have ruined all, I must repair all. Eleanor will marry Courteney if I have to drag her to the altar myself.'

Augusta's lips quivered with amusement. 'I scarcely think that violence will be necessary.'

Tiffy met her eyes and grinned. 'Of course not. She is as anxious to wed as Courteney, only with her, appearances are everything.'

Augusta nodded and sighed. 'It's at times like this when I wish Courteney were just a little more like Jago.'

'Yes! Jago would never have allowed himself to be rebuffed in such a way. He would have laughed and made her dance with him and *romanced* her out of the crochets. Though not, of course, if it was a quadrille.'

Augusta choked, met Tiffy's eyes, and began to giggle helplessly.

'It's no laughing matter,' Tiffy began, then she also giggled. 'Can you imagine Jago frowning at Eleanor as he frowned at me during that horrid dance? She would have fled all the way back to Jamaica.'

Lady Augusta sobered, and gave Tiffy a searching look. 'You mock her, yet you think she is right for my brother?'

Tiffy shrugged. 'You know me. I mock anybody who does not behave as I would, which is ridiculous, because I never behave *properly*. I am as you so kindly put it, impetuous. Eleanor, now, is such a dutiful daughter that she is bound to make a dutiful wife. What truly matters is that he wants her, so he must have her.'

If Tiffy's eyes took on a militant sparkle and strayed to

where Jago was flirting with Maria, it was because Courteney was right in divining that the changes in her were superficial. Her basic resolves hadn't altered one iota.

CHAPTER TWELVE

ELEANOR WAS convinced that Tiffy's and Courteney's reunion had made a laughing-stock of her, and as soon as the quadrille was over she demanded to be taken home. Mrs Hunt refused, pointing out that nothing could be more calculated to set tongues wagging again, but the normally biddable Eleanor stamped her foot and threatened to burst into hysterical tears. To avoid this further and conclusive calamity, Mrs Hunt gave way.

Their precipate departure was observed with malicious glee. Tiffy, it was said, had properly put The Beauty's nose out of joint. Gambling gentlemen rushed to their clubs to get the best odds on the marquess marrying the little colonial, and to speculate on Eleanor accepting Lord Horsley as the next best thing to Dalmaine.

The next morning when Courteney arrived at the ruffled Hunt household, the last chance to salvage the situation was lost when Eleanor refused to see him. It was Mrs Hunt's unenviable task to act as her envoy. She told Courteney that while she herself readily understood that Tiffy's lack of breeding was the sole cause of the disaster, Eleanor was too sadly discomposed to be as charitable. If my lord still wished to wed her, he must court her all over again. The world, as well as Eleanor, must be shown who truly possessed his heart. Meanwhile, Eleanor released him from any obligation to honour his understanding with her.

Mrs Hunt's own heart was sinking at this, so she hastily reminded him that Eleanor had waited with uncomplaining patience for his return from Europe. He

THE MARQUESS AND MISS YORKE

only had to prove that his fidelity matched hers for this sorry affair to have a happy outcome.

For Tiffy, a cloud now lay over that glorious victory summer. Her days were full of pleasure but her heart was full of aches. It hurt her to see Courteney having to line up with Eleanor's other suitors, to be refused anything as intimate as a waltz, and to have his floral tributes accepted but not worn.

Jago, too, was causing her a great deal of worry. He was always unpredictable, but lately there was a brittleness about him, a wildness, that boded no good for anybody, including himself. She knew he was playing deep and that his luck was out. Then, one morning, she learned through the servants' grapevine that he and Courteney had quarrelled. But when she tried to charm more information out of Courteney, she was met with a gentle rebuff. Jago, less considerate, advised her not to stick her nose in matters that were none of her business.

She was almost at her wit's end, for it seemed she had been running hard all summer to get nowhere. She was feverishly pondering what else she could do, when Jago acted and in the most decisive manner. It was on a day when Courteney was driving into Essex to visit a great-aunt. Lady Janetta was accompanying him, but Tiffy had declined to go. Jago was driving her to Richmond in his curricle.

When he called for her, she came down the stairs wearing a pale green gown with a green straw bonnet she'd had trimmed with artificial snowdrops especially for the occasion. Jago noticed it immediately, and laughed. 'How appropriate! Did you guess I mean to claim a trophy today?'

'Trophies have to be won before they can be claimed. What makes you think I am in the mood for playing games?'

'My dear Tiffy,' he replied, 'when are you ever in the mood for anything else?'

Farley came through the hall, and Jago paused. 'His lordship will not be back until late this evening, I gather?'

'That is correct, Mr Jago.'

'Give him this when he returns, there's a good fellow.' Jago gave him a letter and walked on with Tiffy.

Outside, she saw that no groom was to accompany them, and her spirits zoomed. They remained high because Jago appeared to have thrown off his cares. He was charming and attentive, and Tiffy, basking in the warmth of his good humour, flirted gaily with him.

His response was so encouraging that it was several minutes after they had crossed to the south side of the River Thames before she looked about her and cried, 'This is not the road to Richmond!'

'Quite right. This is the road to Dover, thence to Paris, Vienna, Rome or wherever else our fancy takes us.'

'Then we are eloping! How exciting,' she responded, merrily entering into the spirit of things.

'I think you will find it more diverting than gazing at those damnably dull deer at Richmond,' he agreed.

Tiffy laughed. 'Much as I can believe you'd be high-handed enough to spirit me away without so much as a change of clothes, I can't believe you would travel in such a fashion. Not even for an elopement. You are always so impeccable.'

He bowed slightly towards her without taking his eyes off the road. 'Very true. My travelling chaise—and baggage!—awaits us at an inn further along this road. I could scarcely collect you in it without advertising our intent, and we mustn't be caught until we have spent a night together. Afterwards, nobody will dream of pursuing us.'

There was such a ring of truth about this that Tiffy dropped her bantering manner and demanded, 'Jago, are you *serious*?'

'For once in my life, yes.'

'Good God! And you're not drunk?'

'Only on your beauty, my pet.'

Tiffy didn't bother to flutter so much as an eyelash at this compliment, but said, 'This is too sudden even for you, Jago! If you *are* serious and you are *not* drunk, then the bailiffs must be after you.'

'They are,' he agreed evenly. 'I am a most unsuitable bridegroom. If you had any sense, you would demand to be taken back to London instantly.'

'Poof! I am not so poor spirited. Only why me? Why not Maria?'

'A new love for a new life,' he told her lightly.

'That's all very well, but do you love me?'

'As much as I am capable of loving anyone. If that is not enough, you must teach me to love you more.'

'What a cunning thing to say. You know I can never resist a challenge.'

Jago laughed. 'You wouldn't be half so fascinating if you could. Well, Tiffy? Are you willing to chance your luck with me?'

These were the words she had been yearning to hear for so long that she savoured them for a few seconds before answering, 'Yes.'

'May we neither of us regret it,' Jago murmured.

'You devil!' Tiffy objected. 'I was expecting something more lover-like than that.'

'I shall make up for your disappointment when I have you in the privacy of my chaise. There is a limit to what I can accomplish in an open carriage and with a frisky team in hand.'

Tiffy, seeing the sense in this, snuggled against him and leaned her head on his shoulder. Eventually she said, 'Jago, about the bailiffs . . .'

'Do they bother you?'

'Of course not,' she scoffed. 'Bailiffs are always about, like measles. I'm surprised, that's all, that

Courteney hasn't rescued you. I thought he always did so, on account of you being his heir.'

'Not this time . . . I'm dipped to the tune of several thousand. That's nothing new and I would have recovered eventually. Now, alas, that Dalmaine is home and strongly tipped to be on the point of marrying you . . .'

'Oh, that silly gossip!' Tiffy broke in.

'I could call it something stronger than that. It has made my creditors so nervous they are demanding payment. God knows how many distraint orders will be made against me before the week is out.'

'Yes, but Courteney . . .'

'Refuses to advance me a groat unless I abandon my present way of life and enter a profession.'

'Hell's bells,' Tiffy breathed, unable to think of Jago as anything but a gentleman of leisure.

'Precisely. There is the Church . . .' He stopped as she giggled, then smiled. 'Yes, unthinkable! There is also the Foreign Office, but since I never learned the knack of tolerating people I dislike, I'm scarcely cut out to be a diplomat. That leaves the army, and a fine fool I'd look if I joined up now that the war with France is over. All in all, I prefer to quit the country and restore my fortunes abroad.'

'Anyone would,' Tiffy agreed indignantly. 'How could Courteney have been so unreasonable? It is so unlike him! Why didn't you apply to Lady Janetta? She approves of your way of life.'

'Only so long as it costs her nothing. Believe me, Tiffy, I know my tight-fisted grandmama. The moment I became a charge on her would be the moment I ceased to be her favourite.'

'Running off with me will scarcely please her.'

'I hope to weather that. Lady Janetta's main aim is to get Courteney married. Eleanor can hardly remain suspicious of you after you have eloped with me. With any luck, by the time we return in a year or two,

Courteney will have his precious heir and I shall be forgiven.'

'Ingenious,' Tiffy said admiringly.

'It's damned risky. However, I've got nowhere by betting on certainties this past year, so it's time to play the long shots.'

'Oh? You seemed pretty certain I would elope with you.'

Jago, glancing down, saw that she had tilted her head and was regarding him flirtatiously through her eyelashes. 'Tiffy, if you will look at me like that, the sooner we are in the privacy of my chaise the better . . .'

Tiffy laughed, but when they reached the small and rather dilapidated inn where his chaise was waiting, his coachman came running to say there had been a hitch. One of his leaders had cast a shoe, and his groom had taken it to the next hamlet where there was a blacksmith. As he had been gone for nearly half an hour, and the hamlet was not above a mile along the road if the morons at the inn were to be believed, the groom should be back at any minute.

Jago's eyebrows drew together, but since there was little he could do, he tossed the reins to his coachman, climbed down and helped Tiffy to alight. He was still frowning as he looked from her to the inn, and said, 'This isn't the sort of place frequented by the fashionable, which is why I chose it, but I didn't think we'd have to risk the interior ourselves.'

'You are too nice by half! You'd be surprised at some of the places I've frequented.'

'Ah! Life with your father, I collect,' Jago replied, ushering her inside.

Tiffy chuckled, thinking of the Tin Flute, and said demurely, 'If it pleases you to think so.'

'A hint of mystery. I like that. I have so many of your secrets still to learn.'

Tiffy, ever practical, retorted, 'I think I'll be a great

deal more comfortable if I don't attempt to learn yours.'

Jago's eyes gleamed. 'I begin to think we were made for each other, my love.'

'What a slow-top you are. I've always known it.' She turned as the landlord entered and bade him dust a bench so that she might sit down.

This he did with the corner of his long apron, apologising profusely to Jago for the lack of a private parlour, there being no call for one, on account of Quality being as rare as snowballs in summer in these parts, preferring as they did to use the regular posting-houses. Jago cut short this effusion with a half-sovereign and a request for beer for himself and lemonade for the lady. The landlord took the hint, returning shortly with a tray bearing a tankard of home-brewed ale, a glass of lemonade and a plate of biscuits contributed by his unseen spouse. He put the tray on a table by the freshly-dusted bench and departed.

Tiffy sat down, took off her bonnet, placed it beside her on the bench, then fluffed up her crushed ringlets. Jago put his tall beaver hat on the table, took the tankard and strolled over to the empty fireplace where he turned and surveyed her, leaning an elbow on the high mantelshelf. He looked very incongruous in that homely taproom. His tall, powerful figure dwarfed everything in such a confined space, and she perceived that although she was used to roughing it, he would not be at all happy if he were obliged to do so.

Following this train of thought, she said, 'I do wish you had warned me! I have somewhere between two and three hundred in ready cash I could have brought with me.'

Jago drank some of his ale. 'Are you afraid we'll be obliged to swim the Channel? Don't be. I have a few hundred pounds to tide us over.'

'That's all right then,' Tiffy replied. 'When shall we be getting married?'

'As soon as we receive your dowry, my sweet.'

'Jago, if you think any of my relatives will put up so much as a penny, you should be locked up in Bedlam. They'll be glad of the opportunity to wash their hands of me.'

'So I believe. I have not, however, applied to your relatives.'

'But there's no one else.'

'Yes there is, my love,' Jago corrected her coolly. 'There is Dalmaine.'

'*Courteney?*' Tiffy gasped.

'Don't sound so incredulous. Believe me, he will be only too glad to pay up, and pay up handsomely . . .'

'Jago, no! It is outrageous. Courteney is no kin of mine. He is not obliged to bribe you to marry me.'

'He will think so. Having somewhat quixotically engineered your elevation into Society, and embroiled Lady Janetta to that end, he will feel very much obliged to protect you both from the consequences of it. This becomes a trifle tedious, but I really must remind you that I am his heir and you are under his grandmother's protection. If we do not marry, you will be a fallen woman; I a blackguard for not doing right by you. Stigmas neither of us will ever overcome. Dalmaine will not permit that. He will pay for an immediate marriage.'

This silenced her momentarily, then she objected, 'He will know that we shall marry anyway.'

'Why? I have a reputation for being something of a devil, and you for not caring what is thought of you. No one can be certain what we will do. However, in the letter Farley will give him this evening informing him of our flight to France, I have pledged my word to marry you once the dowry of ten thousand pounds is paid.'

'He is supposed to trust the word of a blackmailer?'

Jago's eyes gleamed dangerously. 'Don't play the prude with me, Tiffy Yorke! *You* are not slow to grab what you want from life. You are adept at inducing others to pay for your pleasures. Nor do you refuse trinkets from your admirers that more fastidious girls would never accept.'

'Oh, well, if men like to make fools of themselves . . .'

'Why not encourage them to do so? Precisely.' Jago took an enamelled snuffbox from his coat pocket, flicked open the lid and took a pinch. 'Can you wonder if I am not impressed by your sudden show of scruples?'

She turned away. He was right. She had never encouraged either Jago or Courteney to cherish any illusions about her, believing that this would give her the freedom to act precisely as she pleased. And yet . . . And yet . . . she did not feel free. She stamped her foot in frustration and burst out, 'Hell and damnation! My cursed Achilles heel.'

'Your *what*?'

'Courteney. I can't do this to him. To anybody else, yes, but not him. He *trusts* me.'

Jago raised his eyebrows. 'More fool he!'

'Yes,' she agreed bitterly. 'Only this time it is more fool *me*. I never meant it to happen, God only knows, but he is the one person who *can* trust me. More or less. I stretch his trust sometimes, but I never break it. I *can't*.'

Jago thrust himself away from the mantelshelf. 'I never gave any credence to the rumours about you two. Was I a fool? What exactly are you and Dalmaine to each other?'

'Everything and nothing,' she babbled incoherently. 'You will not understand.'

'Try me,' he invited ominously.

Tiffy began to pace about the room, gesticulating wildly, as though actions could express what words could not. 'When we first met we were both bedevilled by misfortune. We were good for each other. Companionably, not romantically. Even when we didn't need each other any more, the bond between us remained. That is why he has been so kind to me and why I cannot treat him as if he were of no account. I harmed him enough by setting Eleanor against him. I cannot harm him further. He would never harm me.'

The ugly look left Jago's face and he said dismissively, 'Maudlin nonsense.'

She stopped her pacing and faced him miserably. 'I knew you wouldn't understand. No one ever does. It makes no odds. I can't take money from him in this way.'

'You won't be obliged to. The transaction is between Dalmaine and myself.'

'That's splitting hairs.' She went towards him and clasped his hands, looking earnestly up at him. 'We do not need his money. We have so much else besides. Our looks, our talents, our *ton*. We can live comfortably on the money you have by you while we set about making our fortunes.'

'Comfortably? Tiffy, my sweet, we are used to living *exquisitely*! Can you imagine us pinching and scraping? I can't.'

. She tightened her hold on him. 'We have each other. Nothing else matters.'

'Enchanting nodcock! You can teach me all about romance—but only after I have taught you all about money.'

Tiffy pulled her hands out of his. 'Don't patronise me! I am not a *nodcock*. I mean what I say. You must listen.'

'Tiffy, you are being a dead bore. We need money. Dalmaine has it. All you stand to lose is his good opinion. I might lose my grandmother's fortune. Which of us is sacrificing most?'

'If you loved me, you wouldn't be talking about sacrifice,' she answered stormily. 'If you want money, run away with Maria. I can only offer myself. If that is not enough, you are not the man I thought you were.'

A lazy smile curved his lips. 'Are you so sure about that?' He put his hands on her shoulders and ran them caressingly down her arms. He felt her tremble, and laughed softly. 'There isn't a lot of you, but every inch is woman. I've wasted precious time reasoning with you when this was all that was necessary . . .'

His arms went about her and Tiffy was clamped against his strong body. His lips came down to claim hers. She turned her head away and began to struggle fiercely, certain that if she did not make him heed her now, she would never be able to do so.

'Stop it,' she gasped, as he turned her head back to his.

His lips came down on hers again with the unhurried expertise of a man certain of his mastery. She yielded, but it was against her will, and she reacted violently when he raised his head and said with satisfaction, 'That's better. I prefer promise to prudery any day.'

'Damn you, Jago Harwood,' she told him furiously. 'If you think one kiss can turn me into your slave . . .'

He cut off her words with another kiss. It was more demanding, more brutal, than the first, and her reasons for resisting him became hazy. She was no longer sure whether her real triumph lay in winning this battle or losing it. Then, suddenly, the issue was resolved for her. Jago was pulled away from her so violently that she staggered backwards, came up against the bench and sat down abruptly on her bonnet.

She gasped and blinked in disbelief, for it was Courteney who had hold of Jago. He was swinging him round to deliver a savage punch to his chin. Jago reacted swiftly enough to avoid the full force of the blow, but he was off balance and went down with a crash that reverberated round the taproom.

The landlord came running. Courteney tossed him a gold coin, and said with quiet authority, 'We desire some privacy. You have nothing to fear. Any damage will be made good.'

The landlord, looking from Courteney to Tiffy and

Jago, hedged, 'That's all very well, sir, but I can't have no murders here.'

'There will be nothing more violent than a thrashing, I promise you,' Courteney assured him, stripping off his swallow-tailed coat. Jago got up and began to follow suit.

The landlord looked relieved, as though brawling in his taproom was too common an occurrence to make a fuss about. He voiced only one further qualm, 'The lady . . . ?'

'. . . is leaving.'

'I am *not*!' Tiffy felt too weak with reaction to get to her feet, but her voice was strong enough. Nobody, however, took the slightest notice of her. The landlord bowed and left. Courteney and Jago began to push the furniture back against the walls. They appeared to know precisely what they were about.

Stripped to their breeches and shirts, there was nothing to choose between them. In size and build they were identical. With the same intent expressions on their faces, they even looked alike. Both Harwoods, of a certainty, and another certainty was that they were getting set to punish each other. Jago's brown eyes had never blazed more passionately, nor Courteney's grey ones more icily.

Panic brought Tiffy to her feet. 'No!' she exclaimed. 'You mustn't fight. I won't have either of you hurt. I *won't*!'

They both ignored her, and together moved the bench she had just vacated back against a wall. She stuttered indignantly, 'S—stop it. Stop it this instant!'

She felt a hand on her arm. It was Tobias. He thrust her bonnet at her, took her arm, and began to propel her towards the door. Tiffy tried to free herself, protesting, 'How dare you! Let me go. Jago! Courteney! Make him let me go! I *will* not be thrust out of the way like a piece of furniture.'

Courteney's controlled voice cut across her furious one. 'This is no place for you, Tiffy. Tobias has my orders. Kindly go with him.'

She tried to forestall Tobias by throwing herself on the floor, but he caught her round the waist and began to half drag, half carry her through the door. 'Jago!' she wailed.

He smiled sardonically, 'A maiden does not appeal to the dragon she is being rescued from.'

'Don't talk such fustian,' she panted, clinging to the door frame. 'I won't have you two fighting. I—I am not worth it.'

'Oh, but you are,' Jago contradicted, as Tobias picked her up bodily, causing her skirt to slide up to her thighs. 'I've never seen shapelier legs in my life. Have you, Dalmaine?'

Tiffy never heard the answer to such deliberate provocation, because Tobias carried her outside and slammed the door. She swore with stable fluency as he carried her across the yard, kicking her legs and pounding at his chest with her fists, exhausting herself to no effect.

'Give over,' Tobias scolded. 'You're only giving the yokels something to gawk at. Behave like the lady you're supposed to be.' Thrusting her into Courteney's carriage, he climbed in after her. He closed the door, rapped on the roof and, as the carriage moved forward, sat opposite her, back straight, arms folded, as though he were riding in his rightful place on the box.

'How dare you!' she gasped.

'Begging your pardon, miss, but I ain't having you jump out the first time we slow for a corner. His lordship has ordered me to get you back to London.'

'Tobias, we are friends. I never thought that you would be my gaoler . . .'

'I never thought you'd cause my master this much

trouble, neither, after all he's done for you. Shame on you, Miss Tiffy.'

'A pox on your hypocrisy! If you really cared for his lordship, you would be stopping that fight. He will be dreadfully hurt. Mr Jago is not a man to cross. He is a Corinthian. He excels at all the sports. He boxes with Gentleman Jackson. He does all kinds of things his lordship does not.'

Tobias snorted disparagingly. 'My master doesn't play the part of looking after himself, he lives it. No need to fear for him.'

Tiffy was startled. 'You mean he can *beat* Mr Jago?'

'I wouldn't go that far. Normally they fight each other to a standstill, and feel the better for it. Howsoever . . .'

'Good God! They've fought before?'

'Since they was in shortcoats. That's only natural, being as how they're chalk and cheese. *Howsoever*,' he stressed, returning to the point where she had interrupted him, 'with Mr Jago in his cups, it's my master as has the edge today.'

'Mr Jago is sober!'

'Strewth, he must have been drunk for a sennight to step this far over the line.'

Suddenly she knew he was speaking the truth. She remembered what Jago had said when she'd asked if he were drunk: *'Only on your beauty, my pet.'* She bowed her head, seeing through a haze of misery the crumpled bonnet Tobias had thrust into her hands. The snowdrops were crushed. Her fingers strayed sadly to them. An unworthy trophy. For an unworthy man.

A man who needed to be drunk to elope with her because he didn't truly love her. There was no romance in that. Perhaps he'd chosen her only as a way of getting back at Courteney for refusing him a loan. He was more of a devil than she knew, Jago Harwood, only that didn't ease the ache of loving him.

Her head drooped further. Tobias, watching her

uneasily, said, 'You're never going to cry, Miss Tiffy? Not you.'

His words had a bracing effect. If Jago was not yet tamed, neither was she. 'No, I am not,' she replied purposefully. 'Tell me how it was that his lordship came to catch us. He was supposed to be taking Lady Janetta into Essex.'

'We'd got no farther than Islington Spa when we met a courier from Lady Pepswyck saying she was ill with bronchitis and couldn't receive visitors. We turned back, arriving home only minutes after you set off. Lady Janetta went straight upstairs, and Farley gave his lordship Mr Jago's letter. The chaise was still harnessed and the horses fresh, so off we goes after you.'

'Then everybody knows! There will be a scandal anyway.'

'No, there won't. His lordship was obliged to tell me and Henry-coachman what you were about—and Farley, because he was to say Mr Jago had had an accident with his curricle and we was bringing you home. None of us will talk, and Mr Jago's servants know better than to prattle about his business. His lordship will bring you off safely, never fear.'

'I'm supposed to be obliged to him?' Tiffy asked. 'I'd rather be loved than safe!'

'If Mr Jago loved you, he'd have married you decent and proper.'

'He—he was indulging my romantic nature,' she defended. Tobias didn't look impressed, and so she added, 'There would have been difficulties. I am not a suitable bride.'

'Nor him a suitable bridegroom until he's mended his ways. You're well out of it, Miss Tiffy, as you'll come to see in time.'

'I'd much rather be on my way to France with Mr Jago than sitting here listening to your scolds. Don't think I'm penitent, because I'm not. Nor am I *out of it*, as you say.

When we get to Dalmaine House, how are we going to explain away the fact that neither Mr Jago nor his lordship is with us?'

'Mr Jago was concussed, and his lordship is staying with him until he's recovered,' Tobias replied promptly.

'Very inventive, but I don't see how Mr Jago's travelling carriage is going to be accounted for.'

Neither did Tobias, but he said confidently, 'His lordship will think of something.'

'If Mr Jago hasn't knocked him senseless. Oh, I wish I knew what was going on . . .'

CHAPTER THIRTEEN

Tiffy was kept in suspense until the evening. She had dressed for dinner before receiving a message that the marquess had returned and would see her in the yellow salon. It was too much for her volatile state to find Courteney calmly straightening the folds of his neck-cloth before a mirror as though nothing untoward had happened. She snapped, 'You're mighty cool! Where have you *been* all day? What has *happened*? How dare you leave me so long without news! Where is Jago?'

The heavy emphasis, the flashing eyes, the hasty footsteps, were so like her that Courteney had to smile, albeit wryly. When had she ever been shaken by a situation that would have prostrated any right-minded female?

'Well?' she demanded. 'What have you to say to me?'

'A great deal; but first we must get our stories straight. Lady Janetta might walk in on us at any moment, and it won't do for us to be saying different things.'

'I am not interested in stories! I want the truth.'

He took her arm and led her to a couch. 'You shall have it, if you will stop talking. I am very pressed for time.'

Tiffy pulled away from him. 'My time, of course, is of no importance. I have been kept twiddling my thumbs, imagining the horridest things, and . . .' She broke off as she noticed a bruise on his scarred cheek. 'So! You did not have it all your own way. Is Jago hurt?'

'No more than he deserves. He bears me no grudges. Will you be as generous until you have heard me out? It's as much in his interest as yours that today's events are covered up.'

Tiffy threw him a smouldering look, but she allowed herself to be seated on the couch. She waited until he sat beside her, then turned towards him and scoffed, 'I don't see how a travelling chaise piled high with baggage can be brought back to London without somebody seeing it and asking awkward questions.'

'That was the biggest difficulty, but we have thought of a way round it.'

'*We?* You mean Jago is with you on this?'

'He scarcely wants his folly advertised to the world. Indeed, he is dependent on your co-operation.' This silenced her, and he went on rapidly, 'We are going to say the curricle overturned in a ditch. You were thrown clear, but Jago suffered bruises and cracked ribs. This is necessary so that we can invent a doctor to prescribe several days' rest, thus enabling me to summon his chaise to convey him to Dalmaine.'

'The castle? Why should you send him there?'

'I feared he wouldn't rest properly if he returned to the metropolis.'

She glowered at him, but admitted, 'Clever.'

'It will hold up, provided nobody enquires too closely, and there's no reason why anybody should.'

'You've rusticated him to keep him away from me, I suppose?'

'No, to keep him from being thrown in the Fleet. He'll be safe at the castle until his affairs are sorted out.'

'Oh. What about the curricle?'

'I drove it back to London this afternoon.'

'What?' she exploded. 'Where have you been all this time?'

'In the City thwarting distraint orders. I left his agent and mine trying to unravel the extent of his obligations. He consigns all his bills to the fire until he is actually dunned.'

Tiffy saw no sin in this, and was about to say so when Courteney continued, 'All in all, it's been a busy day and

I'm not finished yet. I must get changed for dinner and then go on to White's. Jago made a last bid to restore his fortune by gambling on credit last night. He promised to redeem his vowels this evening. I must do that for him or he will never recover his standing. His supposed accident will account for his inability to redeem them himself.'

'You mean that if he'd won, he wouldn't have eloped with me? I—the dowry—was his last resort?'

'I'm afraid so, Tiffy.'

His sympathetic eyes goaded her into boasting, 'At least it was *me* he wanted. Had it merely been money, he would have run off with Maria Burroughs.'

'There was never any chance of that. Under the terms of Burroughs's will, the handsome income Maria enjoys reverts to his family if she re-marries. Maria is much too worldly to ruin herself financially by marrying Jago, or socially by living openly with him.'

The warm blood in Tiffy's veins turned to ice. Jago had told her: *A new love for a new life* when he had known Maria wouldn't go with him. The instinct to defend—whether herself or him she knew not—was still there, however, and she said, 'He still risked losing his inheritance from Lady Janetta by eloping with me.'

'That's debatable. My grandmother loves a rake, but only up to a certain point. While she lived quietly in Bath, he was able to conceal his wilder dissipations. Unfortunately for him, this Season in London has opened her eyes. Jago is also approaching thirty, the age at which she believes a man should settle down. She has told him so. He has taken no notice, causing friction between them. Jago knows that, fond of him as she is, she will not leave her money to be thrown away on the gaming tables, yet he has been unable to check himself. Now that a change of lifestyle has been forced on him, he might be able to retrieve his position, but he was well aware when he eloped with you that his chances of inheriting her fortune had dwindled to almost nothing.'

This further example of Jago's perfidy was so crushing that Tiffy flinched. Courteney took her hand and clasped it comfortingly. 'I would have spared you this, but it wouldn't be kind to conceal what sort of man Jago really is.'

She snatched her hand away, exclaiming wildly, 'He's my sort of man! At least, he will be when I've taught him not to make a fool of me. I don't care if he's a rake and a gamester and—and unscrupulous. So, too, am I.'

'Not unscrupulous enough to extort money from me,' Courteney said positively.

'Jago told you the dowry was all his doing?' she asked eagerly. 'Well, then, that proves he must care for me. I knew he did.'

'Jago said nothing about the dowry,' Courteney corrected her. 'He didn't have to. I already knew that was his touch, not yours, just as I knew the elopement was sprung on you. You see, Tiffy, you have a need Jago doesn't share—to justify your actions, if only to yourself. You could not have done that without leaving a letter of explanation to me. Before I set off after you, I went up to your room. There was no letter, and your mother's miniature was still on your dressing-table. You'd have taken that with you had you known you weren't coming back.'

In her perverse way, she was not gratified to find he regarded her as Jago's victim rather than his accomplice, and she retorted sulkily, 'I shall write a letter now, so that it will be ready the next time I run off with Jago. And I shall, you know.'

'He will not attempt to elope with you again.'

Her eyes blazed violet fire. 'I suppose that was your condition for paying his debts?'

'In part.'

'Only in part? What's the rest of it?'

'He is going to join the army.'

'So that's what you meant about *a change of lifestyle has been forced on him*. Pooh! I don't believe it! He's foxed you. He's only pretended to go to the castle. He's on his way to France.'

'I hold the mortgage on his estate, a precaution I took the last time I was obliged to pay his debts. A landless gentleman has no consequence or any means of raising credit—two things Jago could not live without. I will foreclose unless he joins the army. He has no choice but to do as he is told.'

There was a stern note in his voice Tiffy had never heard before. It almost made him seem a stranger. She gasped, 'You've humiliated him! I despise you for that.'

'Jago respects me more when I exert my power than when I withhold it. He believes it is in the nature of things for the weak to be trampled underfoot, as he tried to trample me today. He either learns to live responsibly or I wash my hands of him. It's his last chance.'

Tiffy jumped up from the couch. 'I see how it is! This is the Marquess of Dalmaine laying down the law. Playing God! We lesser mortals must fall on our knees and quake. Jago's punishment has been meted out, and mine, I suppose, comes next. Well, damn you, *Marquess*, I'm still on my feet and mean to stay that way. I don't care a rush what you do to me. I am sorry for *nothing* save that wretched dowry. I love Jago, devil though he is, and I mean to have him.'

Courteney rose to his feet. 'Tiffy, this infatuation will not last. It . . .'

'Infatuation? What do you know about it? You don't know what love is because you have never felt it. My love is flesh and fire and passion. It isn't the meek and mewling emotion you feel for Eleanor, otherwise you'd never be content to worship her from afar while she plays off her airs and graces on you. You'd want to grasp her—and hold on! And if she loved you, she'd make damned sure you did.'

Because she was hurting so much herself, Tiffy wanted to hurt him, and she succeeded. It was some seconds before he could reply, 'You are talking about lust. That lasts no longer than infatuation.'

'Don't play with words. I know how I *feel*, and I couldn't care two pins for anything else. Not honour or duty or respectability or any other of the stupid things you set so much store by.'

Courteney walked towards the door. 'We shall talk again tomorrow, when you are calmer.'

'Running away, my lord?' she mocked. 'From flesh and fire and passion? Shouldn't you stay long enough to tell me what my punishment is for daring to be *human*?'

'There will be no punishment. I blame myself for not taking better care of you. If I hadn't been so immersed in my own affairs, I would have seen what was happening weeks ago and stopped it. It was my fault you were nearly ruined.'

'Oh, go away,' she answered irritably. 'You are ridiculous. Next you will be blaming yourself for Jago's sins as well as mine. No, wait! Are we forbidden to meet?'

Courteney had opened the door but he looked back at her. 'I am not so Gothic, nor can I think of anything more likely to drive you back into his arms. Once he is in a position to support a wife, there is nothing to stop him applying to Lord Swayle in the regular way for your hand in marriage.'

'Jago would never do anything so tame!'

'If he loves you, Tiffy, it is in your power to make him do anything you wish.'

'That's fine, coming from you! You can't get Eleanor to consent to a betrothal, far less a marriage, and she is supposed to love you. Practise what you preach if you want me to heed your sermons. Until then, I'm better able to manage my life myself!'

Tiffy swept past him and went upstairs to her room. Regrettably, her triumph lasted only as long as her temper, and that had burned too fiercely to sustain her for long. She excused herself from dinner, pleading the shock she had suffered in the supposed accident as an excuse for having a tray sent up to her room. She picked at her food, wondering wretchedly if Jago were thinking about her, and finding little comfort there. He was far more likely to be thinking about himself. He would hate army life. Would he hate her, too? She had difficulty in swallowing a morsel of chicken, and didn't try to eat any more. When the tray was taken away, she decided to go to bed. She put a branch of candles on the bedside table and tried to read. Her eyes took in the words, but her brain couldn't absorb them. It was too busy exploring the bittersweet paths of might-have-beens.

The large four-poster with its pretty pink and white drapery made her feel lost, a princess without a prince. As the hours passed, her resilience against the anguish that consumed her lessened. Thoughts she had deliberately kept at bay crept in and desolated her, particularly the dispassionate way Jago had been prepared to exploit the very real passion they had for each other. God knew she didn't want to be worshipped, but she didn't want to be cheapened, either.

She hadn't taught him anything about love and she had been so certain that she could. Tiffy, her confidence gone, felt genuinely frightened for the first time in her life. It was as though the foundation-stone that gave her so much assurance, and supported all her hopes and dreams, had been pulled away. She was falling . . . falling . . . and there was nobody to catch her, nobody to save her. She knew that if Jago were in London, she would get up and run through the night to him, not caring whether he loved her or not, not caring for anything save escaping this soul-destroying solitude. But Jago was not in London. There was nobody she could turn to.

Except Courteney. She sat up abruptly, her eyes

brightening. *Of course, Courteney!* He had never repulsed her no matter what she had said or done. If she
went to him, she could tell him how sorry she was for her
spitefulness. He would forgive her—he always did—
and then perhaps she would feel better.

Tiffy got up, slipped on the white silk peignoir that
matched her nightgown, thrust her feet into her flimsy
high-heeled slippers, and hurried across the room. Peep-
ing out of her door, she hesitated when she saw that the
candles in the wall sconces along the passage were still
burning. Somebody, then, in the family wing, had not
yet gone to bed. It could not be the dowager. She had
heard the distinct thud-thud of her cane going past a long
time ago. It must be Courteney.

The thought of retreating into her bedchamber to
endure so much as another five minutes of her own
company was too much for her. She threw caution to the
winds and hurried along the passage, the thick carpet
muffling her footsteps, only pausing when she came to
the corner. She looked round it and saw Marlowe, the
ancient valet, coming out of Courteney's suite. He
walked away and disappeared round another corner,
presumably heading for a secondary staircase that led to
the servants' quarters.

She hurried on and tapped softly at Courteney's door,
creeping in when there was no answer. The huge room
was deeply shadowed. The valet had drawn the curtains
across the windows and round the massive four-poster
bed. The only light, from a six-branched candelabrum
placed on a table beside the empty fireplace, illuminated
a tray of decanters and, next to it, an armchair where
Courteney lounged, staring down at a glass in his hand.
His fair hair looked guinea-gold in the softly flickering
light, and the shadows were not responsible for the
gloom of his expression.

Shimmering out of the darkness in her white silk, Tiffy
breathed thankfully, 'Courteney . . .'

He stared at her, nonplussed, then put down his glass and came to his feet. 'Tiffy! Have you lost your senses? You should not be here.'

'I am so miserable! I don't know what to do with myself.' She cast herself into his arms and buried her face against the dark cloth of his dressing-gown.

Courteney found himself holding an armful of sheer seductive silk with, beneath it, the even more seductive warmth of Tiffy's slender body. For a second she was like the answer to a prayer, and he clasped her with a savageness he hadn't dreamed of, then he recollected himself and thrust her just as savagely from him. He turned away, picked up his glass and drank his brandy, not trusting himself to speak.

Tiffy felt bereft. She held out her arms to him and pleaded, 'Courteney, don't send me away. I know I said a lot of horrid things, but I didn't mean them. It was my temper talking, the way it always does when I am in the wrong. I want to say I'm sorry, and . . . and . . .'

He glanced at her, and just as swiftly away. 'Go back to your room. You should never have come here. Even if it were not for that, I am not fit company for anybody this evening.'

Her arms dropped to her side and she said, bewildered, '*You, too*? Why?'

'We shall talk in the morning. Pray go now.'

But Tiffy, forgetting her distress in his, went towards him and lifted a hand to turn his face to hers. She knew only one reason for the torment she saw there, and whispered, 'It's Eleanor, isn't it? What's happened?'

His hand clenched on his glass. 'The Hunts were holding a soirée tonight. I went there after I'd concluded Jago's business at White's. I asked Eleanor to marry me. Now, without any further prevarication. She refused.'

Tiffy gasped, but before she could say what she was thinking, he went on, 'Wellington has asked me to accompany him to Vienna for the Peace Congress. It's an honour I can scarcely refuse, even though it means I must stay on his staff a few months longer. I wanted to take Eleanor with me. I thought we could make a honeymoon of it. Eleanor, however, remains adamant that she will not marry a serving soldier.'

'And if you sell out?' Tiffy asked.

'I have permission to propose to her again, but that's not enough. Damn it, it's not enough!' He hurled his glass into the fireplace, where it splintered into a thousand pieces. The sound shattered the quiet of the room.

Tiffy stared. Never had she heard Courteney utter the mildest curse before, or ever imagined him with his emotions out of control. She said, aghast, 'This is my fault. My lamentable tongue! You heeded the spiteful things I said and, indeed, you shouldn't have. I was really talking about myself, what I expect. Eleanor needs gentle wooing because she is a proper lady. I thrive on passion because I am not. I don't know what it is about me that is so very different. I think I should have been a man.'

In her flowing white silk she looked the embodiment of all that was feminine and alluring, and he said unsteadily, 'Tiffy, you rogue. You—always think of something that will make me laugh. I . . .'

He got no further because there was a discreet yet determined tapping on the door. Tiffy gasped when Courteney caught her up in his arms. He thrust her through the scarlet velvet curtains round the four-poster and dropped her with little ceremony on to the matching velvet bedspread. He heard a further gasp and a giggle, hastily suppressed, and walked back to the fireplace. He glanced at the bed. The disturbed velvet had stopped shivering and completely hid its secret. He said languidly, 'Come in.'

A footman entered, the candle-snuffer in his hand attesting to the fact that he was putting out the lights in the passages now that the marquess had retired for the night. He said diffidently, 'Do you require assistance, my lord? I heard glass breaking.'

'Thank you for your concern, Billings. I was careless enough to drop my glass into the fireplace. It can be cleared up in the morning. I'm going to bed now.'

'Very well, my lord.' Billings bowed and withdrew.

Courteney picked up the candelabrum, strode over to the bed and swished back the curtains. Tiffy was kneeling on the scarlet coverlet, her impish face wearing the apprehensive expression of an urchin caught out in a misdeed. There was, however, nothing urchin-like about the rest of her.

Her white peignoir had fallen from her shoulders and her satin nightgown clung to the curves of which she was normally so proud and now seemed entirely unaware. The candlelight picked out copper highlights in her tumbled mass of black curls, and her lips pursed into a soundless whistle. 'That was close! How dreadful if I had compromised you, Courteney.'

He shook his head at her. 'Do you never think of yourself? When I consider the exhausting day I've had trying to protect your reputation, only to have you fling it away in my bedchamber, I could . . .' He stopped, lost for words.

Tiffy supplied them for him. 'I know, you could wring my neck. Put those candles down. If you drip hot wax on me I shall scream, and that will be both our reputations gone for ever.' She piled up the pillows at the top of the bed and patted the place beside her. 'Do sit down. I shall have to wait a few minutes until the servant has left this wing, and you were telling me about Eleanor.'

He stood irresolute, but her very unselfconsciousness made it easier to do as she suggested than to point out the dangers of her situation. He put the branch of candles on the bedside table, and leaving the curtains open on that side of the bed, sat beside her. After a moment he sighed and leaned back against the piled-up pillows.

Tiffy also sighed and stretched out beside him, resting her head against his shoulder. 'How cosy this is. I was dying of loneliness in my room. Do you know how it is when you cannot sleep and your thoughts are going round and round, and you feel sad and angry and all manner of confusing things, until you yearn for daylight —only daylight never comes?'

It was a *cri de coeur* Courteney recognised, and he put an understanding arm round her shoulders. She snuggled up gratefully, murmuring, 'My best and truest friend. I knew you would make me feel better. Am I doing the same for you?'

He ruffled her hair affectionately. 'I do not feel as desperate as I did.'

She tipped back her head so that she could look up at him, her slanted eyes warm, her full lips smiling. 'Strange, how *good* we always are for each other. I suppose it's because, not being in love, we can be entirely natural. Love confuses everything so dreadfully. It's because I cannot be like this with Jago that we are so often at daggers drawn. It must be the same with you and Eleanor. What will you do?'

'Go to Vienna. I have a foolish wish for Eleanor to want *me*, the man, not the marquess.'

'You're thinking of something I once said, and you shouldn't, not if it is going to make you unhappy.'

'It will scarcely make me happier if she marries me for the wrong reasons. Surely, if she loves me, she would marry me as I am and not how she wishes me to be?'

'Oh, Courteney,' Tiffy said huskily. 'You're hurting as much as I am! Today Jago thought only of what *he* wanted, and not of how I felt. He wanted money as well as me, which made me feel so cheap. It seemed so wrong when I have so much love to give him. That should be enough, shouldn't it?'

He bent his head and kissed her cheek. 'Yes, Tiffy, it should.'

They lapsed into a silence so understanding that no further words were necessary. Their private anguish lessened in a shared burden which, by degrees, became no burden at all. Each took from the other the pain, the emptiness, of loving more than they were loved. They pursued their individual thoughts, but were so very much in accord that when one felt a need, the other responded instinctively. Thus it was that when Tiffy sighed and snuggled more closely still, both his arms enfolded her so that she felt even more secure.

A euphoric state of content crept over them, heightened by their isolation in the great bed, enclosed as it was on three sides and with candlelight glowing softly on them from the fourth. Beyond that was the hostility of the endless night, but nothing outside their haven had any reality for them just then.

Their emotional rapport, their physical closeness, made it seem the most natural thing in the world for Tiffy to kiss his neck, which was the closest part of him her lips could reach. He responded by kissing her curls and resting his face against them. Both nuzzled each other, lazily, affectionately, and then lay still.

After a while Tiffy moved slightly, and her head slid from his shoulder on to the pillows. Courteney propped himself up on one elbow and ran a gentle finger down her tilted nose, murmuring, 'That's the part of you I like best. It is so very much . . . Tiffy.'

She pulled a face at him, and touched the scar on his cheek. 'That's the part of you I like best. It is so very much . . . Courteney.'

He kissed her nose. She kissed his scarred cheek and they smiled at each other. He bent his head closer to kiss her cheek, but she moved her face slightly and his lips brushed across hers. There was so much sweetness in the touch that they drew slightly apart and stared at each other. Slowly their lips drew together again and clung.

There was so much tenderness, so much honesty, in their kiss that there seemed no danger, and it was only natural for them to seek more solace. Lovingly, he kissed her cheeks, her eyes, her ears, her throat, while she moved her face this way and that to kiss him back when she could. They were lost in a magic that appeared to have no beginning, and therefore neither of them questioned the end.

It was by accident that Courteney's hand slid down her silk-clad back. A most delicious shiver tingled through her, and as she felt the vibrations in his body, she clung to him. His gentle hands became urgent, sliding over her, exploring, awakening such waves of desire that she melted wherever he touched.

She felt him shrug himself out of his dressing-gown and then slide her nightgown from her shoulders. She kicked it away from her, impatient of any restraint, needing the feel of his flesh on hers to extinguish the fire consuming her. But the touch of his naked body on hers only fuelled the flames, and she knew no relief until their bodies fused. She clung to him, loving him and being loved, knowing at last supreme happiness and supreme content.

When he collapsed against her she cradled his head on her breast, smoothing his fair hair. The passion had gone but the tenderness had returned and she was intoxicated still. She knew it should have been a dark head she was holding against her, and tomorrow that might matter. But tonight it didn't. She closed her eyes and slept.

Tiffy awoke in her own bed. She was loosely wrapped in her peignoir, and her nightgown was on the pillow beside her. Vaguely, because she had been so very sleepy, she remembered Courteney carrying her back in the grey light of dawn, kissing her as he placed her under the pink and white quilt, and promising they would talk in the morning.

She stretched languorously and smiled, unable now to picture Courteney in such a romantic role, although she recalled vividly enough the delight she had discovered in his arms. The feeling of well-being persisted. Her despondency was gone, her optimism was back. She was herself again, and once more all things were possible.

Talk . . . had he said? What was there to talk about? Their need, like the night, was gone. Now it could only be a case of least said, soonest mended.

Tiffy flung off her covers, clutched her peignoir about her and padded barefoot to her dressing-table, thrusting her face close to the mirror. There was nothing in her reflection to show that she had crossed the threshold between maidenhood and womanhood. The difference, then, was in how she felt—and she felt very good indeed. No misery, no depression, only an eagerness to resume her battle with Jago. She had new knowledge to assist her, and after last night, she should be able to coax a certain favour out of Courteney . . .

She went back to her bed and tugged the bell-rope vigorously for her maid. Some half-hour later, demurely dressed in sprig muslin and with her curls brushed artlessly *à l'Anglaise*, she was running down the stairs calling for Farley. He came out of the breakfast parlour, bowed, and bade her a good morning.

'It's a beautiful morning,' she replied exuberantly. 'At least, it will be if my lord has not yet gone out. I particularly want a word with him.'

Her cheerfulness, considering that her elopement had been foiled not twenty-four hours previously, surprised Farley, but he merely said, 'That is fortunate because his lordship desires a word with you, and charged me to tell you so. He has had his breakfast and is in the library.'

When Tiffy entered, Courteney was not, as she'd supposed, busy at his desk with his odious papers. He was standing by one of the tall windows, his arms folded, his brow furrowed as he gazed out at the quiet square. At the sound of the door closing he came swiftly towards her, taking her hands and lifting them to his lips. 'Dearest Tiffy, I am sending the announcement of our betrothal to the papers. We shall be married as soon as it can be arranged. Any unseemly haste will be explained by my attendance at the Vienna Peace Congress.'

'M—married?' Tiffy stuttered.

'Of course. Honour demands it.'

'My honour doesn't,' she retorted. 'You do me a shocking injustice if you think I came to your room to trap you!'

'I think no such thing. You came to me for comfort, and I seduced you. You must permit me to give you the protection of my name.'

'Oh, is that all! Truly, Courteney, the way you always take the blame for everything I do is becoming tiresome. If anyone was seduced, I rather think it was you.'

'I have taken advantage of you, an innocent girl under the protection of my roof. Good God, yesterday I thrashed Jago for doing less. You *must* marry me.'

'Well I won't!' she exclaimed indignantly. 'If anybody's honour is gone, it's mine, and if I'm not bothered, why the devil should you be?'

'My dear, you are not thinking straight. We *must* marry.'

She flounced away from him and sat on a chaise-longue. 'I am thinking very straight, thank you. This is me, *Tiffy*. I have no martyr instincts. You might be prepared to sacrifice yourself on the altar of honour, but I'm damned if you are going to sacrifice *me*.'

'Would marriage with me be so very dreadful?'

'Of course it would! I don't want to marry you. There was no talk of marriage between us last night. Why should there be this morning? We have been naughty and must be punished, is that it?'

He was aghast. 'No! I have much to offer you, Tiffy. You would be the Marchioness of Dalmaine.'

'I would rather be Mrs Jago Harwood,' she flashed. She saw him flinch, and all her old tenderness for him welled up. She pulled him down beside her and gently kissed his cheek. 'Courteney, don't let your conscience spoil what happened between us. Last night we were both in despair. We needed each other, and so, for a little while, we loved each other. We made each other happy. Where is the sin in that? Why should we spend the rest of our lives paying for something we both wanted at the time?'

'You make it a lot simpler than it is.'

'You make it a lot more difficult,' she countered. 'Do you want to make me unhappy?'

'No!'

'Good, because I don't want to make you unhappy, either. Let's talk no more of marriage.'

'We must. There might be . . . issue.'

Her smile vanished. 'You mean I might be pregnant? Grief, what a phantom to frighten me with! If I go to Jago less innocent than I should be, that's his fault for wanting more than me alone. But a child! Fate could not be so cruel! If I might be pregnant, there's just as strong a chance I might *not* be, and I'll gamble on that. I shall know in a very few days. In the meantime, don't degrade what happened between us with regrets.'

'I shall always feel I should marry you.'

'Then the sooner you marry your Eleanor, and I marry my Jago, the better.'

He stood up and walked back to the window, frowning as heavily as when she had entered the room. 'Jago will not make you a good husband.'

Tiffy chuckled. 'When was I ever interested in anything that was good for me? I am the infamous Miss Yorke, remember.'

Courteney turned back to her. 'Don't be flippant. If

last night proved anything, it is that your judgment isn't yet to be trusted.'

'Behold me, not only a fallen woman but a wiser one,' she mocked, pulling a face at him. The wrath this kindled in his eyes surprised her, and she added rapidly, 'All right, I shall not tease, only you mustn't lecture me. I am not in the mood for sorrows and sermons today. I am sorry I did not make you as happy as you made me, because . . .'

'You made me very happy, Tiffy,' he interrupted.

Her face softened. 'I'm glad, because I particularly wanted to beg a favour. May I, if I promise to be all propriety, visit Jago at Dalmaine? You know my word is to be trusted. The promise I made to cause no scandals while in Lady Janetta's care applied only while I was in Bath.'

'I am aware of that.' He thought carefully before he continued, 'It wouldn't be wise to visit Jago. All his schemes have come undone and he will want to lick his wounds in private. He's a very proud man.'

'Damn! You're right, of course. He will love me less if he sees me now, and perhaps more if he doesn't. Much as I hate doing nothing, I suppose my best course is to wait until he comes to me.'

'Your best course is to avoid him altogether.'

She wrinkled her nose, her eyes sparkling with mischief. 'I'm not rising to that bait. I want my breakfast.' She went over to him and gave him one of her impulsive hugs. '*Dearest* Courteney, do stop looking like a condemned man. You have offered for me and I have refused. Your honour is vindicated. All you have to do now is ruffle my curls so that I know all is well between us.'

He did so, and Tiffy, not noticing his reluctance, kissed him quickly on the cheek and went away to the breakfast parlour. She had no idea she was leaving him—as Jago was left—to lick his wounds in private.

A few mornings later she was able to tell him, quite cock-a-hoop, that she wasn't pregnant, so they were free to pursue their own chosen partners. And, as though on cue, Jago returned to London. He joined the Life Guards—the Hyde Park Saunterers, as they were known—and was able to continue living in his old lodgings in Duke Street. Since his military duties were none too onerous, he resumed something of his former social life, and with all his old assurance. Humiliated he might have been. Chastened he was not.

The first time Tiffy saw him in his scarlet and gold uniform, she fell in love with him all over again. She had tactfully decided not to refer to the elopement, but he had no such scruples. He called her his little prude and laughed when she was furious. He was so patently certain she was still his for the raising of his little finger that she was almost, but not completely, glad when the dowager decided she had had enough of London.

Lady Janetta, loathing strangers about her as she did, now regarded Tiffy as so much a part of her household that she swept her off to Bath without a quibble. They stayed there for a few weeks and then set out once more on a round of visits to the great houses. Jago, apart from a furlough neatly arranged to take in the hunting in Leicestershire, remained in London. Courteney went to Vienna without a bride. Eleanor had not relented.

For her eighteenth birthday, Courteney sent Tiffy amethyst earrings, writing that the violet stones so closely matched her eyes that they seemed an obvious choice, and for Christmas shortly afterwards he sent her a fan decorated with seed pearls and delicately painted with violets. Tiffy, confounded once again by what she could give a man who was rich enough to buy an abbey, had laboured long, and with much colourful language, on embroidering a pair of slippers for him. She loathed needlework, and sent them off with a note admitting that they were hideous but hoping he would appreciate the effort.

Once Christmas was over, Tiffy began to look forward to spring and a new Season that would bring her back into Jago's orbit. Then, in March, while she and the dowager were deciding which gowns should be packed, disaster struck. The entire household was laid low by a particularly virulent strain of influenza. As if that were not enough, Napoleon escaped from Elba and all Europe was in a turmoil again.

Tiffy was over the influenza in a few days, but the dowager, who prided herself on never being ill, was seriously stricken. Pneumonia set in, and since she loathed all doctors and preferred Tiffy's swearing to her servants' hushed solicitude, Tiffy became her chief nurse. Together they muddled through the crisis and the long haul back to health, but by the time the dowager pronounced herself fit, the better part of the Season was over.

London, in any case, had become meaningless for Tiffy. Brussels, Wellington's headquarters as he mustered the Anglo-Netherlands army to meet the new Napoleonic threat, was the place to be. Jago's regiment was quartered outside the town, but he had lodgings within it. Courteney, who had left the Staff to return to his regiment, was staying at the house his sister had hired in Brussels, whenever his duties permitted.

The Hunts, Maria Burroughs, Lord Horsley—practically everybody Tiffy knew—were making merry in Brussels, while she racked her brains in Bath for a means of getting there. The opportunity she was seeking occurred one morning in June, when the dowager, reading through her mail, suddenly exclaimed, 'Neither of my grandsons will oblige me by marrying and producing more Harwoods, but here's Augusta doing her duty by Stanleigh again. He's bringing her and the boy home for safety's sake, which ain't at all to her liking, but

Dalmaine means to take over the hire of the house in Brussels for the time being.'

Tiffy, fitfully tidying the skeins of tangled silks in the dowager's embroidery box, raised eyes blazing with excitement. 'Why don't we go there? Courteney won't need a whole house to himself.'

The dowager glared at her. 'You'd see me in my box to get to Brussels, wouldn't you?'

'Yes,' Tiffy admitted, 'although you're much too stubborn to be boxed up before you see a *Harwood* heir. Of course, if you're frightened by the news of the French gathering on the Belgian frontier, there's no more to be said . . .' She let her words hang in the air, waiting for the explosion.

It came immediately. 'What, me scared of a Corsican commoner and his republican rabble! That will be the day.'

Within the hour, the dowager was calling for her writing-tablets and informing Courteney he could expect her and Tiffy a day or two after his receipt of this letter.

Tiffy was *aux anges*. Once more fate had intervened to bring her closer to her heart's desire. She had no thought of danger, and neither, apparently, did the better part of the cosmopolitan visitors to Brussels. Those who were prudent had already retired to Antwerp, Ghent or the impregnable safety of England by the time Tiffy and Lady Janetta arrived on the eleventh of June.

Although the proximity of the French naturally gave rise to constant rumours and counter-rumours, Brussels was still very much a city *en fête*. Talking about anything as serious as war was considered bad *ton*, and nobody observing the promenading, the parties, the picnics and the balls would have suspected that Napoleon's legions were preparing to fight their way to the city gates.

The house Lord Stanleigh had compelled Lady

Augusta to vacate because of her delicate condition belonged to a merchant. Lady Janetta was gratified she could find a great deal of fault with it, but it was elegant enough and in the best part of town.

By fortunate circumstance, shortly after they arrived Courteney rode in to spend the night in Brussels. Tiffy gave a shriek of joy when she saw him, launched herself into his arms and hugged him, all the time pelting him with questions she gave him no chance to answer. The dowager put an end to these transports by ordering Tiffy to take a damper, then she asked, 'Where's Jago?'

'At Liedekerke, near Ninove, where he is quartered. He will be in Brussels tomorrow for the Remptons' ball. I'll have a note sent round to his lodgings to tell him of your arrival,' Courteney told her.

As Lady Rempton was one of the many callers received by Lady Janetta the following morning, she and Tiffy were given invitations to the ball. Jago arrived to pay his duty call while Tiffy was dressing for it, and spent half an hour closeted with the dowager in the privacy of her boudoir.

Tiffy, who had bribed the porter to let her know when he arrived, was lurking at the top of the stairs when he came out, ostensibly on her way down to await the dinner gong. She was carrying the train of her lavender crepe ball-gown over her arm, and she was, she knew, in her best looks. So, too, in his magnificent scarlet and gold dress uniform, was Jago. She exclaimed, 'Jago, of all people! How you surprised me.'

'Did I?' he mocked. 'I rather thought I had been waylaid. But you wouldn't do that, would you, my little prude?'

Tiffy glared at him. 'Don't call me that! You know I hate it.'

'Perhaps I shall make amends by waltzing with you this evening.'

She shrugged, and he laughed as he walked with her

down the stairs. When she paused at the entrance to the green salon and he strolled on to the front door, she asked, 'Aren't you dining with us?'

'I shall have enough of my family at the ball this evening.'

'I'm not family!'

'Nor will you be until you break your childish bond with Dalmaine. I will not share the loyalties of a woman with any man.'

Tiffy's violet eyes gleamed. 'Jealous, Jago?'

'Disappointed.' When her eyebrows rose questioningly, he explained, 'Prudes are always disappointing, Tiffy.'

He laughed as she flounced into the green salon and slammed the door, and he was still laughing at the ball later that evening. If he had a care in the world, it was not evident on his handsome face. He waltzed with all the prettiest girls, and as Tiffy had more partners than ever, she was able to reply in kind. The most pleasing part of the ball from her point of view was to see Eleanor waltzing with Courteney not once but twice—a clear indication he was in favour again.

As for herself and Jago, she found the game between them becoming a trifle tedious. She hoped he thought so, too, for then she was certain he would end it.

CHAPTER FOURTEEN

JAGO AND Courteney spent the next two days with their brigades, and Tiffy had to wait for the Duchess of Richmond's ball on the fifteenth of June to see them again. Everybody was asking if it were true that the French had crossed the frontier and fallen upon the Prussians, but during the day a reassuring number of senior officers rode in to attend the ball, so it was felt that nothing serious could be happening.

Tiffy wore her finest gown, white silk with the neck cut low enough to reveal the promising curves of her young breasts. Her hair was twisted into a Grecian knot at the top of her head, from which her black curls cascaded to the nape of her neck. She carried a posy of hothouse violets thoughtfully provided for her by Courteney, and in her ears she wore the amethysts he had given her.

In her cool white silk on that hot airless night, a perfect foil for her exotic features and colouring, she had never looked lovelier. She attracted more partners than she knew what to do with, and when Jago arrived later with Maria on his arm, she was able to throw him a look of justifiable triumph. He acknowledged it by raising his fingers to his lips and blowing a kiss in her direction.

He waltzed twice with her during the course of the evening, calling her not his little prude but his little witch, and she knew he was once more blowing hot towards her. At midnight she was in the garden surrounded by admirers when a young officer rushed out exclaiming. 'It's war all right, by Jove! Wellington's just arrived and confirmed it. The army's under orders. I'm for Braine-le-Comte. Tiffy, your hand! I wish to kiss it for luck.'

She held out a hand that was suddenly cold. It was seized and kissed by all the young officers, and then they flocked into the ballroom in search of more news or to make further farewells. Tiffy remained where she was, shivering on that balmy mid-June night. War had always seemed remote to her. Unthinkable . . . and one naturally did not think about the unthinkable. Now she was forced to, and she was filled with dread.

She sought out Lady Janetta, who took one look at her white face and rasped, 'Yes, it's true. My last two grandsons in the same battle, and not an heir between 'em!'

'Where are they?' Tiffy whispered through dry lips.

'They took their leave of me some minutes ago. They are bound for Ninove, where our cavalry is mustering.'

'Gone? Without saying goodbye to me? I don't believe it!' She ran out of the ballroom towards the front door. Before she reached it, a hand grasped her arm and she was pulled into an anteroom.

She gasped, and what little breath she had left was stifled by Jago's arms. His hand seized her curls and pulled her head back while he demanded, 'Kiss me, little witch. If I'm to be a damned hero, I'll have a proper hero's farewell.'

His lips crushed hers, but she was so frozen with unreality that none of the usual wild passion flowed through her. She felt as if they were actors in a play. Soon the curtains would close, the audience would applaud and they could go home and be themselves again. It was the stupidest feeling, but she couldn't do anything about it. She couldn't melt and say all the things she should be saying.

When Jago released her, she wondered dazedly whether he would finally declare his love for her, without any conditions or reservations, but it was to somebody behind her that he spoke, and with laughter. 'What, still prowling, coz? You flatter me. Tiffy's safe enough for the time being, there being a limit to what even I can manage at a ball.'

Tiffy turned her head and saw Courteney, but Jago laughed again and looked down at her. 'I'm very good at taking care of this precious skin of mine, so don't fear for me. Fear for yourself. I mean to settle all the unfinished business between us when this little mêlée is over.'

He flicked one of her straying curls back from her face and strolled towards the door. When he reached Courteney, he paused. Tiffy, looking at Jago so splendid in his Life Guards' scarlet, and Courteney so distinguished in his Hussars' dark blue, felt as if her heart would break. She saw them shake hands and that, as nothing else had, convinced her they would soon be fighting for their lives. She closed her eyes, and when she opened them again Jago was gone.

She went blindly towards Courteney. Before she reached him, there was a flurry of footsteps and Eleanor burst into the room. Her beautiful face was ashen, her eyes dilated and her musical voice pitched higher than usual. 'My lord, don't tell me you are going, too? Oh, no, you must not. You will be mutilated again. I can't bear it, I can't!'

Rage flickered through Tiffy, but for once she fought and controlled it. When she stepped towards Eleanor it was to say in a rallying tone, 'That is not the way to send a man off to war! You do it with a smile and a kiss and a promise to be waiting when he gets back.'

Eleanor covered her face with her hands and burst into tears. Tiffy gave her a little shove into Courteney's arms, saw him catch and hold her, and walked away.

'Tiffy . . .' It was Courteney's voice. As she turned, he went on, 'We haven't said goodbye.'

She saw Eleanor's head buried in his shoulder, watched her hands steal up to clutch at the braid on his jacket, and was surprised how much pain there was in this unreal world that had claimed her. She forced a smile, and replied, 'It's not my way, remember? I'll wait until I can say hello again.'

She whisked herself away, a deep unease within her that was quite separate from the war, and when she wondered whether Eleanor would at last say the words Courteney had waited so long to hear, it was with a certain vagueness. She couldn't seem to come to grips with anything.

When she went back into the ballroom she passed Maria staring blankly at the pink roses climbing over the trellis on the wallpaper. She hesitated, then walked on. She knew the same stricken look was on her own face, and there was nothing anybody could do about it, except call off the war. The dowager, maintaining with a lifetime's authority that it was the duty of women to carry on as normal while their men went off to fight, insisted on staying for supper and was in no hurry to leave afterwards.

By the time they got to bed, the drums were beating for war and bugles were calling the soldiers billeted within Brussels to arms. Baggage-wagons rumbled over the cobbles, horses neighed, orders were shouted, soldiers called to each other or sang as they marched towards the gates.

Sleep was impossible. Tiffy, in as much a turmoil as the town itself, got up again. She felt compelled to go to Courteney's room, which was the silliest thing, because tonight he was not there to comfort her. She went anyway, wrapped in her robe and carrying a lamp. She did not know what she was seeking, but she found his dress uniform flung across the bed as, in haste, he had changed into his service uniform.

She touched the heavy braid on the jacket, remembered Eleanor doing the same, but felt no guilt of trespass. Courteney would understand, if Eleanor did not. She sighed and put the lamp down on his dressing-table, seeing as she did so a package with her name on it.

Wonderingly, she sat down to open it, and a familiar blue velvet pouch fell into her lap. She loosened the drawstrings, took out her mama's necklace and a note. Courteney had scrawled it hastily, but with care in case other eyes than hers might read it:

> No violets in the dew for me, my dear. I always think of you smiling and, whatever happens, I would like to think of you smiling still. I am returning the property you entrusted to my care, with my thanks for all the richness your friendship has given to me.
>
> Courteney

'Oh!' Tiffy gasped. She bowed her head over the note and the necklace and gasped again, 'Oh!'

The door opened, and more light flooded into the room. The dowager stood there, holding aloft a branch of candles. She demanded, 'What are you doing here?'

'Crying, and I wish you would go away.'

'Foreigner!' the dowager barked contemptuously. 'A proper English girl don't weep when the men go off to war.'

'You should have seen Eleanor at the ball. She wept all over Courteney and begged him not to go because he would be mutilated again. I could have mutilated her!'

'I don't deny she's foolish, but what's it to you? I ain't so old I don't know it's Jago you have a *tendre* for, which makes you as foolish as Eleanor. What's that in your hand?'

'My mama's necklace. Courteney was holding it in —in trust for me, but he wants me to have it back. I—I fear he has had a premonition.'

'Bah! He's a soldier, not a seer. I can't think why he's given that necklace back. You can't wear a fake among the *ton*. Don't gape at me, girl! I know all about it. I picked it up when it fell from his pocket the day he gave you two thousand for it. I knew as well as he that it was mere trumpery, but he swore me to secrecy. Said it would destroy your faith in your father if you discovered he'd had it copied, or some such drivel.'

'But—but Papa held it in trust for me,' Tiffy stammered.

'Then you've learned a good lesson. Never put your trust in gamblers. Sooner or later the cards or the dice betray the best of intentions.'

Tiffy held up the necklace. 'It looks so real.'

Lady Janetta took it from her and scraped one of the stones against the dressing-table mirror. 'Glass don't cut glass. Good God! It *has* cut.' She studied the necklace under the light of the lamp, and exclaimed, 'Damme if Dalmaine ain't had it copied again, and in real diamonds. Why, when he's already two thousand down on the deal?'

'Because it's just the sort of lovely thing he would do,' Tiffy said huskily, taking back the necklace and holding it tenderly. 'I only wish . . .'

'What, that you'd asked more for it?'

'No, you disagreeable old harridan! I only wish Eleanor knew what a fine man she is getting.'

'If he lives.'

'Don't say that! He *will* live, and Jago, too. When something is in doubt, you have to fix in your mind what you want to happen—and it will, if you believe in it enough.'

'Moonshine!'

'You just like to be miserable. I am going to bed. Very likely I'll wake up to find Napoleon has been *rompéd* and all is well again.'

She was over-optimistic, but Brussels was quiet when she woke some time after noon. A steady exodus of people were seeking by road or river the safety of Antwerp or Ghent, and midway through the afternoon guns sounded to the south of the town. They continued until late in the evening, but nobody knew what was going on.

The following day, the seventeenth, the wounded began to arrive, many of them collapsing in the scorching sun to lie where they fell in the streets, unable to drag themselves a step farther. There were not enough doctors, and Tiffy and Lady Janetta joined other ladies who forgot their squeamishness and went out with flasks of brandy and water, lint and bandages, to do what they could to ease the suffering. The sun vanished, lightning flickered through the sky and thunder rolled continuously. People opened their doors to get the wounded under cover, and when the storm broke, the rain lashed down.

Tiffy and the servants continued to work among the wounded in the green salon while the dowager, sitting on a straight-backed chair in the middle of the room, directed operations. Towards evening, Tiffy was checking on two Highlanders propped against a wall in the hall, one with a head wound and the other with a bloodied and broken arm, when there was a knocking at the door.

She answered it, and a distraught Eleanor tumbled in. She moved forward to clasp Tiffy's hands, then drew back with a squeal of horror. 'Ugh! You have blood on your dress.'

Tiffy was bone weary. She had fetched and carried, acted as a human crutch for soldiers who could not walk unaided, tackled with ignorance and inadequate means hideous injuries, fought nausea and despair, and all the time dreading that Jago and Courteney might be lying somewhere without even such makeshift help as she could offer. She looked down at the stains on her muslin dress, up at Eleanor's aghast expression, and replied between gritted teeth, 'Injured men can't help but bleed. They don't do it to be disobliging. Have you come to help?'

'Mama would never permit me. We have given what sheets and blankets we could spare when there was a collection, and she says that is enough. Besides, I *couldn't.*' She caught sight of the wounded Highlanders, looked hastily away, and dropped her voice to a whisper. 'Do you know they are naught but common soldiers?'

Tiffy replied caustically, 'They are bearing their pain with uncommon bravery. I'm very busy. What do you want?'

'There's no need to speak to me like that. I am on a mercy mission of my own. We are leaving Brussels at dawn, and Papa offers you and Lady Janetta his protection if you want to come with us. Oh, that we have not delayed too long! Did you know the Prussians have retreated and our army is falling back?'

'Yes, so that communications can be maintained between them. Supplies are still moving *forward.* There's no need for alarm.'

'No need . . .' Eleanor gasped. 'It's being said that Napoleon has given his soldiers permission to sack the town. There will be pillage. Rape!'

'Pooh! Rumours put about by Bonapartists to frighten muttonheads like you! I'll tell you something, Eleanor. Anyone who got hold of you would soon let you go. You haven't enough spirit to interest a Frenchman.'

'How dare you!'

'How dare you think of leaving when Courteney may be needing you. It's infamous to run away from him a second time.'

Eleanor's eyes filled with tears. 'I cannot stay. You haven't thought! Courteney might have lost a limb or been hideously scarred again. I cannot be expected to bear that. I have too much sensibility.'

Tiffy's temper exploded. She lashed out and her open palm caught Eleanor a ringing slap across the cheek. Eleanor screamed and burst into sobs. Tiffy pushed her out into the street, saying bitterly, 'You use sensibility as an excuse for thinking of nobody but yourself. You don't know what it is to feel love or even compassion. You are a selfish, spineless little toad. Don't stop running until you are back in Jamaica, or I swear to God you'll wish the French *had* got hold of you.'

She slammed the door on her and turned to find Lady Janetta standing in the doorway of the green salon. Tiffy's chin lifted. 'I meant every word.'

The dowager stared at her for an inscrutable moment, then stomped back into the salon without uttering a single blistering comment. Tiffy, quivering with rage and something else besides, took this as criticism and shouted after her, 'She's not fit for Courteney. She's just not fit.'

The eighteenth of June was overcast but dry. The wounded had been moved to their billets or to the hospital tents, where Tiffy spent most of the day. It was exhausting work, but she was glad of it, for there was little news to relieve her anxious mind. As the day progressed, all that was known was that Wellington had drawn up his army some twelve miles outside the town, close to the village of Waterloo, and was there disputing Napoleon's intention of being in Brussels in time for dinner.

When Tiffy returned home that evening, she had no thought of dinner. She went to the stables, where she issued precise orders before entering the house and going up to her room. A little later she walked in on Lady Janetta, wearing the best suit of the Belgian stable boy who had been hired with the house. She was booted, and a footman's hat was pressed firmly atop her pinned-up curls. She said without preamble, 'I am taking your carriage to Waterloo.'

The dowager's knuckles whitened on the cane she clutched. 'Have you heard something about Dalmaine and Jago?'

'No, but I have just tended a wounded trooper. He's a

Peninsula veteran and knows what's what. He said he's never known a battle such as this. A pounding-match he called it, and asked me if I've ever heard of a battle in which everybody was killed because neither side would give up. He told me the French cavalry was walking round the British squares as if they were their own, because there's too few of our cavalry left to chase them off.'

'Good God!'

Tiffy pulled on her gloves, and continued grimly, 'It's too much to hope that both Courteney and Jago have escaped injury. I believe those horrid bumpy carts the wounded are being brought back in are killing off many who might otherwise survive. That is why I want the carriage. To bring back Courteney and Jago, if—if necessary. I cannot trust the servants to go alone. They might turn back if things are difficult.'

'That disguise ain't good enough for close scrutiny. You might drive straight into the French. You'll be raped for sure.'

'I have my papa's pistol, and the coachman and grooms are armed.'

The dowager muttered, 'Wild blood, the Yorkes. Too wild, I always thought, but now I'm glad of it. Take the carriage—and bring 'em back. Alive. Corpses are no use to me.'

'You will be left without transport if the battle has gone against us.'

'Bah! I don't mean to join the rabble on the road to Antwerp.'

Tiffy nodded and swung towards the door. The dowager called, 'Wait, you baggage. I might not see you again, and I want to know. Which one is it with you? Dalmaine or Jago?'

'It was always Jago—I thought. Now I don't know. I only pray I don't find out too late.'

*   *   *

The pace of the dowager's powerful horses was reduced to an oxen-like plod as the road through the forest to the battlefield resembled nothing so much as an obstacle-course. The spilled or plundered loads from abandoned wagons were strewn everywhere. To add to the confusion, dusk fell. It was a mild evening but the fitful moonlight was unreliable and the lanterns on the well-sprung carriage cast strange lurching shadows over the road and bordering trees.

It was only Tiffy's forceful and frequently blasphemous presence on the box beside him that stopped the dowager's old coachman from turning back. He clearly thought her mad, feared her more than the French he was convinced would fall upon them, and called upon the good Lord to deliver him from his plight. Tiffy scarcely heeded him. Goaded on by the most frightful anxiety, she was undeterred by anything that barred her way.

Every so often she stood up on the box and held aloft a lantern to peer down into a cart of wounded, feeling sick with relief when the beam of light failed to pick out a beloved face. They seemed doomed to pick their way along a road that never reached a destination, and, indeed, they were still some miles short of Waterloo when Tiffy was once more forced to stop the carriage while the footmen cleared baggage from an overturned wagon.

She climbed down with her lantern to give more light, and saw two horseman approaching at a walking pace. She went towards them, anxious for news, when something unmistakable about the squat and solid shape of one of the riders made her exclaim, 'Tobias, by all that's wonderful!' Then she saw the big frame of the man on the far side of him and, running forward, she cried joyfully, 'Courteney! Oh, thank God!'

'Rather thank his opposite number. I have more dealings with him,' answered a lazy drawling voice.

'Tiffy, my little witch, what devil's broth are you brewing now? And in breeches, too.'

'Jago . . .' Tiffy skidded to a halt. The dreadful fear that had driven her here engulfed and overwhelmed her, for she could think of nothing except death that would part so faithful a watchdog as Tobias from his master in time of danger. She had the curious feeling she was turning to stone, and before her lips became paralysed, too, she forced them to whisper, 'Where's Courteney? He's not—not *dead*?'

Then she thought what a stupid question that was, because she didn't want to hear the answer. Never wanted to hear it. While she didn't positively *know*, she could continue with her journey. She could pretend she would find Courteney a little further on. He would be safe and well. He would take her into his arms and make everything all right again, the way he always did.

Because that was what she wanted . . . her dear friend who had become so much more without her ever realising it. She was glad Jago had survived. The world would be a drabber place without him, but it was Courteney she needed so very much to live.

She wouldn't believe them if they told her he was dead. She wouldn't even listen. She . . . But nobody was paying any attention to her. Jago was swaying in the saddle, and Tobias, steadying him, was shouting to the footmen, 'You two. Give a hand here.'

In that instant Tiffy seemed to become two people. One of them was dying painfully with Courteney; the other was trying not to notice by carrying on as normal. *This is madness*, she told herself, and welcomed it. If being busy would keep reality at bay, then she would be busy.

She piled up the pillows she had ordered to be put into the carriage, and instructed the footmen to prop Jago up against them so that his legs could be stretched along the seat. They left the carriage as Tobias climbed in, and

Tiffy opened Jago's red coat. It was thrown loosely across his shoulders and she was able to study the bandage just below his shoulder without disturbing him. It was spotted with dried blood but showed no sign of fresh bleeding.

'He'll do,' Tobias grunted beside her. 'He had no nasty bits of metal to be dug out of it. It's a neat clean sword-thrust, too high to touch the lung. It's loss of blood what caused him to swoon. Ay, and exhaustion and brandy. He wouldn't get into a *common* tilt-cart, if you please, so there was nothing for it but for me to ride with him, his lordship having ordered me to see him safe to Brussels.'

Tiffy, lifting a bag of medical supplies, dropped it and swung round on him. 'His lordship? He's *alive*?'

'Of course he is,' Tobias answered in an aggrieved tone. 'I wouldn't have left him otherwise.'

'Oh, I could box your ears. I thought you'd l-left him because he was d-dead.'

'As if I wouldn't be guarding his body, God forbid, instead of fooling around making sure Mr Jago don't break his neck. There's no need for you to take on so. Three times his lordship was brought down today when his horses were killed under him, but he's nothing worse than cuts and bruises to show for it. The French are beat, and it's the Prussians what came up late in the day as are chasing them, our lads being too tired to do aught but drop where they stand. His lordship is seeing to his men and I thought all our worries were over; now here's you causing more scandals to fret him with. Ain't he been through enough? You should be ashamed of yourself, Miss Tiffy.'

But Tiffy's heart was leaping with joy, and the only reply these strictures earned him was a warm, 'It's so *good* to hear you scolding me again, Tobias!' She picked up the medical bag and took from it a vinaigrette and flask of brandy.

Tobias shook his head. 'Best leave Mr Jago be. It will be a tidy while before you're in town, the road being in the state it is. The longer he sleeps, the better.'

'You're right. You ride back to his lordship. Safe he might be, but I'll feel easier in my mind if you are with him.'

'I'll feel easier in mine,' he acknowledged, 'only I don't know as how my master would want me to leave you alone with Mr Jago.'

'Strewth!' Tiffy exclaimed, midway between tears and laughter. 'This is not an elopement. The minute I am back home, I shall change into my skirts and not do a single thing his lordship would dislike.'

'Seems to me there's a world of difference between your notion of what his lordship would dislike and his,' Tobias grumbled, but he climbed out and helped to get the carriage turned before he rode away.

Tiffy supported Jago until the carriage was set on its return journey, then she sat on the opposite seat and studied him. With his black hair falling across his forehead, his face no less handsome in sleep, and his scarlet coat open to reveal the bandage gleaming whitely against the dark hairs of his chest, he looked the most romantic figure in the world.

Knowing now that it was the quixotic and gentlemanly Courteney who was the true romantic, she none the less smiled affectionately at Jago. It was the kind of affection a girl retained for a favoured toy she had outgrown and no longer wished to play with. Jago had bewitched her, but while he had touched all her senses, it was Courteney who had captured her heart.

Courteney had championed her when nobody else had wanted to know her, shielded her from every possible hurt, and all because they called each other 'friend'. It seemed to Tiffy now that their becoming lovers had been no accident of circumstance, as she had supposed. It had been a natural deepening of the bond between them, at least for her.

Her dazzled eyes had drawn her to Jago while her hungry heart had found love with Courteney, and she had been unaware of the conflict until the war crisis three days ago. Then she had not known which one of them to run to and her dilemma had lasted right up until now, when fantasy could no longer be confused with fact.

All in all, she had got herself into a pretty pickle, and how to get out of it she did not know. But having wasted two years chasing the wrong man, she wasn't going to waste another two chasing the right one! Would Courteney think it very strange of her if she told him, several months too late, that she would like the protection of his name, after all? Or would it be simpler to seduce him all over again?

She was thinking this one through when Jago stirred, groaned, and opened his eyes. After a moment or two they focused on her, and he said, 'Take off that stupid hat and give me some brandy.'

She gave him the flask. 'You may have the brandy, but the stupid hat stays on. Nobody must guess I am a girl. Courteney has the greatest dislike of scandals.'

'Damn Courteney!'

'You mustn't say that to me. We are very nearly in Brussels, and if your wound is not too painful I would like to talk to you.'

'I can think of something better to do. Come over here.'

'No, this is serious. It will be a bit of a surprise for you, but I don't wish to marry you.'

He swung his legs off the seat, lounged back at his ease and smiled. 'It is a surprise. I haven't asked you.'

'How like you to be awkward when I am trying to get things straight,' Tiffy said heatedly. 'You spoke of settling the unfinished business between us, and what else could you have meant? I know I have pursued you like a—a shameless baggage, but it was all calf love. It wasn't *real*. These past three days have made me see that. I have grown up.'

Jago eyed her narrowly. 'Have you, indeed? Come here.'

'It won't do any good.'

'Come here.' He leaned across and pulled her towards him so that she fell on her knees on the floor of the carriage. He turned up her face, kissed her slowly and searchingly, and then angrily. When he released her, he said, 'Who is it?'

Tiffy got up and sat opposite him once more. 'Does it have to be someone?'

'Most assuredly it does.'

She sighed. 'Very well. It's Courteney.'

Jago stared at her, then exploded, 'You cunning little minx. You were after him all the time. What was I? A means of making him jealous?'

'It must seem like it, but it wasn't that way at all. You were a challenge, and so precisely a young girl's idea of a hero that I naturally thought I loved you. Only you delayed too long, and I discovered I really loved Courteney.'

'I see. The fact that he's a marquess has nothing to do with it?'

'Nothing. I told him once I'd rather be Mrs Jago Harwood than the Marchioness of Dalmaine. And I was so wrong!'

'Very touching, but most unrealistic. The man's a crushing bore.'

'Oh, no!' Her eyes filled with sudden tears. 'I could tell you of a hundred—a thousand!—things that have made me love him, but you would only think me mawkish.'

'I would,' he agreed. Then, 'What will you do about Eleanor?'

Tiffy's jaw jutted. 'Murder her if necessary.'

The moodiness vanished from Jago's expression, and

he laughed. 'Tiffy, you'll be wasted on my cousin. Are you sure you wouldn't rather marry me?'

'I'm sure, and you should be grateful for it. I have a common streak, and I would raise merry hell if you did not behave yourself, which we both know you would not. You need to marry a lady bred to turn a blind eye to her husband's liaisons.'

'You speak some sense in with all your nonsense. Perhaps I should lay siege to Eleanor. She's rich as well.'

Tiffy said carefully, 'Maria loves you. I saw it in her face after you left the duchess's ball.'

Jago drank again from the flask, and said wickedly, 'How good of you to remind me of Maria. Instruct the coachman to call at the Hôtel de Belle Vue. We shall take her up before going on to my lodgings. She will know precisely how to make me—ah—comfortable.'

The motion under the wheels changed, and Tiffy, looking out of the window, saw that they had passed through the gate and were in Brussels. It was not much past midnight, and there were plenty of people about. Anxious, she guessed, to ask any incoming vehicles for news. She rapped on the ceiling of the carriage, and as it stopped, she said, 'I'd better get back on the box. Nobody will take the slightest notice of me up there, but they will certainly stare if they see a groom in a carriage.' She reached for the door handle, then paused and looked back. 'Jago, can we be what we have never been before—friends?'

'No, but I promise you we will be lovers when you are bored with domestic bliss.'

'That will never be,' she said with certainty.

He kissed his fingers at her and grinned. 'I'll be waiting.'

She shook her head at him, climbed out and swung herself once more up on the box. She had scarcely settled in her seat when a clatter of hoofs made her twist round.

She saw Tobias and—'Courteney!' she cried.

He came alongside, stood in his stirrups and plucked her from the box. Before she knew what was happening, he had swung her through the air so that she landed astride his horse behind him. As he released her, she threw her arms round his waist to steady herself. Her hat fell off and her hair slipped from its pins and tumbled to her shoulders. 'Courteney!' she gasped. 'What are you doing? You will cause a shocking scandal.'

'I mean to,' he said grimly, and for once succeeded in stunning her into silence. He galloped home with her, where he dumped her on the pavement, swung himself out of the saddle and threw his reins to Tobias.

Lights blazed from every window of the house, and as the porter flung open the door, Courteney picked her up and carried her inside. It seemed to Tiffy, totally bewildered and blinking in the sudden light, that the entire household was gathered in the hall. Maids, footmen, kitchen workers and even Lady Janetta, and all of them gaping as though an apparition had come in out of the night.

In fact, it was two apparitions. Tiffy with her tumbled hair and breeches, and Courteney with his torn and muddied uniform, his dishevelled hair, his exhausted face and icily blazing eyes. Lady Janetta gathered her wits first, and exclaimed, 'Dalmaine! Damme if I ever thought to be so pleased to see you.'

He bent his head in a curt bow. 'Your servant, Grandmama. You may be easy. Jago is safe and the French are defeated.'

'Champagne!' Lady Janetta cried, clapping her hands for the butler, but when Courteney carried Tiffy straight past her to the stairs, she asked, 'Now what's amiss? What do you mean to do with Tiffy?'

'Ruin her,' he answered savagely, and took the stairs two at a time. He carried Tiffy into his room, kicked the door shut behind him and dropped her on his bed.

'Don't look so surprised,' he went on, ripping off his battered blue coat and flinging himself into a chair to pull off his boots. 'Girls who seek ruin invariably find it, but yours will be at my hands, not Jago's.'

Tiffy stared at him with eyes like saucers. 'Whatever have I done to make you so angry?'

'What haven't you done?' He stood up and came towards her in his shirt and breeches and swooped to unbutton her coat and pull it off. 'You let Jago maul you before my eyes at the ball. That is the picture I've carried with me these past days. It's driven me to the edge of madness. I was pushed beyond it when I heard tonight you'd risked your reputation and God knows what else to bring him home.'

He seized her by the shoulders and shook her. 'He's not worth it. Will you never realise that?' He released her just as suddenly, pulled off her boots and tugged off her breeches. As her over-large shirt fell to her knees, he added bitterly, 'I'm tired of waiting for you to come to your senses. You remember he wanted ten thousand pounds to marry you? Did it never occur to you he would just as easily have taken the money to jilt you? That's the sort of man he is. He doesn't know *how* to value a woman or even care for her. If this is the only way I can keep you safe from him, then so be it. I've started this particular scandal and, by heaven, I'll finish it as your husband!'

He was swooping down on her when a knock on the door caused him to check and swing towards it. Tobias entered, his expression as impassive as ever. 'My lord,' he began, 'I know you've good cause to be angry, but this ain't right. You know it ain't. I can't stand by and . . .'

Tiffy turned her tousled head towards him and said clearly, 'Tobias, go away. I am the best judge of whether I want to be ruined or not.'

He stared at her, then a huge smile spread over his

honest face and he hastily stepped outside and closed the door behind him.

'Tiffy . . .' Courteney breathed, and she held out her arms to him. He caught her up and held her close and smothered her face and hair with kisses. 'Tiffy, my precious love, I thought I was going to make you hate me, but I didn't know what else to do.'

She clung to him and buried her face in his chest. 'As if I could ever hate you . . . . I love you far too much. It was you I really came for tonight, you I have always loved. I realised that when I thought you might be dead. I was frightened. Oh, Courteney, hold me tightly! I never want to be so frightened again.'

He kissed her fears away, and when she sighed and relaxed against him, he stroked her hair and asked, 'Why did you push Eleanor into my arms at the ball? All I wanted was to say goodbye to you.'

'I thought you loved her.' She raised her head and gazed anxiously at him. 'Are you sure you don't?'

'I never loved her. I worshipped her, which is something entirely different. She was the perfect image of what I imagined my ideal woman was. Then I met you, and discovered how infinitely more lovable an imperfect woman can be.'

'Oh,' Tiffy gasped. 'You always say the most beautiful things. You will make me cry.'

'Violets in the dew,' he murmured, kissing her. 'I can think of nothing more beautiful.'

Tiffy sniffed, and a latent jealous streak prompted her to say, 'Many people think I am but a candle to the sun of Eleanor's beauty.'

'A candle is so much more beguiling.'

She flung her arms round his neck and turned a radiant face up to his. 'I do love you so! Lady Janetta will be cross and say you have made a beggar marriage, but if you're sure it's what you want, will you please, please, ruin me again?' A doubt shook her. 'That is, if you're positive you don't mind the scandal.'

'Tiffy,' Courteney vowed, 'in future you can have as many scandals as you please—providing they are always with me . . .'